Hotter than Hell

By

Mark Tushingham

*Together, we changed the climate of our world and created Hell.
I am just a creature of that place.*

- **Lieutenant General Walter J. Eastland**,
Commanding General, III Corps.

DreamCatcher Publishing
Saint John • New Brunswick • Canada

"If we are to award Mark Tushingham's dark fascist vision of global warming, humanity's place as a ruler of the earth has to be replaced with an acceptance that we are, at most, the earth's partners."

            – Rev. Bill Thomas,
              United Church of Christ Minister,
              Saint John, New Brunswick,
              Canada

"Despite Tushingham's imaginary future, I hope mankind has enough self-correcting mechanisms to prevent it from ever becoming a reality."

            – Bob Allore, P.Eng.,
              Chief Design Engineer,
              Lepreau Nuclear Power Plant
              Lepreau, New Brunswick,
              Canada

Copy right © 2005 Mark

Tushingham
First Printing - Nov 2005

All rights reserved. No part of this publication may be reproduced or transmitted in any form or by any means - electronic or mechanical, including photocopying, recording or any information storage and retrieval system - without written permission for the Publisher, except by a reviewer who wishes to quote brief passages for inclusion in a review.

DreamCatcher Publishing acknowledges the support of the New Brunswick Arts Council.

Library and Archives Canada Cataloguing in Publication

Tushingham, Mark, 1962-
    Hotter than Hell / Mark Tushingham.

ISBN 0-9739234-1-5
Printed in Canada
1. Title.

PS8639.U82H68 2005 C813'.6C2005-906829-9

Publishing Consultant: Carl Senna
Cover and Typesetting: Hardy & Associates
Author's Photo Dianne & Mark Tushingham

DreamCatcher Publishing Inc.
55 Canterbury Street, Suite 8
Saint John, NB
E2L 2C6

"To Dianne"

Prologue – A Possible Future

There had to be a breaking point. Society was straining under the mounting effects of climate change: increasing numbers of destructive storms each year wrecking our cities, warmer oceans destroying fish stocks, changes in precipitation patterns decimating our farms. Many governments had been ignoring or covering up the excessive human depletion of the world's natural resources for years. There had to be a place where such government neglect of this crisis would eventually fail. That place was Los Angeles, the year I arrived…

Part I

On the Road to Hell

The road to Hell is paved with good intentions.

– **Karl Marx.**

– Chapter 1 –

Los Angeles

California was a fine place to be if you were a cactus. When I arrived in Los Angeles early in the morning, the temperature was already 108°F in the shade. The spring heat wave covered all of the southwestern states from California to Texas, but southern California was particularly hard hit. The world's climate was getting out of hand. After serving as the Army's liaison officer with Homeland Security at the Pentagon for the past four years, I was ordered to Los Angeles as the deputy commander of the liaison field office. I had combat experience in Libya and Siberia; and the Army thought such experience might be needed in Los Angeles. The Army was right. The heat and draconian water rationing had the residents of the city desperate to the point of anarchy.

I installed myself in my assigned quarters in a pleasant house in Pasadena, and the next day I reported for duty. The office was run by Colonel James Huel (or Jimmy, as he insisted everyone call him). My orders were to report to his office at eleven in the morning. I thought at the time that the hour seemed late: eight would have been more appropriate. Nevertheless, I arrived promptly at eleven, and presented myself to his civilian assistant, a young, attractive blonde.

"Major Eastland reporting for duty," I said.

"Are you ..." Is that today, she asked.

The work area around her desk and computer was cluttered with piles of paper. She began typing, as though she had momentarily forgotten I was still there, but in a minute or so she made a puzzled expression. Suddenly she stopped typing. She began to frantically search the disorganized piles of papers on her desk and on the floor, scattering them about. There was none of the military orderliness in her that I had expected. I assumed that she was looking for a copy of my orders, but she never found what she was looking for. She now became flustered, and turned to me.

"Colonel Huel isn't here," she said.

I provided her with my copy of my orders. She glanced at them.

"Like I said," she said, "Colonel Huel isn't here. But Lieutenant Joyita can help you."

With that, she waved her hand, pointing me vaguely down the hall.

Unescorted, I walked down the hall and eventually found Joyita's office. The office was neat and well organized. The young man behind the desk was smartly dressed in a crisp uniform. He promptly stood to attention when he saw me, and snapped a salute. I returned the salute and presented my orders. Joyita invited me to sit while he read them carefully. This was more like what I expected.

"Sorry, Major Eastland," he said, "I was not informed that you were to arrive today. Colonel Huel is meeting with state officials."

Joyita quickly produced my assignment file from one of his well-ordered cabinet drawers. Coronado Joyita was a very short man. He was not quite five-foot tall; and at six feet two inches I towered over him. He had a round, happy face that seemed ageless. I couldn't tell whether he was eighteen or twenty-eight.

At two forty-five in the afternoon, Colonel Huel finally returned to the office. I had waited without going for lunch for over three-and-a-half hours in his office. I have always been a stickler for punctuality: and I expected it of others. But he was my superior officer, so I couldn't say anything. I fumed in silence. The colonel sauntered by me to plop down heavily in his chair with a sigh. As he passed by me, I sensed a faint whiff of alcohol in the air. He flung his cap onto his desk, revealing a mass of well-groomed blond hair. It was definitely not a military cut. Rising unsteadily and with a slight tremor, he stepped gingerly over to me to greet me and to shake my hand. His proximity confirmed that he fairly reeked of bourbon. He smiled roguishly at me.

"You must be Walt," he said. "Welcome aboard."

Turning to his assistant, he shouted: "Please get the major's file for him. Cori will have a copy, if you can't find it."

"Thank you, Colonel Huel," I said. "But I have it here."

I handed him the file that Joyita had given me.

"Great, Walt," he said.

"Walter, sir," I corrected him.

"Never mind," he shouted again to his assistant. "Tell Cori I have it."

I was certain that Coronado disliked the name Cori as much as I disliked the name Walt. I could accept the familiar from my friends, but not from a stranger. I deliberately called Huel, "Colonel Huel."

"Oh relax, Walt," he said, sensing my discomfort at his informality. "Call me Jimmy. This isn't the uptight East. This is California. Relax."

After he had flipped through my file, Colonel Huel eased himself out of his comfortable chair and walked over to me. He sat on the edge of my desk.

"Walt," he said. "Try to enjoy your time here. Everything's under control; there's really not a lot to do. Take a few days to see some of the beaches. Rela-a-a-x."

With the strictest water rationing in California history—with rolling power blackouts from the massive and constant use of home air conditioners—he actually tried to reassure me that things were under control. Politely, I thanked him for the suggestion but insisted that I'd prefer to get to work.

Within a week, Lieutenant Joyita and I were doing all the Army liaison work in the office. The colonel worked a few hours each afternoon, but he did not show up for work at all on Fridays or on a weekend. I did not miss him. The arrangement suited us both.

* * *

As the hot spring turned into a scorching summer, I worked hard at coordinating security work with the staff at the district office of Homeland Security. Most of them were political appointees—none of them impressed me. I also set up regular meetings with the Los Angeles Police Department, the California State Police, the Navy at Long Beach, and the Marines at Camp Pendleton. I had an excellent working relationship with the commander of the Marines' 1st Rapid Deployment Force.

In June, Homeland Security began to plan for a routine, but, nevertheless, significant event in Los Angeles that summer: the announcement by the governor of his candidacy for the Republican presidential nomination at the party's convention. Polls pointed to none of the primary runners as a clear favorite among the Republicans in the primary races. The governor's announcement was to take place at the new convention center in Anaheim, a sprawling complex of buildings with numerous entrances and a long, irregular perimeter—a security nightmare. I anticipated that Homeland Security would ask the Army to provide additional forces to help secure the complex. It seemed to me to be a sensible precaution, given the potential for violent protests getting out of hand, but the request never came. Although the announcement was scheduled for August 3, Homeland didn't think it even necessary to brief the Army until July 22. The briefing of the military took place at Homeland's district offices by the district chief. There were about a dozen people. Colonel Huel and I represented the Army.

As I sat and listened to the presentation, I wasn't pleased. Security was to be an all-civilian affair: police and a few Homeland agents—no Army. The district chief stressed several times that there were not to be any uniformed soldiers.

I asked the governor's aide why not.

"The governor," he said, "wants to show he's a friend of the people. News photos of him behind rows of armed troops will send the wrong message."

I pointed out that there had already been water riots in Carson and Huntington Park, that the mayor of Los Angeles had to call out the Army to restore order, and that eighty-eight people had died in the Carson riot.

"The governor," the aide said, "wants to show people he's in control. They need to know he can end the national water crisis when he is president."

"But sir," I said, "don't you think that the people care more about water than images?"

"Wrong, major," the aide said. "Image is credibility. The governor must be seen as a leader. We want people to trust him, to feel secure when they see him in the news."

"With all due respect," I said, "but we should at least have some Army units discretely in the neighborhood."

"No," he said.

The governor's security chief now squirmed in his seat, as though he, too, had already raised the same considerations and had been overruled as I was just then. But I felt that I had nothing to lose trying again to press my case.

"How about putting some Army helicopters on standby?"

The aide wavered. He seemed to consider my suggestion, until Colonel Huel intervened.

"Relax, Walt," he said. "Let the civilians deal with this. They'll decide if there is to be Army involvement."

I leaned back in my chair, shook my head and kept my mouth shut. The meeting was soon adjourned.

That night I stormed around the house for hours berating the governor's flunkies and the Homeland incompetents. The fact that my overworked air conditioner had broken down didn't help.

I decided I needed a break from Huel and the office. I had been invited to visit Camp Pendleton to meet with the marine commander, whom I had met earlier that week. So I decided to visit him to get away. First thing next morning, I arrived at Camp Pendleton's main gate. He came to the gate and escorted me to his office. After some polite chitchat, he looked at me gravely.

"I know what's bothering you," he said.

"Are they all blind to the mood of the people they represent," I asked.

"I think they're all charged up for the upcoming Republican nomination," the marine commander said.

"Look," I said. "You heard my orders. I can't even warm up a helicopter."

"And so what brings you here," he asked.

"Do you think you could keep your force on standby," I asked. "My orders didn't mention anything about involving marines."

"A fine distinction," he said. "I doubt your colonel would see it that way. Crowd control is not something us marines train for anymore. That's exclusively army business now."

"I know, but if things get bad, it will be more like a rescue operation than crowd control."

"Hmm. Maybe we could do some training on the third. Something that requires us to be ready for quick deployment."

He wasn't any more explicit than that, but we understood each other.

"You know," I said, "if all goes well, no one will ever know of our efforts."

The bulky marine nodded.

* * *

On August 1, wide-scale rioting broke out over severe water rationing in Van Nuys. Order was never fully restored, and sporadic vandalism and looting of supermarkets continued. The temperature on August 2 was a blistering 124°F; that evening it was slightly lower at 109°F. But on Saturday, August 3, the city was poised for trouble.

A fierce sun shone in a hazy gray-blue sky. It was cooler (if you can call it that) than the day before. The air was hot and smoggy. My lungs burnt from the dirty air, although the locals seemed use to it.

I arrived at the sprawling Anaheim convention complex at 10:50 a.m., along with Joyita. I parked a rented cube-van full of loaded rifles for my marine commander's men in case we needed them. The van was parked near a strategic back exit, a precaution that I did not share with Huel. Joyita and I were both dressed in civilian clothes—our orders were for no visible Army presence. Huel arrived much later with his friends from the Governor's Office. I had loaded it full of automatic weapons and canisters of tear-gas. The governor's chief of security seemed relieved when I cleared my actions with him. Joyita and I reconnoitered the complex. Its newly painted white walls were shiny and unblemished. Inside, plush red carpets were everywhere, high chandeliers hung spectacularly from the ceiling of the main room, paintings and tapestries on the walls and exotic indoor plants flanking the stage. Californian and American flags lined the back of the podium. The media was beginning to set up their equipment when I entered the main room. Television cameras, including a new holographic one, were at the back of the room—their high-definition zoom lenses focused on the podium. I left the main room and wandered back outside. Crowds were beginning to form on the far side of the police barricades. Signs protesting the water rationing were already visible. Television cameras panned the scene looking for a newsworthy shot.

There were plenty of police about, but none in riot gear—after all, the governor was, so I had been told, a friend of the people.

A few hours later, I surveyed the service bays. There was a small crowd lined up behind the police barricades. Why were they there? Maybe they thought that the governor would try to sneak into the complex through the back door? The caterers arrived then. Dismayingly, the caterers unloaded the provisions for the night's banquet. It was not so much the boxes of food that bothered me, but the cases of bottled water. I saw the cases and the police saw the cases, but when the crowd saw the cases I heard distinct tones of muted disapproval and resentment. Trouble was brewing. A number of police were at the ready, their faces full of apprehension. The police now faced the crowd. Ironically, the amount of water was within the ration limits for a political event and permitted for the number of people expected at the banquet. Nevertheless, when viewed all together in one place, the amount seemed to the crowd to be a violation of the rationing order. Rumors of political bending of the rules and corruption spread through the crowd as soon as the small pile of cases became a vast mountain of cases. I had a growing sense of impending doom when I left the service bays and returned to the main entrance to await the governor's arrival. I mapped out an escape route from the center to my waiting cube-van.

The governor was scheduled to arrive at 6:30 p.m., but by my watch he was forty-five minutes late. News of minor rioting for water near Long Beach Airport appeared on the television news screens; the newscasters also reported that the governor's airplane had been diverted to Los Alamitos Naval Air Station because of the riots. The crowd outside the convention center became unruly and noisy. Some of them denounced the governor for making them wait. The minutes dragged until the governor climbed out of his limousine and smiled confidently before the angry crowd.

In a few minutes, the speeches from the dignitaries started; they were televised, of course, and many of the crowd outside could view the spectacle on their wrist-watch screens. The front table was a "Who's Who" of the Republican Party in the West: the senior California senator and Majority Leader of the Senate, the senior Nevada senator and chair of the Armed Forces Committee, the governor of Arizona, three California congressmen, plus the mayors of Los Angeles, San Francisco, Sacramento and San Diego.

I was now standing in a corner off to the right side of the stage. Joyita and the governor's chief of security were beside me. Huel was seated with the governor's press aide at one of the back tables. The security chief fidgeted with his earphone and glanced about nervously; suddenly all the color drained from his face. I don't know what he heard through his earphone, but it was obviously not good news. He rushed off to the governor, who had not yet taken the podium. He leaned over and spoke into the governor's ear. The governor's face showed no expression. He remained calm.

News spread quickly: riots had started outside. The security chief's team surrounded the governor while other security teams protected the rest of the VIPs. People were running for the exits to look after themselves. The security teams were all armed with pistols—no one had anything more powerful than that to take down a single shooter. I was not armed at all. No one knew what to do. I worked my way through the crowd towards the security chief. Automatic gunfire sounded outside the hall. Panic filled the faces of the crowd. All the people who had been scrambling to get out turned round and now rushed back into the room. An armed mob ran into the center firing automatic rifles indiscriminately at us. Security fired back with their pistols, but they were no match for the automatic rifles and machine guns of the rioters. The men and women of the security teams dropped like flies. All this was recorded by the television cameras, because no one had thought to turn them off after the cameramen fled.

I reached the head table, picking up a pistol from a dead security guard along the way.

"This way," I yelled to the VIPs around me, pointing to an exit.

The governor, a few senators and congressmen crawled over the dead security guards; they joined me amid the gunfire and screams. Joyita and a few other security officials were with me. We ran to the service exit, through the deserted kitchen, and down some stairs into the vast underground parking lot. The lot had been closed for the event, so there were no vehicles in sight. We ran through the deserted parking lot in the direction of the exit nearest to the van I had parked loaded with weapons. We ascended the stairs and emerged in a quiet courtyard. My van was just around the corner.

We reached the van just in time to see a large threatening mob shouting angrily and approaching us in the distance. I unlocked the back latch and lifted the roll-up door. Throwing the next-to-useless pistol to the ground, I picked up a rapid-fire rifle; I placed a satellite phone and a tear gas canister in my pockets. I ordered Joyita to distribute rifles to the others. The Homeland men didn't wait for the rifles from Joyita, but they jumped into the back of the van and emerged armed. Joyita gave a rifle to a senator who took it with gusto. A young congressman held his rifle awkwardly.

"Point and press," I shouted at him.

One of the governors, however, refused to take a rifle. I had no time to argue with her and left her to do as she pleased.

"We must get to a roof," I said.

With the mob almost upon us, I stepped from behind the van and emptied an entire ammo clip into the ones leading the pack; it was enough to stop the rest of them. The mob retreated, but then began to regroup for another charge at us.

I knew that to reload my empty rifle would have taken me too long and the crowd would have been on top of us.

I dropped it and I grabbed a second loaded rifle from the back of the van. I led my small group to the roof of the hall, a smaller secondary conference hall that, like the parking lot, was closed for the day. I used the satellite phone to contact the marine commander. After a few anxious moments of static, I heard his voice.

"Eastland," he said, "we're already airborne and on our way."

"How soon," I asked.

There was a pause.

"Four minutes," he said. "We saw what happened in the convention hall on TV. How bad is it really?"

"Very bad!" I said. "There are thousands of people trying to attack us. Heavily armed and desperate. Don't underestimate them."

"We'll get you out."

My small group reached the roof without incident, but we were soon discovered. A mob of about thirty fired at us from the windows of a nearby building. One of the Homeland men was shot through the head and a congressman was wounded. When we returned fire and hit some of the mob, the others retreated for a few minutes. I heard the helicopters then. Four of the choppers came into view and quickly landed on the ground around the building; a fifth landed on the roof near us. As it did, a sniper on an adjacent roof killed the other Homeland man. While Joyita shot at the sniper, the senator and I dragged the congressman over to the waiting helicopter. The governor of Arizona followed behind us. Her face was ashen.

Five marines leaped from the chopper and made their way over to us. The marine commander was one of them. A marine medic took over from me and slung the wounded man effortlessly over his shoulder. Two other politicians followed him back to the helicopter. I turned to call to Joyita, but I saw that he lay wounded. I ran back to him and dragged him towards the helicopter. It was then that I was hit. The bullet grazed my forehead. It was not a deep wound, but it bled profusely. Blood flowed into my right eye. I brushed it away, but more flowed in. It looked much worse than it was. I continued to drag Joyita, but soon a marine relieved me: it was the marine commander.

"Get on the chopper, Walter," he said. "You can't fight like that. We're going into the hall to search for others."

Those were the last words he ever said to me. He didn't survive. The helicopter took off with its cargo of survivors and headed back to

Camp Pendleton. The pilot and the brawny medic were the only marines of the 1st Rapid Deployment Force to survive. The marine commander and forty-four other marines were killed by the mob—just a minor statistic considering the events of the next two weeks.

* * *

At Camp Pendleton, a medic eventually tended to my superficial but bloody wound, but it was after midnight when he finally released me from hospital. I was anxious about finding out what was going on, and I wanted to find Joyita and the wounded congressman somewhere in the base hospital. The other politicians, I suspected, in hiding elsewhere on the base, were too busy to see me. I was an out-of-uniform army officer on a marine base. I was a lone civilian for all intents and purposes as far as most people seeing me now were concerned, and so alone I found myself in the officers' club, behind the deserted bar. I was subjected to a news program blaring from a television and a screen image of an aerial scene of flames set against a darkened city. The announcer spoke haltingly. I was horrified to learn that, in the hours since I arrived at the base, riots had spread across Los Angeles. The announcer read names of neighborhoods that were in flames; half of the city was on fire.

Hearing gunfire in the distance, I rushed out of the officer's club. As I stood there in the dark listening, a marine corporal called to me. He told me that the base commander wanted to see me. Together, we ran to his office.

I entered the commander's office, forgetting momentarily that I was out of uniform, and I instinctively saluted the general, a short, beefy man in his mid fifties.

"You're quite a fellow," he said. "I can't believe you made it out. It's hell in there."

I quickly described how the city, not just the convention center, was a battle zone.

"I have your orders," he said. "I was told that they come straight from the top. And you're to leave for Washington immediately."

I was just as surprised as he was. In the current emergency I expected to be assigned to a nearby army unit or placed under the temporary command of the marines.

"Command," he said, sensing my disappointment at the news, "doesn't want to risk loosing you."

He noted that not only was I one of only five witnesses to what went on inside the convention center, but I was the most senior security person to survive.

"No one else," I asked.

I was staggered. There had been over a thousand people in the convention hall.

He shook his head gravely.

"The marine commander is also missing in action," he said. "We have no control of the situation. I can barely defend my own camp."

I was at a loss for words.

"You're dismissed, major," he said. "And good work."

The same corporal who had brought me to the office escorted me to the airfield and to a small unmarked jet waiting for me. The pilot saluted me, and directed me to a seat across the aisle from the senator who refused the rifle. Her face was pale, her hands trembling, and she seemed so self-absorbed that she didn't seem to notice me. Besides the pilot and the co-pilot, no one else was aboard. We took off without incident. And as we gained altitude, I peered out of the window to the city burning below us. No electric lights were visible—just the glow of flames.

* * *

It took more time for the military to debrief me regarding the events of August 3 than it did for them to restore order in Los Angeles. Although I played no part in either the planning or the operations responding to the riots, I replayed the events of the day over and over again. I was ordered to watch video replays of the riots, listen to numerous security tapes and provide my commentary. Army Intelligence wrung every drop of information out of me, at least of what I recalled, and when they were satisfied with my reports, I was given three days of leave.

A three-day leave turned into a month off duty. During that time, the nation and the world learned of the magnitude of what had happened in Los Angeles. Of the nine billion people on the planet, almost everyone saw the images of that day. When the estimates of damage started to come in, the nation was staggered. There were over ninety thousand people dead, including seventeen thousand soldiers. Nearly one million people were wounded and eight million were homeless. The hospitals throughout the rest of California and neighboring states were overwhelmed with casualties. The government of California was smashed. Vast areas of the Los Angeles were gone. Property damage ran into the trillions of dollars. The fires in Beverly Hills, Hollywood and Glendale were still burning out of control, but the orgy of destruction that possessed the citizens of Los Angeles had ended. Of those who survived, all were hungry and thirsty. Finally, the heat-wave subsided and aid flowed in from other parts of the country. The federal government declared martial law throughout California. Ration centers were set up, emergency shelters were built, curfews were enforced, and bodies were buried in mass graves in the desert near Barstow. Soldiers were posted on almost every street. Slowly order returned, but southern California would never recover.

At the end of my leave, I was ordered to report to Army Liaison Command on the first floor of the Pentagon. My duties were light there. It was clear to me that the Army had not decided what to do with me. On November 7, my commanding officer came into my office and silently handed me two envelopes. The first one awarded me a Congressional Commendation for Meritorious Service. The second letter was from the Commander of the Army. It informed me with typical military brevity that I was awarded the Soldier's Medal of Heroism, the Army's highest award for bravery not involving combat and a Purple Heart for my injury. I was overwhelmed with emotion and pride.

With seventy thousand soldiers patrolling California maybe it wasn't such a good idea to be rewarding a soldier for killing Americans, so my award ceremony was a very small and brief affair in an office several blocks away from the Capitol. Only the senator and the congressman that I saved were at the ceremony, where an army deputy commander pinned the medals on me, saluted and shook my hand, wished me well and left the room.

– Chapter 2 –

Egypt

Having served as a major for less than nine months, I was promoted to lieutenant colonel upon receiving the Soldier's Medal and the Army also allowed me to choose my next posting. I decided on the World-Watch Operations Center in Fayetteville, North Carolina. In those days, it was a much sought after post by mid-level career officers, as it almost guaranteed becoming a general in the future.

I watched (via high-resolution, enhanced-color satellite images) as one by one the countries of South America fell into anarchy over water and oil. Satellite images of the last part of the Amazon jungle burning reminded me of the view from my airplane window when I left Los Angeles, only on a much grander scale. Oddly, I remembered from my childhood a picture book of animals from around the world with a picture of jaguars. Now there were no jaguars left in the wild, nor were there any jungles for them to live in if they did exist outside of zoos.

After serving my tour of duty at the World-Watch Operations Center, the Army next assigned me to 11th Tank Regiment of the 34th

Armored Brigade as second-in-command on the retirement of my commanding officer. Receiving my eagles upon that appointment, I was promoted to colonel and given command of the regiment. The 34th was an experimental brigade. We field-tested new armored fighting vehicles for the Army; and under my command, we received our first allotment of new vertical take-off tanks called Grasshoppers. Vertical take-off technology was integrated into a standard battle-tank, and the Grasshopper was the result. Its extended hull included four directional jets that could lift the tank off the ground and fly it for nearly fifteen minutes until the fuel tanks ran dry. In all, the flight could cover eight to ten miles. The ugly tanks flew slow and low and were hard to handle (turning was a tricky skill to learn), but they flew. They could fly over mind-fields, enemy lines, or just peek over a hill to fire. Surprisingly little of the heavy armor had been sacrificed to achieve this. The use of new composite armor provided the weight reduction necessary. With the overwhelming numbers of inexpensive self-guided missiles that were available to a modern Army, it was essential to have something that could take multiple missile hits. In theory, the Grasshoppers could take several missile hits and remain operational—something no helicopter or fighter drone could do.

The Army was eager to assess these new tanks in battle, when, conveniently, war broke out between Egypt and Libya. My 11th Tank Regiment was activated and deployed to aid the Egyptians. Originally we had planned to land at the airport outside of Matruh, along with other elements of the Second Infantry Division (to which we were temporarily assigned). However, with the recent Libyan successes at the border, the Egyptian Army was forced to abandon its western desert. My regiment therefore had to land at Al Alamein, a city in western Egypt, while the rest of the division landed farther west at Alexandria. The Egyptian armor had been badly mauled, so our presence on the battlefield was a priority. The war had been underway for nineteen days, but in the last two days the Egyptian lines had crumbled. For some unknown reason, the Libyans had paused and not taken advantage of the Egyptian collapse. At the time, it was thought this was due to the heat, which had reached 130°F. Every breath I took scorched my lungs. At least the tanks and vehicles of the regiment had air-conditioning.

I ordered the regiment to take positions five miles inland of the Mediterranean Sea and twenty miles back of the Egyptian lines. We were the Egyptian Army's only reserves in this area.

My first meeting with the Egyptian general commanding this sector was not auspicious. He was a large bulky man. His sharp eyes kept darting around the tent, but never once did he look directly into my eyes when we spoke. He seemed to me to be a man more used to having his enemies behind him, instead of in front. As I was the subordinate, I placed on the bulky translator headset over my ears.

"Colonel Eastland," he said (as translated by the machine), "please move your regiment to this point."

He pointed to a place on the map-screen before us where he wanted me to leave my strategic position and take up a defensive position less than a mile behind his front lines.

"Sir," I said. "That would leave my tanks vulnerable to infantry anti-tank fire. I need to stay mobile. The best way to use my tanks is to—."

"Colonel, I need your tanks there. My men must see that they have armored support."

I now understood. His lines were barely holding and the morale of his men was crumbling. The Egyptian general, who was about to make a classic mistake, was more concerned about stopping panic in his own Army than starting panic in the enemy. My tanks should have been used to hit the enemy, break through their lines and hit again from behind.

"General," I said, "that's a mistake."

I started to explain why I thought so when my cultural liaison officer gently tugged on my sleeve. She indicated that she needed to talk to me. I knew what she was going to say. I had made a cultural error.

"Not in front of his men," she whispered. I lifted the translator headset slightly.

"Ask for a private meeting." I said.

Too late! The general had to keep face with his men.

"Colonel," he said. "I order you to deploy your tanks here. You're dismissed."

I stormed out of the tent with my staff trailing after me. But I was angry with the general—and myself. I had years of experience as a liaison officer, and yet I handled the Egyptian general very badly. I had only myself to blame. I should have done much better—not that it would have made any difference. Nevertheless, I was not going to let this oaf destroy my regiment. I resolved to call my commander back at divisional headquarters.

I reached my communications vehicle and ordered a corporal to call headquarters. It turned out that my commander was at a meeting in Cairo and couldn't be reached. I spoke to his deputy, a woman at the rank of Brigadier General. I explained the situation and recommended that the commander issue orders countermanding those of the Egyptian command.

"Colonel Eastland," she said. "We are here at the request of the Egyptian government."

She reminded me that the Egyptian general was the senior officer in my sector and that I had to comply with his orders.

"If I move to where he has ordered me," I said, "and the Libyans attack, my regiment will be badly out of position."

I knew that I would get bogged down at the front and wouldn't be able to maneuver, and I wouldn't be able to plug the holes in the Egyptian lines. There wouldn't be an Egyptian government if the lines were broken.

"The rest of the division will be moving up," she said. "If there are holes, we will patch them up later."

"Later!" I said. "There will be no stopping the Libyans once they are through. This is the last real defensive line that the Egyptians have!"

"I'm sure," she said, "our division will be able to push the Libyan Army back without too much difficulty."

I don't know where she got the idea that the Libyans would be a pushover. They had torn the Egyptians to pieces and were eager to press their advantage. I refrained from telling her that she was being overly confident; instead, I offered a compromise.

"General," I said, "I could split my regiment. The 55th Battalion could stay up close and the 57th and 60th could position further back, ready to counterattack."

"No, Colonel," she said. "The Egyptian general is your commanding officer."

I could see then that I was getting nowhere with her. The general had ordered my entire regiment to the front, so that was where I had to take them. She was insisting that I factor in political considerations into my military decisions.

"Political considerations!" I exploded. "I'm only concerned with military ones."

"Colonel," she said. "You have your orders. Carry them out."

The radio went dead. I threw down the headset in disgust and left the communication vehicle in a rage.

Making the best of a bad situation, I spread my tanks out in a triangle formation, with only the apex at the place to which Egyptian had pointed. The rest were spread out to the rear—as deep as I could get away with. I also placed all of my anti-missile batteries to guard my rear-left flank where I expected the Libyan infantry to attack. The Mediterranean Sea was less than two miles to my right and that would do as protection for that flank. I fully expected the Egyptian lines to the south to be penetrated and for my regiment to become outflanked and surrounded. I started planning ways to extricate my regiment if the Libyans struck, and I sent my drones flying over the enemy lines while the reconnaissance platoon reconnoitered the desert behind us.

The images taken by the drones showed little activity by the

Libyans, except in one instance. My intelligence officer Captain Sean Wycross (a bright young man) showed me some low-level computer images taken from one of the regiment's reconnaissance drones. I peered at the blurry black-and-white images, but I couldn't make anything of them.

"What am I looking at," I asked.

Wycross took off his helmet and ran his fingers through his sandy-blond hair.

"Sir," he said. "I think this image shows pipe-laying equipment. And this one shows pipeline parts."

"Pipelines? For fuel?"

"I don't think so," he said. "They're too big and they're not connected to anything—at least not yet."

"If they're not pipelines for fuel," I said, "why are the Libyans taking so much effort to camouflage them?"

We saw that the equipment was invisible to any high-level drones or satellites. What were the Libyans hiding, I asked him then. Was he sure it was pipe-laying equipment? Could it be something else?

Wycross shook his head.

"I don't think so, sir," he said. "It's pipe-laying equipment all right, but why they are hiding it is a mystery."

As it turned out, Wycross had stumbled across the Libyan's big secret of the war, but neither he nor I, nor anyone else, understood just then the significance of the pipe-laying equipment and the pipeline parts. I radioed the Navy's task force, sailing out in the Mediterranean, and suggested that they bomb the location (just because the Libyans were taking such efforts to hide the equipment). However, the Navy planes had other priorities, and the site was never attacked—not that it would have made any difference to the outcome of the war.

I didn't foresee the full extent of the disaster that lay ahead; no one in their wildest imagination could have guessed what was going to happen two days later. With the world's attention on Egypt's Western Desert, no one noticed Israeli tanks emerge from the Sinai

Desert. This was what the Libyans had been waiting for. The Libyans and Israel had formed an alliance against the Egyptians. The Israelis soon crossed the Suez Canal and started to move on Cairo. The Second Infantry Division (except my regiment) was turned around and rushed east across the Nile Delta to hold the northern flank of the eastern line. An Egyptian Army Division pulled out of the line against the Libyans and rushed eastward. The western line, which was fragile before, was now untenable.

It was now, of course, when the Libyans attacked. The Egyptian lines disintegrated (as I predicted) and the Libyans broke through. I was cut off before I received orders from Egyptian command headquarters to pull back. My regiment had not yet fired a single shot and already the battle and the war were lost.

I called a command meeting. I told my officers that it was time to see how the flying tanks worked. With scattered elements of Egypt's Sátt-a Division holding to the west, I decided that two-thirds of my tanks would hop over the Libyan forces to the east, swing round and hit them from behind. Meanwhile the remainder of my tanks and my mobile anti-missile batteries and infantry support units would attack from the west—a classic pincer movement, and a long shot that depended on how prepared the Libyans were for our tanks' unusual ability.

My deputy commander took the 55th and 57th battalions charging through the desert. The 60th Battalion and the infantry and anti-missile support followed three miles back, while I followed just behind in the command vehicle, surrounded by the supply vehicles. No one was left behind.

I deployed most of my drones out ahead of the 55th, with the rest over the various elements of the regiment. I called for air-support from the Navy, but I couldn't get through with all the jamming and counter-jamming; it was a wonder the radios worked at all. Fortunately, the Libyan Air Force was nowhere to be seen either. My drones were the only aircraft flying in our air space. Some of my drones were armed for counter-drone action and others for attacking tanks. Most, however, were armed just with cameras. These provided me with an excellent view of my regiment, as it charged towards the Libyan lines. It was an exhilarating sight. The tanks threw up a dust cloud that was visible for miles—just as I anticipated. The Libyans prepared to engage. At the last moment, my deputy commander turned his forces towards the sea and lifted off. As planned, he swung them around the end of the Libyan line and curved in behind them. The tanks of the 60th then came out of the dust cloud and hit the Libyan lines. The Libyans attention focused on the 60th. They let off a barrage of anti-tank missiles at the tanks; however, my anti-missile batteries were ready and returned fire. The Libyan missiles were easily intercepted, there being fewer enemy missiles than I expected. My commander had nearly completed his maneuver when the Libyans realized what was happening, and struck at his tanks with their few remaining anti-tank missiles. He was out of effective range for my anti-missile batteries to protect him. Four tanks were hit several times each and fell into the sea; one more crashed the beach. Good men lost. My deputy commander's own tank was hit once but thankfully remained operational.

The surviving tanks landed behind Libyan lines and turned to attack. The Libyans were not prepared for tanks in their rear and their infantry soon disintegrated. But with the two halves of my regiment joined, our victory was complete— it was only temporary. We had only just finished refueling when Libyan tanks appeared: elite armored brigade descended on my isolated regiment. My maneuver had caught the Libyans off guard and had given us a chance. If we had not attacked, the Libyans could have taken their time to get their tanks into position and cut us to pieces at their leisure. As it were, they had to react to us destroying their infantry.

We held them off for three hours, but we were heavily out numbered. With our smart shells, we destroyed five tanks for every one they destroyed. They could afford the losses; we couldn't. We were surrounded and the Libyans thought we were not going anywhere.

They became more cautious. Who wants to die on the eve of a victory? This gave me the respite I needed. I reformed the remnants of my regiment. The 55th and 57th battalions were down to two tanks a piece; the 60th had six. My anti-missile batteries were spent or destroyed. My strength was down to less than a hundred men. With the 60th covering, I refueled the tanks of the 55th and 57th.

I radioed to the Navy to send helicopters to extract my men. Unfortunately, my regiment was not the only American force to suffer that day. The Libyans had sent a barrage of over two thousand missiles at the American fleet standing off-shore. This explained why there were so few missiles with the Libyan units attacking my regiment. The overwhelming number of missiles had swamped the fleet's anti-missile defenses. Unlike the Army, the Navy had underestimated the tactical impact of cheap, mass-produced self-guided short-range missiles. Three anti-missile frigates disappeared in a ball of fire, and a mini-carrier was slowly sinking. An old ultra-carrier, the centerpiece of the fleet, was badly damaged and on fire. With the ultra-carrier limping back to Taranto, Italy, the remnants of the fleet, which now centered on a helicopter carrier, moved farther out into the Mediterranean. The Libyans had prepared for fourteen years to take their Egyptian rivals down in the struggle for Arab leadership. They now had a military victory beyond their wildest dreams.

The Navy's ground-support officer on one transport carrier radioed me that we were now out of range for the transport helicopters to reach us. I asked him how far the helicopters could come towards shore. After a pause, he informed me that eight miles was the limit. I told him to send the helicopters. He was very surprised when I told him how we would come out to meet him. The Grasshopper's unique abilities were not widely known in the Army—let alone in the Navy.

Three of the more heavily damaged tanks were placed in automatic fire mode and left to cover our retreat. They would shoot anything that moved within a certain arc, and when their ammunition was expended they would attempt to ram the nearest enemy vehicle. I ordered the two remaining drones to be armed and the support equipment to be abandoned. With these hasty preparations complete, I got my men onto the surviving tanks. These tanks would act as flying platforms to carry my men to safety. This was certainly not what they were designed for.

My men clambered onto the seven remaining tanks. Each tank carried its crew of four inside with nine or ten men hanging precariously onto its hull. I climbed aboard a tank. I confess that I was not too keen on becoming a Libyan prisoner. The tanks rolled steadily towards the Mediterranean at a modest speed so as not to shake the men off the hulls. We reached the coast without incident and became airborne. The noise of the tank's jets was deafening; the vibrations shook you to your very core.

Behind us, the three remaining tanks were automatically engaging the oncoming Libyan tanks. They didn't last long. When the last one was destroyed, I indicated to my drone operator, who was crouched beside me, to send in the last two drones. They each destroyed a Libyan tank. After that, we were defenseless. We couldn't fire our guns because of the men on the hulls. Our only option was to get out of range quickly. With no further resistance, the Libyans charged to the shoreline and fired their guns and their last salvo of missiles. There were several near misses and then two missiles simultaneously hit the tank next to mine. It was my deputy commander's tank. Already damaged from earlier combat, the weakened tank exploded, killing all inside and on its hull. Shrapnel flew in all directions. Most of the men on the tanks on either side were wounded, including me. A piece of metal tore through my left arm, which was the one I was using to hold on to the tank. I lost my grip and nearly fell off the hull. A soldier on board pulled me back up.

Cruising some two hundred feet above the sea, our tanks finally flew out of range of the Libyan guns. Thankfully, we had lost only that one tank. The plan was simple: fly straight and slow (conserving fuel as much as possible), set the tank on the surface with the last drop of fuel, and get off quickly. I had no idea if the tanks would float for a few minutes or immediately sink like a stone.

The lead tank was the first to set down on the sea. As I flew over it, I watched the men on the hull dive into the water and scramble out and away from the bobbing tank, until its back end disappeared into the water and its gun barrel stuck straight up. Slowly it slid beneath the surface. I realized that we stood a better chance of being seen if we stayed together. I called down the hatch and ordered the tank leader to land. He relayed the message to the other tank commanders. One by one, the tanks settled on to the sea and the men jumped off. One by one, the tanks sank back-end first. When my tank landed, I waited for the crew to emerge and then I leaped into the water beside them. The water was very warm, but we had no lifeboats or life-jackets—not the standard issue for a tank regiment. I felt myself being pulled under. I struggled to remove my boots. The men around me were doing the same. Once relieved of weight, we floated easily in the warm, salty water.

With the last of the tanks gone, all was quiet—except for the ringing in my ears. I called my men to me and we waited. Two mammoth transport helicopters arrived ten minutes later. They settled onto the surface and we swam over to them. The helicopters took us back to the transport ship. When I stepped on to the flight-deck, an unpleasant realization hit me: I had gone into Libya with an elite tank regiment, but I had come out with nothing—not even my boots. The Army would not be happy. But happy or not, the Army would have to admit that I had saved seventy-nine men from torture in Libyan prisons.

My men and I flew back to Italy. And the true magnitude of the debacle unfolded there for us in our debriefings. The Libyans swept eastward with little resistance from the Egyptian Army. The Israelis drove westward, stopping at the Nile. Cairo and then Alexandria fell and the Second Infantry Division (minus my regiment) was trapped. The division surrendered, fortunately to the Israelis. The few American units supporting the Egyptians against the Libyans were never heard of again.

Why did this happen, I asked myself. What drove the Israelis into the "Unholy Alliance" as it was dubbed by the media? The images of the pipeline equipment that Captain Wycross brought to my attention were the clue. The Libyans and the Israelis coveted the same thing: the waters of the Nile. The Libyans had depleted their great inland aquifers at Kufra and in the mountains of Al Hasawinah. They were desperate for fresh water, as were the Israelis. The two governments had reached a secret agreement to share the precious resource of the Nile. The only obstacle in their way was the Egyptian Army and its supporting American units.

Unfortunately for the members of the Unholy Alliance, the pipelines that were supposed to bring water back to their parched countries were never completed. The pipelines were continually sabotaged by Egyptian partisans. Not only that, but other countries were equally covetous of the Nile's water. Algeria attacked Libya, and Palestine and Jordan attacked Israel. Soon the entire Middle East and North Africa were ablaze. The whole region, which had suffered economic collapse after the introduction of fuel rationing in the western countries, descended into bloody anarchy. It was far worse than what was occurring in South America. Neither the General Assembly of the United Nations nor the Security Council was able to reach a consensus about what to do. The United States, with its own riots over water, food, medical and fuel rationing, and now a military bloody nose, could do little—even if it wanted to. Because we had internal problems of our own, there was no longer any desire to become involved in messy international conflicts. The United States was now retreating from global military interventions.

– Chapter 3 –

West Point

There was considerable debate about what to do with me within the bureaucracy of the Army. I had, after all, lost an entire elite regiment equipped with experimental—and very expensive—technology. Some of the brass wanted to reward me; others wanted to punish me for abandoning my post and losing the tanks. In the end, both sides got something: I received my medals (again in a small private ceremony), but I was put out to pasture to a minor teaching role at West Point.

I was a forty-three year old colonel, with twenty-two years of military service. It was clear that the Army expected me to quietly serve out a few more years and then retire. I surprised them all—and myself. I enjoyed West Point. It was not the punishment that some had wanted for me. I found it rewarding work to mold the young, receptive minds of future officers. Besides that, I enjoyed being home each night. I left promptly at 7:50 each morning and returned each evening. I was originally assigned to teach a course on liaison work. Later, I managed to add a military history course that I designed during my spare time called Strategic Economic Resources and Their Impact on Army Operations. At the end of my third year at West Point, in addition to my teaching duties, I became the Assistant Registrar for the school. The Commandant was suitably impressed with me that he eventually asked me to teach the prestigious course Tactics for Occupying Armies.

It was a hard time for the Army and the country. The extreme environmental policies that the government had put into place following the Los Angeles riots began to take effect. The government had panicked. It decided that there was no time for gradual changes; everything had to be done at once. The result: chaos, just months before the economy collapsed. One international agreement followed another. Kyoto, Caracas, Shanghai, Lisbon—what did they achieve? A slightly slower growth than we would have otherwise had. The agreements bought us what? A few years? A decade at most? Even if we stopped polluting the air and warming the earth without rationing measures, we were still going to suffer from heat, droughts and violent storms for the next three hundred years. Of course, I knew that you can't do what the government was trying to do all at once. You have to phase it in. Maybe fifty years ago, we could take our time—maybe even thirty years ago—but now it's too late. We were facing economic collapse.

There were widespread food shortages now on a daily basis. Fuel was rationed, electric power failed routinely, and the economy spiraled downwards. Massive unemployment led to desperate people roaming the streets. Shanty towns sprung up like weeds across our once rich country. The government patched up one crisis only for two more to take its place. The Army's budget was slashed, but it was nowhere near as much as the other services. Even then, some in power realized that the Army would be necessary to maintain order.

In my oasis of calm and order at West Point, there was one advantage of all this social disruption: the college continued to receive a great many applicants and could be very selective on who it accepted. With the Army's reduced budget, only the brightest and most-dedicated cadets were chosen, and I, as Assistant Registrar, had a significant role in selecting them. I got to know the young men and women very well, which was an enormous advantage to me when I eventually took command of III Corps.

Throughout the outside turmoil, I enjoyed a quiet life—at least as well as I could with all the blackouts, food shortages, gasoline rationing, and frequent news of rioting in one city or another. I even took up sketching with charcoal as a hobby (oil paints were impossible to get) and I attended plays put on by the cadets, which became an excellent replacement for the frequent loss of electrical forms of entertainment. I developed into quite the connoisseur of amateur theater.

It was also the time when the real trouble began, when the crops on the Great Plains failed. It was too hot for the seeds to germinate. The massive irrigation projects of the recent past had depleted the aquifers under the Great Plains. There was nothing left. For the first time in history, the United States became an importer of food. However, we were in stiff competition for supplies with over one-and-a-half billion Chinese and a similar number of Indians. Riots became more frequent.

Mayhem and food riots soon broke out in Atlanta—almost as bad as that in Los Angeles—and the government passed a controversial 44th Amendment to the Constitution. This amendment on emergency powers included new authorities for the Army, requirements for media censorship, suspension of legal processes in certain circumstances, and many other clauses. The passage of this amendment was a wake-up call for me. Things must really be bad if such an amendment could get through Congress. I decided that I had remained hidden in my oasis long enough. I became restless and was determined to do my part to bring back order and stability to my country.

I kept in contact with old acquaintances, the junior senator from California, and Mike Waverly, the mayor of Albany. Eva Micklebridge had become a colonel in the National Guard. Jane Sykerman was buried away in a Washington think-tank, a Foundation for World Resources and International Affairs. Jane never told me what she or anyone else at the Foundation did. Every report the Foundation produced was classified, "Top Secret, Level Red" or higher. I started to lobby my contacts. I wanted to do something meaningful.

* * *

It was my duty to help my country and I could offer more than just being a teacher. Over one meal and meeting, I managed to coax Mike Waverly to go to bat for me, and the gambit paid off.

Albany had not suffered as much destruction as larger cities had, but nevertheless crime was rampant and shootings frequent. Fortunately, Albany had not had any large scale riots. The underground organizers of the really big riots in this area focused their attention on New York City. Consequently, the cities in upstate New York had experienced only small, spontaneous food or water riots. Mike had managed to keep the number of police at a reasonably high level, but had to sacrifice schools, roads and hospitals to do so. Nevertheless, the citizens of Albany believed themselves to be better off than people in other cities. Mike became the rarest of persons: a popular politician.

While I was on my way home from teaching a class, I received a video call from Mike's assistant. The assistant informed me that Mayor Waverly would be available for dinner on that next evening. It turned out that Mike was on his way back to Albany from White Plains. He had been attending a state-wide meeting on urban law enforcement. As luck would have it, Eva Micklebridge was attending the same meeting as Mike and she was pleased to attend.

The next day, a colleague mentioned that Captain Sean Wycross was in town—Wycross, my intelligence officer in Egypt and the first person to see the Libyan pipe-laying equipment. Like me, Wycross couldn't get a promotion after the Egyptian fiasco; unlike me, he couldn't get a pleasant teaching post or a Defense Superior Service Medal for consolation. Wycross was presently an intelligence officer at Fort Drum with the Tenth Infantry Division (no longer called the Tenth Mountain Division since the recent Army reduction and reorganization). I had not seen him since we flew back from Italy six years ago. He accepted my invitation to my dinner.

Wycross naturally arrived on time, as he knew my expectation for punctuality. While waiting for the others to arrive, we reminisced about our time in Egypt and discussed what happened to my men.

"Have you kept track of the men in our old regiment," Wycross asked.

"Most are no longer in the Army," I said.

Our colleagues indeed had either left the service or were forced out in the Army reduction. I really didn't care to talk about the men I had led in Egypt; I wanted to know how he was doing and how was the Tenth. My first combat mission was with the Tenth in Siberia: such excellent men.

"The Tenth," I said, "was a great division."

"Not anymore, sir," he said. "The division is barely at half-strength. Equipment isn't being replaced, fuel's hard to come by, morale is bad and getting worse."

But as bad as his story was, I had a feeling that he was hiding something even worse. However, before he could tell me any more, Mike Waverly and his wife arrived. Carrie Waverly was a stunning woman, quite a bit younger than her husband. Her carefully cut blonde hair framed a smiling face with near-perfect features.

We stood around chatting about trivia. Mike and Carrie had a gift when it came to small talk. Finally Colonel Eva Micklebridge and her husband Karl arrived. They were late, and we had just decided to start dinner without them. Eva and Karl didn't look at each other. I sensed tension between them and that Eva was putting on a brave face.

I ushered my guests to the table. As we sat and quietly talked amongst ourselves, the meal progressed and the talk became more serious. I remember we discussed the upcoming elections, the riots in Atlanta, and the dismal state of readiness of the armed forces. I was impressed with Carrie Waverly's encyclopedic recall of every congressional race in New York State. She was a politician's wife to the core. Mike was going to run for Governor of New York.

Mike had been doing his homework on me, and it was he who bought up the subject of my current lack of prospects.

"I'm being wasted here at West Point," I said. "I can do more for my country. There must be order in the streets so citizens can feel safe again."

I had also done my homework: this was the same sentiment that Mike Waverly had expressed in his election campaign for mayor of Albany. We understood each other.

The others silently listened to us.

"If Governor Cole wins next year's presidential race," Mike said, "things will change for the better. We can always use a man of clear thinking."

Mike Waverly and Martin Cole, ex-financier and current Governor of Pennsylvania, were political allies as well as close friends.

First, Mike wanted me to get out of West Point and back into the mix. He knew the senior senator from California well enough that he expected she would lose her re-election bid. He figured that no one could survive the numerous food-ration scandals that swirled around her. The guy who might just take her seat from her, he said, was someone I had rescued from the Los Angeles Riot. He assured me that I would be remembered favorably by the winner of the election and that I should leave everything to him. He knew how to make things happen for good people, he said, and he would have something for me in a matter of days of the election.

I nodded my appreciation. The dinner was a success. Now, I had to wait to see if Mike's wheels rolled smoothly or whether they became stuck in the Army's mud.

Three months later, I received a letter from the Army Personnel

Department. I was to return to the World-Watch Operations Center in Fayetteville, North Carolina. Because of Mike's influence and a glowing recommendation from the Commandant of West Point, I finally got some action. The next assignment was not all that I had hoped for but it was a start. I suspected that if I proved myself useful there would be better ones in the future—possible even a promotion. The Army owed me a general's star.

I reported for duty that winter. My quiet life had ended.

– Chapter 4 –

Fayetteville

The World-Watch Operations Center in Fayetteville focused on what was going on in the world. I was given the command of the Asia Department. It was not a large or important department anymore. The Navy had closed its base at Diego Garcia because of budget cuts, and there was chaos in Japan and a revolution in the Philippines, once our staunchest allies in the Pacific, but no more. The United States lost interest in Asia. China had its own internal problems and was no longer considered a threat. I wondered if the Chinese were thinking the same about us.

I had no experience in Asian affairs. So why was I given this department? Simple Army expediency. The previous department head had retired and no one wanted to be the head of such an unimportant department; so I was slotted in. It was the best I could obtain. I had a small staff of ten people: my deputy, an intelligence officer, two image interpreters, three satellite operators, and two administrative staff and a computer interface technician. This was quite a change from teaching hundreds of students at West Point or commanding a front-line regiment in Egypt. Nevertheless, I was in the midst of events again—or at least no longer completely out of them.

My small staff was competent and the department ran smoothly. During the first few months, I had little contact with my commander. Her focus was entirely on events in America—but that now changed.

My intelligence officer asked for a staff meeting to brief me on some unsettling events in India. The meeting was held in my office, with two other officers who were image interpreters.

The three officers entered and saluted smartly. Their uniforms were crisp and spotless. I had quickly stamped out the informality that my predecessor had permitted to creep in. I returned the salute and permitted them to sit.

"Colonel," my intelligence officer said. "There are some interesting developments in India. With your permission, sir, we will start the briefing."

The first image interpreter stood up and turned on the wall-screen. An image of central India appeared on the screen. The tiny woman pulled out a pointer from her pocket and pointed to the image. She could barely reach the image.

"This is central India," she said.

The young woman seemed nervous. She touched the image and it slowly zoomed in on India's west-central region.

"These are the two regions of India affected," she said. "The river here between them is the Tapti River, or rather it was."

The river before us on the screen was completely dried up. For the third year in a row the monsoons had missed the western coast of India and had tracked northward through the Bay of Bengal instead of northeastward through the Arabian Sea. The Tapti River was the principal source of water for the entire Tapti Valley—a significant source of crops for the west-central region including the city of Mumbai. The Narmada River to the north was now running very shallow and would likely dry up within two or three weeks. There were probably more than three hundred million people relying on these two rivers for food and water, now that the underground aquifers were depleted.

She touched the screen and the imaged zoomed in on a city north of the Narmada River.

"This is the city of Indore," she said. "Population nine million. The image was taken three days ago. Here is today's image."

She touched the screen and the city was obscured by smoke. She moved the pointer and the computer deleted the smoke from the image. The city was on fire—not various parts of the city, but the entire city. She moved to the next image.

"Here is the city of Mumbai," she said, "and its outlying satellite cities of Thane and Ulhasnagar. Total population is forty-five million."

There were fires everywhere. She zoomed in to focus on lines of refugees that were pouring northward along the coast.

This is far worse than Los Angeles, I thought in horror.

When she had finished her presentation, she sat down. On cue, the other image interpreter rose to his feet. The tall, lanky, bespectacled man had no problem reaching the screen. He touched its surface and the image of pathetic refuges disappeared. A map of east-central India appeared in its place. In a deep, booming voice, he started his presentation.

"We are seeing some extraordinary military movements," he said, "in the states of Andhra Pradesh, Chhattisgarh, Orissa and the eastern half of Madhya Pradesh."

He touched the screen and the imaged zoomed in on a road filled with military trucks.

"This is the main road north from Jabalpur," he said. "These are elements of India's Third Armored and Twelfth and Fourteenth Infantry divisions."

As we could see, they were heading north—not south or west, which was what one would expect if they were going to restore order in Indore.

Next he moved to another image.

"These are the bridges," he said, "across the Mahanadi River at Sambalpur. Elements of the Twenty-seventh Infantry Division are turning southwest towards Cuttack."

He slid the image northward.

"Here are some movements," he said, "on the main highway to Calcutta. Mixed elements of the Fourth and Fifth Armored, and Fourth, Eighth and Twenty-sixth Infantry are moving northward."

Just then there was a knock at the door and one of the satellite operators entered. He whispered into my intelligence officer's ear and handed him a piece of paper. Reading the paper, he looked astonished.

"This is new information," he said, "but it confirms my analysis."

He touched the screen and a downward-looking image of a fleet of helicopters appeared.

"These are elements," he explained, "of the elite First Air Mobile Division near..."

He referred to the piece of paper.

"Kanpura," he added.

By my reckoning, the number of helicopters we were looking at was most, if not all of the helicopter assets of the division. We watched the image in silence. The troop-carriers landed while the attack helicopters circled. A group of helicopters moved off to the north. My intelligence officer instructed the screen to track them as the choppers launched a barrage of missiles at a complex, the headquarters for India's IV Corps.

"Sir," he said, "all the active divisions here have men from the central states of India, including the First Air Mobile Division. This is the opening move of a civil war."

By his analysis, he concluded that the objective of the eastern force was Calcutta and the western force was driving up the Ganges Valley to attack Delhi.

To me the scenario was somehow familiar. All this activity centered on a great river. It was Egypt all over again.

"Captain," I said, "I agree with you that there will be a drive to

Calcutta, but the western force is too small to take Delhi."

The force was attempting to hold at Kanpura. The objective wasn't to take cities—it was to take the Ganges River. The war was about water.

He looked thoughtfully and then adjusted the screen show to all of India. He pondered new possibilities. Then he instructed the screen to show symbols of the two forces, major roads, principal cities and principal rivers. The thickness of the river was scaled to current volume of flow. The lines representing the rivers Ganges in the east and Indus in Pakistan to the west were thick. These rivers were choked with meltwater from the Himalayan Mountains. There had been serious flooding over the last decade. The lines representing the rivers to the south were thin or dotted (to represent dried-up rivers). The picture was startlingly clear: there were inadequate supplies of water in central and southern India to support the half-billion people who lived there.

Finally, thanking him and the two lieutenants for the presentation, I dismissed them. I then made an urgent appointment with my commanding officer. The general in charge sat and listened, but her mind was elsewhere. Events in faraway India didn't concern her. She was dealing with demands for images and interpretation regarding the devastation of Oklahoma City by twin super-tornadoes, both F5-plus in strength and coming within four hours of each other. She was also dealing with an armed standoff in Miami between the Army and Caribbean refugees from Hurricane Leslie, the first Category Six hurricane. I tried to stress the seriousness of the situation, but she wasn't really interested.

For three weeks, the only Americans concerned with events in India were my group, a few low-level officials in the State Department and some analysts in the Central Intelligence Agency. We watched with surreal detachment as the battles ebbed and flowed. Calcutta fell easily, but Kanpura and Patna were reduced to ruins through constant fighting. Kanpura fell that week and the Army of the New Central Indian States (as it now called itself) started its drive towards Delhi. It was then that the world's attention focused immediately on India.

I was walking back to my home after a long day when I received a call on my wrist phone. The speaker shouted excitedly: "They've nuked Hyderabad!"

I ran back to my office. My officers joined me moments later. We had the main screen divided into quarters, showing various scenes. The one in the upper left caught my attention immediately. It was an oblique view of several spreading nuclear mushroom clouds. Nothing like this had been seen since the ban on above ground testing a hundred years ago.

I called my general and informed her. Moments later, she was in my office staring at the screen. For over a hundred years, mankind had managed not to use such weapons, and now in a moment of panic and desperation some faction within the rump of the Indian government had attacked its own people. Hyderabad and its satellite city of Secunderabad were gone. The principal city of the central Indian rebels was destroyed. I now had my commanding officer's full attention. She immediately called the Pentagon from my office. We were summoned to a briefing that would take place early the next morning.

Over the next few hours, through a tragic comedy of miscommunications, the situation became worse.

* * *

I arrived at the Pentagon with my general early before the break of dawn. We made our way to the main briefing room of the Joint Chiefs of Staff. We waited in the large room in silence. A sergeant arranged our presentation material and prepared the main and secondary screens for us. One by one, others entered the room. There was little talking. The National Security Advisor and the Secretary of Defense entered the room together. They both looked deeply troubled. No one had slept that night.

The meeting began immediately. Around the table were the top military and intelligence brass, representatives from the White House, Homeland Security, and the State Department. The representative from the State Department and I were by far the most junior people in the meeting. We expected to say nothing; we were only there to provide detailed technical information to our respective bosses, if asked.

"Let's see it," the National Security Advisor said.

My commander pressed a few buttons on the console before her and the main screen showed a replay of the numerous nuclear mushroom clouds growing over Hyderabad.

"This is an image of Hyderabad seven hours ago," she said. "We estimate the total yield to be ten megatons, plus or minus. They really wanted that city destroyed."

"Number of dead," the White House adviser asked.

"Five million from the initial detonation," she said. "Another five million within a week or two, and another two million in a year or so … although we are still refining the estimates."

"What assets do we have in the area," someone asked.

"Two missile frigates and the mini-carrier," someone said. "The ships are visiting Perth, Australia. We also have an attack sub patrolling in the Gulf of Bengal."

"That's it," the Secretary of Defense said.

A Navy admiral present just shrugged.

"How the hell are we supposed to intervene," the Secretary of Defense said.

He knew as well as the rest of us that a full-scale nuclear war would produce fallout that would reach our west coast. The situation in California was already bad enough without fallout there.

"Everything depends on how the Pakistanis will respond," the National Security Advisor said. "Have we made contact with them yet?"

The Assistant Secretary of State looked puzzled and quietly conferred with an aide.

"No, not yet," he said.

The aide beside her looked completely bewildered.

"Are you asleep over at State? Get on to it!" the Secretary of Defense shouted.

"What assurances can we give the Pakistanis," the White House adviser asked. "Can we stop them from retaliating?"

"I doubt it," the Secretary of Defense said. "We'd retaliate immediately."

"It's not in Pakistan's interest to do anything," a general said. "Why would they start something over this internal India affair?"

The Secretary of Defense's face turned bright red.

"Internal!" he said. "I'm sure five million Pakistanis don't see it that way. Keep your opinions to something you know about."

The penny then dropped. I had to speak out.

"It's clear," I said, "we are not all talking about the same city."

The nuclear attack, I explained, was launched on Hyderabad in the central Indian state of Andhra Pradesh—not Hyderabad in southern Pakistan. It was, in my opinion, the final, desperate act of a civil war between northern and central Indian forces. Hyderabad was the headquarters of the central Indian forces.

The entire atmosphere of the room changed. Two-thirds of the people in the room looked visibly relieved. I remember hearing a sigh of relief from someone off to my left. The Secretary of Defense sheepishly offered an apology. People talked rapidly amongst themselves.

The meeting settled back to order then.

"Obviously," the National Security Advisor said, "some of us have not received the correct information."

He assured us that he would get to the bottom of how the information became mixed up later. For now, he asked that we provide him with a quick briefing of what was going on in India.

The committee finally decided that we should not and could not intervene militarily. Our submarine in the Bay of Bengal was to be hastily withdrawn. The White House would make some offers of aid to the stricken and dying citizens of Hyderabad, and then let India sort out its own problems.

* * *

Over the next few months, my group continued to watch developments in India. The desperate nuclear attack had achieved what the northern Indians had wanted. The central Indian forces, with their command structure vaporized, were thrown in to disarray. The drive on Delhi faltered and then failed. Almost immediately civilians panicked: the population of the north feared a reprisal attack, while the population of the central states feared a repeat performance. Riots spread to most cities, including ones in southern India that had so far been spared. Organized fighting continued up and down the length of the Ganges Valley for a while, but then divisions and regiments started to act independently. The command structure for both armies disintegrated. To make matters worse, millions of refugees from Bangladesh's flooded lands took advantage of the vacuum in organized authority to move into northeast India. My small group watched these events from a safe distance. As the initial interest by the politicians waned, we were left to ourselves. No one asked for briefings—not even my commander.

One day in December I received a tantalizing call from the Deputy Director of Intelligence at the CIA. I had met Bryan Cressy briefly at the Pentagon meeting on the nuclear attack on Hyderabad. His call sounded urgent, but Cressy refused to elaborate over the satellite video-phone. He asked for a private conversation and insisted on a secure land-line. I had no idea why he was calling me directly. It was certainly outside the normal communication pathway. I left my office and went to the secure communication room. I informed the officer-in-charge that I had a call coming through and ordered him to make the arrangements. I put on the headset and waited.

Five minutes later, I heard Cressy's voice.

"Colonel," he said, "there's a situation developing that I'd like you to monitor. For reasons I can't elaborate on, this request must be unofficial and outside the normal command chain."

"Go right ahead, sir," I said. "I'll certainly hear you out."

"Fine then," he said. "This is nothing that is outside your operational sphere, and if you notice anything you can brief your commander. I just want you to brief me first on whatever you find."

"You have my word, sir."

A colonel who wants to become a general doesn't unnecessarily disappoint a powerful man when that man asks him for a favor. What he was asking me for was outside operational protocol, but I was willing to hear him out.

"Colonel," he said, "what I'm about to tell you must remain between you and me. I've a private contact within the Australian government."

His contact was in communication with someone high up in the Indonesian Theocracy whose leader, Ayatollah Pemalang, was apparently growing concerned about a military coup. The information suggested that he might be planning something drastic to counter it. For reasons no one yet understood, the Australians were very worried about this development. Cressy wanted us to take a really close look at what was happening on the ground in Indonesia.

His request was not unreasonable and within my operational mandate, so I agreed.

I returned to my office and called in one of the satellite operators. I ordered him to download all images of Indonesia over the past week to my office computer and to send me daily updates. I wanted both regional and local images. Over the next two weeks, I poured over hundreds of images, both photographic and video. I enjoyed the hands-on work. The island of Sumatra was quiet, but on the main island of Java food riots were occurring in most major cities. The city of Bandung was in flames. There was a long line of refugees heading northwest towards Jakarta. I searched for any response by the military, but I could only find a handful of military units on Java. It was not until I examined the images from Indonesia's smaller eastern islands of Bali, Lombok and Sumbawa that I found the bulk of the Indonesian Army. There were large military camps surrounding the airports on these three islands. At the airports themselves long lines of aircraft sat in orderly lines. This was not unusual since the collapse of international travel, but it was strange that military and civilian aircraft were mixed together, and it was highly unusual that the aircraft were being refueled. Clearly, the Indonesians were going to use these aircraft. But for what?

I studied the images and watched the activity. Units were training; planes were being maintained. I didn't understand until I hit the zoom-out button by mistake. There, in the bottom-right corner was the northern coast of Australia. In a flash it came to me: invasion! I immediately placed a call to Bryan Cressy. I told him that I had something, and again he insisted on secure communications. I went to the secure communication room and was soon talking to him.

I told him about the strange troop placements and the activity around the airports.

"There are only two possibilities," I said.

Either the Indonesian Army was going to fly those planes to another part of Indonesia as part of a coup, or they were going to invade another country. The former option was unlikely as the operations were too overt. The latter was more likely and the prime target, in my opinion, was Australia. It has food, at least on its east coast. Australian grain production had not suffered as badly as ours or China's.

"That wily old ayatollah," Cressy said. "If he wins, he is a hero and keeps his people happy. If he loses, he gets rid of most of the military and keeps power by default. Thank you, Colonel."

In my general's office, I briefed her on my findings, but not on my conversations with Cressy. She listened attentively and then dismissed me with orders to monitor the situation. I went back to my office and called my group together. I explained our new priority. I was no longer working alone on the analysis of images from Indonesia.

Christmas Eve the Indonesians stirred themselves. We had just finished our meager Christmas office luncheon party, when my intelligence officer rushed back into the room.

"The Indonesians are airborne," he said.

We all rushed back to the satellite imaging room. The satellite was operating in night-vision mode and there was a slight greenish tint to the images. The aircraft were taking off.

"Which airport is that," I asked.

"Matarm," he said.

"Let's see what is happening at Denpasar," I said.

The technician operated the controls and another image appeared. More aircraft were taking off.

"Where are they heading," I asked.

My officer pushed some buttons and the computer projected its prediction of the flight paths. The many lines headed southeast—in a direct line to the fertile southeast corner of Australia.

I left the room and made a direct call to Cressy's private number on my wrist phone.

"Our friends are up," I said. "Destination as expected,"

Cressy thanked me, but said nothing more. I then headed to my general's office. She had left for the day, so I had the sergeant-on-duty locate her. Once the sergeant had found her, I spoke to her briefly via video-phone. She listened without interruption and then ordered me to continue monitoring the situation. I sensed that there was much more going on than I was aware of.

Events unfolded quickly. The first wave of civilian-marked aircraft tried to land at the airport at Brisbane and Canberra. They were swiftly shot down. After that, the Indonesians abandoned landing at airports. They started to drop soldiers by old-fashion parachutes—at least one hundred thousand in the first wave alone. The airports at Brisbane and Newcastle were quickly captured, but those at Sydney and Canberra held out for hours. After the first wave had captured the airports, the follow-up aircraft landed. They discharged their solders and supplies and returned to Indonesia. Many aircraft were shot down. The attacks on Adelaide and Melbourne were defeated. The Australians started to hold their ground. Their government moved rapidly and efficiently from Canberra to Melbourne. It was clear that the Australians were ready for the onslaught—or at least as ready as they could be. During the first week, the Indonesians consolidated their hold on areas north of Canberra and received regular supplies from Indonesia. However a vicious counterattack by the Australians driving north from Melbourne and the brutal Battle of Bombala ended the supply flights. We watched in amazement as the aircraft remained motionless at the Indonesian airports. By this time nearly half a million Indonesian soldiers were in Australia. Once it became clear that an easy victory was not going to happen, their government abandoned them. It was as Bryan Cressy predicted: Ayatollah Pemalang had solved his problem of a potential military coup.

Over the next few months, the abandoned Indonesian solders lost cohesion. Armed bands pillaged and looted the cities and countryside. Only in Brisbane to the north did the Indonesian command retain some control. The Australians, weakened from the initial battles, could do little to dislodge the enemy. Sydney lay in ruins, and the land from Canberra to Newcastle was a no-man's land covered with the blood of Australians and Indonesians.

Back in Indonesia, the theocracy's iron grip weakened. The population, led by relatives of the lost soldiers, finally overthrew the theocracy after four decades of suffocating rule. Chaos and anarchy reigned. The few remaining soldiers in Indonesia fought armed clerics on one side and starving civilians on the other. The wily ayatollah fled the capital and escaped into the highlands of northern Sumatra. He disappeared from history. It seems God (or the Devil) looks after His own.

However, all this happened when the activities in Asia were no longer my concern. In early January President Cole was sworn in, and in late January I was promoted to brigadier general. I had my general's star at last.

– Chapter 5 –

England

I was sent to the Command and General Staff College at Fort Leavenworth, Kansas, for my mandatory command training. The old buildings were run down and in desperate need of repair, but I didn't care. The training material was interesting, the teachers were engaging, and my general's star was shiny and bright.

I had been provided with an old but well-appointed house on the base, and I had a driver, a chef and a maid. They were retired soldiers who were paid a pittance by the Army, but for them life was better (and safer) inside the base than outside. For me, life had taken a definite upswing. I was delighted about it all.

I spent six pleasant months training at Fort Leavenworth, but I was impatient for my first command. I hoped it would be an armored brigade. I heard rumors that the commander of the 15th Urban Brigade was soon to retire. The 8th Armored Brigade might also become available. As it turned out, neither was offered to me. The Army dusted off my liaison qualifications and assigned me to the upcoming international summit on world security. It was not what I had hoped for, but nevertheless it was very prestigious. I was to accompany top military chiefs on the President's trip to the summit. It was to be held in Birmingham, England, in the latter half of July, and was planned to be the largest meeting of world leaders ever in years.

The day of departure finally arrived. I was looking forward to the trip. I boarded the small Air Force jet at the base's decrepit airport and left for Washington. The air-conditioned cabin was a welcomed relief from the suffocating heat blanketing Kansas. The flight was uneventful and we soon arrived at Andrews Air Force Base outside Washington. I entered a larger plane, which would take me to England. It carried the cream of the military. Across the aisle from me sat a rear-admiral; in front of him were a Marine major general and his aide. At the very front of the plane sat the Chairman of the Joint Chiefs of Staff and the new commander of the Army. When I maneuvered down the aisle past them, they were deep in conversation, whispering in low tones and nodding gravely. Both men looked old and haggard.

Air Force One slowly taxied past my window, gleaming in the setting sun. Onboard were President Cole and his entourage. Once Air Force One had taken off, our plane moved towards the runway and headed into the evening sky.

The flight over the Atlantic Ocean was swift, as there was a strong tailwind pushing us along, and was uneventful except for a few minutes of bone-shaking turbulence over Ireland. The landing however was very unsettling. We had arrived over Birmingham before dawn. The darkness outside the window was lit only by the airplane's lights reflecting off thick clouds. Streaks of rain ran horizontally across the window. The pilot informed us that he expected strong turbulence as we landed.

He had said some turbulence earlier, but now he said strong turbulence. I didn't like the sound of that.

But what could one do?

The airplane bucked wildly. Up and down; side to side. I don't know how the wings stayed on. It was the worst turbulence that I had ever experienced in my many years of airplane travel. The rear-admiral threw up. I confess that I nearly did as well. Without warning there was a mighty bump. The plane lifted sharply and a then a moment later there was a second, smaller bump. We had landed. I let out an audible sigh. The others beside me looked as white as a sheet.

As the airplane taxied to the airport gate, I took my first look at England. The rain was pouring down. What would the farmers back in Kansas give for all this rain? The bright yellow lights of the airport pierced the gloom. They looked welcoming.

We left the plane and were greeted by the military of the European Union. They ushered us to a line of buses. I was surprised to notice as I entered the bus that it was armored. The bus looked normal from a distance, but up close there were the telltale signs of armor plating. No doubt the windows were bulletproof. Our bus started off and we left the airport in a convoy with armored personnel carriers escorting us. The English were either expecting trouble or were just being cautious—I hoped the latter was the case. For the first time, I felt uneasy.

I was surprised to discover that we had landed at Cosford Air Force Base on the west side of the city. Prior to departure, I had been informed that we would land at Birmingham International Airport on the east side, but as we stepped on to the bus we were told of the change in the itinerary. It was part of a security misinformation campaign by the English to deter (or at least delay) the arrival of the inevitable protesters. Officially, we were to land at Birmingham International Airport and hold the summit at the nearby National Exhibition Center. In actuality, the politicians were to hold their half of the summit at Weston Park Hall, four miles north of the Air Force base, while the military were to hold their half at Himley Hall, ten miles south of the base. The two old estates, with their stone walls and extensive, open grounds, were far easier to secure than the crowded, urban setting of the exhibition complex.

When we arrived at Himley Hall, we were greeted by a representative of the English state government. After receiving my information package, an orderly led me to my assigned quarters. I was lucky to be in the house itself. Aides and other low-ranking officers were in trailers on the grounds. My room, however, was on the top floor in the old servant quarters. It was microscopic in size with a sharply sloping ceiling (on which I banged my head several times). The bed was comfortable. I had slept in worse conditions.

* * *

My official role at the summit was as chief liaison officer for all American forces (including Marine, Navy and Air Force). The aides of various generals and admirals reported to me, and briefed me on the informational needs of their commanders. I arranged off-line meetings between our officers and officers of other countries. I also worked with my European counterpart on the flow of information between the politicians at Weston Park Hall and the military at Himley Hall. He held the rank of brigadier (the European equivalent to my rank of brigadier general).

Attendance at the conference was disappointing. America and the European Union were well represented, as were Canada and New Zealand. But Australia, fighting for its life against the abandoned Indonesian Army, sent only its apologies. In contrast, the United Republic of Korea sent a sizable delegation as did the Moscova Republic. South Africa was the only African nation present. There was no one attending from the ruins of the Middle East. India sent two foreign ministers: one from the north and one from the New Central Indian States. This made for some awkward moments. China sent a small staff of low-level officials, as did Siberia. Japan continued in its isolation and sent no one. The Argentinean president arrived only to find that he had been deposed in a coup while he was in the air. The two generals accompanying him rapidly disappeared. No other Latin American country managed to send anyone. That was it.

One day, halfway through the summit, I was sitting in The Ewe House, a makeshift pub on the grounds, with a Canadian brigadier general. We carefully nursed our half-pints of beer while waiting for the arrival of a few colleagues.

"Just got back from Weston Park Hall," a British brigadier announced in an exaggerated flourish when he sat down. He then told us his news.

He had been sitting at the back of the summit room when a short, gaunt man in shabby clothes entered who claimed to be the foreign minister of the country of São Tomé and Príncipe, a tiny island group off the west coast of Africa. How he managed to make it to England was a mystery. But because the man had the appropriate diplomatic credentials and documentation, the guards at the main gate let him in and once inside, he poured out a pitiful tale of rival gangs from Gabon and Equatorial Guinea invading his county. According to him, the armed gangs had mistakenly heard that the islands had vast stores of chocolate and sugar. When they found only fields of withered cocoa plants, they burnt the crops and slaughtered the people. There was nothing left alive on the small island of Príncipe. On the larger island of São Tomé, some of the citizens had cordoned off the central part of capital and were desperately holding out. The foreign minister begged for help from the other countries at the conference, saying that the invading gangs were eating his people. But no one could verify his account, nor make out the details very clearly so uncontrollably was he sobbing. The translator set missed a lot of his words.

Next, the brigadier said, the British Prime Minister made some vague promises about sending food, and President Cole promised to send ships. But the American admirals exploded profanely when told that they would have to find some ships and the fuel to sail them.

Nothing will get done, I thought.

Just then, a Russian general barged her way into the pub. She had to be the shortest, ugliest woman I ever met, but she was as tough as nails and cunningly bright. I would not like to meet her on a battlefield. She shouted excitedly to us in Russian. We automatically reached behind our ears and turned our translation sets on. It was amazing how small these sets had become. They were a quantum leap from the bulky sets that I had used in Egypt. It struck me as ironic that only now—with the world disintegrating about us—that we could all finally understand each other.

While we were fiddling with our translator sets, the woman sat down and extracted her private flask of vodka from her jacket pocket. She never touched the English beer—whether because she didn't like it or couldn't afford it, I never discovered.

"Have you heard," she asked via the translator set.

"The São Tomé affair," the Canadian said.

"No," she said. "The Chinese situation. The entire south has declared independence. Beijing will have to do something now."

China was disintegrating. When Tibet declared independence a month ago, the Beijing government did nothing. Taiwan was next and still nothing. Last week, it was Hong Kong and the neighboring province of Guangdong. Now, the rest of the southern provinces were in revolt. With the famines in the northwest and in the lower Yangtze and Yellow valleys, China couldn't afford to lose control of any more land, particularly agricultural lands in the still fertile south.

"There will be civil war," I said.

"The Koreans are already at the airport," the Russian said. "Although how they will take off in this wind I don't know. And the Siberians are packing."

"Where are the Chinese delegates" the Canadian asked.

The Russian threw up her arms in an exaggerated gesture.

"Who knows?" she said. "Hidden away. Deciding on sides, I suspect."

Delegates began leaving the conference early. First the Asians, and then the rest. By the last day, only the Europeans, Americans and Canadians remained. President Cole and other heads of state released a rosy statement about how the nations of the world would help each other in this time of international crisis. They pledged food and peacekeeping forces. No one believed them. In America, many large cities were ungovernable and food was in desperately short supply. The Europeans were drowning in torrents of rain, after a bitterly cold winter and a scorching summer the previous year. They were also desperately holding back the flood of refugees from the Middle East streaming into Turkey and the Balkans. Thousands a week were dying in the camps in central Turkey. No, nobody believed the leaders—not even themselves.

* * *

The morning after the summit ended, I left my tiny room and made my way down to the waiting bus that would drive us back to our Air Force Base. The top political leaders and military commanders had left immediately after the summit. All flew out by helicopter. The hordes of protesters made ground travel unsafe for them. For us lower officials, an armored bus with a heavily armed escort would have to do.

I had been very busy before the summit, and my focus had been on world affairs. I had not paid much attention to what was going on just outside the guarded perimeter of Himley Hall. But now congregating about outside the walls were many protesters. I no longer ventured outside the perimeter. When I climbed on board the bus, I assumed everything was under control. I took my seat in the middle of the bus and watched the English soldiers outside make final preparations. All wore armored jackets and riot gear. The convoy finally got underway. The three armored buses were sandwiched between armored fighting vehicles. To the front, there were two urban fighting vehicles of European design and an armored personnel carrier; and to the rear, another set of armored cars. Leading the convoy was a large ten-wheeled tank of a design I had not seen before. I overheard someone behind me say it was a new urban tank with considerable array of armaments for a variety of riot-control situations. He added that our army was considering ordering a hundred of them.

Our convoy pulled away from Himley Hall and headed down the long driveway to the main gate. We drove through the gate without stopping. The mob had been forced away by the two large water-cannons mounted on either side of the gate. We traveled quickly through the village of Himley and into the English countryside. Our route avoided urban areas. Rocks were thrown at our bus, but they bounced off harmlessly. At the Hilton roundabout, when the convoy slowed, someone threw a fire bomb at the bus in front. The urban tank turned its water-cannon on the bus and the fire was quickly dowsed.

Soon after Hilton, we turned right on to a smaller road. It was not until we reached the outskirts of Albrighton (less than a mile from the Air Force Base) that we ran into trouble. This was the only urban area of significance on our route. We moved through deserted streets. All was quiet. The town's shanty buildings were ominously empty. We drove rapidly through its downtown section. Suddenly, there was a large explosion. A derelict four-story office tower collapsed onto the street. The bus driver screeched to a stop—throwing us into the seat in front. When the dust settled, rubble covered the front half of our escort and the lead bus. Our bus and the one behind reversed frantically. The soldiers leaped out from the rear armored car, and fanned out to cover our retreat. The mob appeared from its hiding places. Dozens of fire bombs were thrown at the buses. The surviving armored car opened fire, as did the soldiers. Some in the mob returned fire, but most ran back into the ruined buildings of downtown Albrighton. The armored car and the two buses found a place to turn around and then searched for an alternative route. Our bus's paint and rubber tires were on fire. It became very hot inside the bus and smoke started entering the interior. The bulletproof windows couldn't be opened.

We reached a road block and had to turn around again. By this time, the armored car had collected its soldiers and caught up with us. We drove down another street. An armored vehicle suddenly disappeared into a hidden pit. Its crew scrambled out and ran towards the other vehicle. Shots were fired from the buildings and two of the crew fell dead. With our bus now in the lead, our driver searched for a way out of this nightmare. Another road-block! Bullets bounced off the windows.

The two buses were just about to turn around again, when the road-block burst open. The urban tank had survived the collapsing building and had found us again. I was impressed with both the vehicle and the commander inside. The tank turned its water-cannon on the remnants of our convoy and extinguished the fires. The tank backed out of the ruined road-block and we drove through the gap.

We tore through the streets towards the Air Force base. With the fire out and the mob gone, our driver opened the front and rear doors to vent the smoke. I was considerably relieved when we sped through the main gates of the base. As we entered, half a dozen armored vehicles left the base on their way to rescue any survivors from the front half of our convoy. It turned out that of all the officials in the front bus, only an admiral survived. He had been covered with rubble and not noticed by the mob

It was a complete debacle. The organizers of the convoy should have been court-martialed, but our drivers and escorts should have received commendations for their exemplary performance. They saved us all.

As for myself, I was unhurt and unaffected by the event. I had seen combat before. What a world this had become!

– Chapter 6 –

Fort Drum

In October of the following year all my career aspirations were fulfilled. I drove through the main gates of Fort Drum in upstate New York as the commander of the Tenth Infantry Division.

I was now promoted to the rank of a two-star major general in command of a combat division after serving as a brigadier general for just over a year. I was well connected in the Cole administration. Hidden wheels had turned.

My orders regarding my new command were simple: fix it. The Tenth was broken—actually, shattered was a better description. Its ex-commander had been corrupt. Under his command, black-marketing of food and fuel had run free—much to the financial gain of the ex-commander. He even had a protection racket going that terrorized the surrounding civilian communities. He had been a little too successful and therefore too noticeable. In one of the Army's frequent anti-corruption purges, the Army made an example of the ex-commander. He had been court-martialed and sent to a penal regiment as a private and a laborer. I would have had him shot for the shame he brought to my division.

One night, a week before I officially took command, I met secretly with Captain Wycross. He had been with the Tenth since after Egypt. The double stigmas of the retreat from Egypt and now being associated with the Tenth had condemned him from ever being promoted or transferred.

We met in a hotel room in Syracuse, south of Watertown. I offered him a way to become the soldier he always wanted to be. In return, I expected absolute loyalty and complete honesty. Sean Wycross saw his way out and took it. He talked throughout the night about what happened, how it started, and more importantly who could be trusted and who could not. As for his own involvement in the fort's corruption, he told me some of the things he had done. He had followed orders given by his commanders, as had most in the division. A few officers and men had stood up to the corrupt commander and his cronies, but they had been quickly sent off to the penal regiment that was part of the Tenth. Wycross expressed his shame at not being one of those who had tried to do something. He was torn between obeying orders and obeying his conscience, as have many soldiers throughout history. His training won out and he obeyed his orders. I accepted his word and didn't press the matter further. I needed someone on the inside to trust. I judged that no matter what Wycross had done for his old commander, he would be loyal to me. I was fully justified in that conviction.

When I entered Fort Drum, I didn't come alone. The Army provided me with the 1st Infantry Regiment as my support troops. The soldiers of this regiment were once part of the now-disbanded First Infantry Division. That division had been smashed in the battles around Pretoria when the United States pulled its last embassy out of Africa four years ago. With its command structure gone and casualties of over eighty percent, the First Infantry Division had effectively ceased to exist. The surviving battle-hardened veterans had been combined into the 1st Infantry Regiment. This elite regiment had been posted to various bases by the Army and was now to be permanently incorporated into the Tenth. In the future, it would serve as a model for what I planned to do with the rest of the Tenth, but for now it was to serve as my police force and bodyguard.

I led the 1st Infantry through the gate and to the command center. I arrested some officers on the spot and immediately released others from the penal regiment. There was no resistance; everyone had either accepted their fate or had deserted soon after the arrest of the corrupt commander. For the rest, I called an assembly of all available officers and men on the parade field. The division was woefully under strength, so only nine thousand men faced me when I gave them the same offer that I had given Captain Wycross. Most of the men looked relieved.

Over the next week morale noticeably improved. I started a physical training program that was brutal by any Army measure for officers and men. I didn't want anyone to have the leisure to think about the past. I felt obliged to participate as often as I could. It was strenuous exercise, but I have never before or since been so fit. I promoted a healthy competition between men of the 1st Infantry Regiment and the rest of the division as to who were the toughest soldiers.

The Army had given me some broad powers, so I used them. I immediately promoted Wycross to major. Some of the officers who had stood up to the commander also received promotions. I demanded of the Army Personnel Department that certain other officers be transferred to the Tenth. Major Joyita, then at a dull post in the Pentagon, I promoted to lieutenant colonel and put him in charge of the division's administration. I brought in several promising officers I had known in my days as Assistant Registrar at West Point. It wasn't as simple as it sounds, but over the next several months the old division was made anew.

In mid December, I announced to the men that the division was returning to its old name: the Tenth Mountain Division. Before the bureaucrats at the Pentagon would approve the re-designation, I had to promise them that I would not be asking for any additional supplies. The Tenth Mountain was still to be classed as a light infantry division with no special mountain fighting capabilities. I only changed the name—but it was an important change for the men. Formal acceptance of the new designation didn't arrive on my desk until February—long after everyone on the base had forgotten that there ever was a Tenth Infantry. Every use of the name Tenth Infantry on the base was either covered over or removed. On New Years Eve, the old sign over the main gate with the previous name was ceremoniously burned on the parade field. I threw it onto the bonfire myself. It was an important symbolic gesture. For the men, their time with the Tenth Infantry was in the past. The Tenth Infantry gave them nothing but shame; the Tenth Mountain would give them back their pride.

With morale improving and the division back on its feet, I had time to devote my attention to three other problems: the penal regiment, the alarming supply shortages and our dreadful relations with the surrounding communities. Eventually, after a lot of hard work and long hours, I managed to solve all three.

I had inherited the 10th Penal Regiment, as did my predecessor. As hard as I tried, I couldn't get the Army to take it off my hands. I was stuck with it. Like the commander before me, I used it for my own purposes; unlike him, I used it to strengthen, not destroy, the division. I brought in an effective team of two army psychiatrists. I met with them in my office and gave them a single specific task. I wanted them to sort the prisoners into four categories: intelligent and dangerous, intelligent but not dangerous, unintelligent and dangerous, and unintelligent but not dangerous. These were not professional psychiatric categories, but they knew what I wanted.

My plan (which I later adopted) was to make the unintelligent-not-dangerous group into laborers with minimal supervision, while the unintelligent-and-dangerous group would be kept under heavy guard in the base's prison. The men in the intelligent-but-not-dangerous group would be offered a release on the condition that they agreed to be integrated into the division's regular regiments. It was the intelligent-and-dangerous group, by far the smallest group, on which I focused my attention. I formed them into the 1st Special Support Unit. Later, this unit became infamous as the dreaded SSU; however, initially they were formed to do dangerous tasks that I didn't want to assign to my regular soldiers. I wanted to challenge their intellects and provide a focus for their abnormal behavior. I put them under command of a tough officer from the 1st Infantry Regiment, Major Kal Khanan. I had hoped that he would influence them, but it turned out that the opposite occurred. "Killer" Khanan, as he was known, was a cunning but brutal officer. His experiences in Johannesburg had twisted him in ways not easily noticed on the surface. In hindsight, maybe I should have had the psychiatrists assess Khanan prior to giving him the command, but if I had done so I would have lost a valuable tool. Khanan and the SSU provided me with effective ways to deal with difficult situations.

The supply situation (my second problem) was dismal. There were constant food shortages, and fuel supplies for the vehicles were nonexistent. I could do little about the lack of fuel, but I could mitigate the food situation somewhat. I encouraged soldiers and their families to start private garden plots, an activity prohibited by my predecessor, who wanted to control the food supplies. As time went by, our food stocks slowly increased. A mild winter meant that our first harvest in April was good, but early summer crops failed from the heat.

Water supply and lack of irrigation equipment were continual problems. I battled with the bureaucrats in the International Joint Commission for Great Lakes Water Resources. Since the disastrous summer, the commission had the last word on the use of the waters of the Great Lakes, but so much water was taken from the Great Lakes for irrigation that lake levels dropped alarmingly. It became impossible for the ships carrying European grain to the Midwest to sail up the St. Lawrence River, thereby worsening the food shortages. Whenever the St. Clair and Niagara rivers dried up, the hydro power stations along the Niagara River had to be shut down. The commission had to juggle all the competing demands for the waters of the Great Lakes: now precipitation levels were low, evaporation was high, there was no winter runoff, and illegal siphoning was rampant. I got nowhere with the commission, so Fort Drum had to make do with its barely-adequate allocation.

On a second front, I permitted soldiers with farming families nearby to help out on their farms. For other soldiers, I asked for volunteers to work for up to three days per week on farms in Jefferson County. Those who volunteered were exempted from training on the days they worked on the farms. Given my harsh training regime, there was no shortage of volunteers. My soldiers provided the farmers both labor and security from the gangs that roamed the area, offering welcome security—not the protection racket that the ex-commander had run. In return, the farmers paid the division in food.

Over time, this relationship with the local farmers helped reduce the bad feelings for the soldiers of the Tenth among the citizens of Watertown and Jefferson County. As the citizens came to understand the changes that I had enacted, relations improved. To further help with community relations, I set up a security liaison committee involving the Sheriff's Department, the local office of the State Police, security forces of the nearby First Guard Division, and my own military police battalion. Initially, this was simply an information-sharing committee, and it worked wonders in reducing misunderstandings. All of these groups came under my direct command. My earlier work allowed for a smooth transition.

One problem that I couldn't overcome was the supply of fuel. With the chaos in the Middle East and South America, the only supplies of oil that were available to America came from Alaska and western Canada—and only by tanker ship. The faster overland pipelines had been abandoned when their foundations disappeared into the vast quagmires formed by the melting permafrost. The reserves in the

Beaufort Sea had long-since peaked and were rapidly in the decline. Oil from the Canadian Tar Sands was available but couldn't keep up with demand. The oil fields in the Gulf of Mexico and the North Sea were depleted, and the Europeans took everything available from Central Asia. Fuel rationing was a way of life. The farmers and freight haulers were allocated most of the fuel, and politicians tried unsuccessfully to keep the civilians happy by giving them some fuel as well. The Army had a fraction of what it needed, and the urban brigades always had priority. The Army put little importance in providing fuel to a disgraced division in an out-of-the-way base in upstate New York. The Navy and Air Force received almost nothing.

To get around the fuel problem, I had to start thinking more broadly. In September I arranged for a divisional training exercise now that the extreme heat of the summer was over. In the spring, we had held a brigade-level exercise and a number of regiment-level exercises, but nothing larger. I had been in command of the division for nearly a year, and in that time we had never worked together as a division.

I was to command the division during an exercise that my deputy commander had designed and organized. He acted as the chief observer and post-exercise analyst of the mock battle. He was one of those officers that the corrupt officers had imprisoned and that I had subsequently released. He was always grateful to me for that. The mock battle involved some of the division's support units acting as an enemy force defending a wide front. I had also some men from the First Guard Division to assist my supporting units in their role as the enemy. Under my command, the rest of my division would attack and hopefully take the objectives. There had to be a considerable number of rules of engagement, but nevertheless it would be a useful exercise.

It was the second day of the three-day exercise. Events were going well—a little too well. While 1st Brigade was pinning down the enemy, I had ordered 317th Cavalry Battalion of 2nd Brigade to swing around the left flank and probe for any weaknesses in the enemy's position. Officially, the 317th was designated a reconnaissance battalion, but in reality few of its scout vehicles were operational. Furthermore, to conserve the division's fuel stocks, I ordered that this exercise was to be executed entirely on foot. There were to be no vehicles or helicopters involved, except for those of the observation staff.

The battalion commander, a woman I had admired for her efficiency, reported that the 317th had successfully moved around the flank of the enemy. The battalion had not only taken its first objective but elements of it were moving on toward its second. I was puzzled as I stared at the map on the wall screen. There was no way her battalion could have covered that distance so soon. The most likely explanation was that she had become lost and confused her objective. It happens all too frequently in spite of the intermittent coverage of old global positioning satellites. When questioned over the radio, she was adamant that the battalion was where she said it was. The force's positioning system agreed with her, so I couldn't disagree. She was insistent that I come out into the field and look for myself. She said that there was something I had to see. Since she was a good officer, I accepted her invitation.

If we had indeed broken through, I needed to act decisively. I ordered my reserves, the 10th Aviation Regiment, to follow after the 317th. The aviators of the 10th Aviation grumbled about slogging through the dusty fields on foot with the rest of the division, but they followed their orders. The purpose of this exercise was to provide simulated combat experience and to form a team spirit within the division. I decided to travel with the aviators. Instinct told me that this was a critical moment in the battle.

With the aviators of the 10th Aviation Regiment, I reached the first objective and found elements of the 317th quietly holding it. A captain of the 317th came up to me and informed me.

"We've taken the second objective," he said, "and are holding while awaiting reinforcements. The battalion commander will meet you there."

Something is going on, I thought.

I continued my march along side the aviators. We reached the second objective without incident. The deputy battalion commander greeted me.

"The general's here," he said into his headset.

Turning to me, then, he said: "The lieutenant colonel has something to show you."

The remainder of the 317th, who were mounted on horses, burst out of the undergrowth. The lieutenant colonel charged toward me, pulled up her horse expertly, hopped off it, and gave the reins to a waiting private. I scanned the surrounding soldiers mounted on their horses. There was something incongruous about soldiers mounted on horses wearing camouflaged jackets and helmets with communication headsets, their rapid-fire rifles slung over their shoulders.

"This is a cavalry battalion," she said.

Explanations would come later. At this moment, the 317th were at attention.

"Congratulations," I said. "You have done well today. We've got the enemy off balance. Now let's crush them."

Her men cheered. I pointed in the general direction of the enemy and ordered the men of the 317th Cavalry and the 10th Aviation to hit the enemy's headquarters and supply depot.

After the men were underway, I took her aside, as she walked beside her horse. I demanded an explanation. With fuel rationed and most of the vehicles non-operational, her battalion had lost mobility. They were reduced to foot patrols and operations.

"Last March," she said, "I inspected a small farm north of the base. They were about to slaughter and eat Bones, my horse."

She patted her horse on his nose. The animal whinnied in appreciation.

"Bones," she said, "looked at me with his big, gentle eyes."

The emaciated horse had won her heart, so she couldn't let it be killed. She offered the owner a trade, the horse in exchange for her help protecting their farm —a security-for-food program. They liked the idea, so they gave her the horse, and she discovered that she liked the mobility that the horse provided. Over time, she made the same arrangement with other farmers. Eventually she acquired enough horses to mount most of her A Company. Volunteers were easy to come by, and what her troopers lacked in riding ability they made up for in enthusiasm. At first it was nothing more than a hobby, but when she heard of my divisional exercise, she thought that she would show me a way to recover the mobility that we had lost. It was a wonderful idea.

I patted the horse. He was a nice, gentle chestnut gelding that responded to my stroking. I was pleased. My division – at least part of it – was mobile again.

The actions of the lieutenant colonel and presence of the horses of the 317th started me on a long process of thinking about mobility in an era of fuel shortages. I had always had a passion for military history, so I began to review historical accounts of armies that had to deal with fuel shortages. I found two interesting examples: the Moscova Republic three decades ago and the Germans way back in the last century. Interestingly, both armies made extensive use of horses and bicycles. With my whole-hearted backing, the battalion commander acquired enough horses to mount the rest of the 317th.

I next turned my attention to the rest of the 2nd Brigade, which was to become the mobile half of my division. My division's supply officer acquired enough bicycles for the entire 14th Regiment. I didn't ask how he did it; I thought it best not to know. The theory was that the regiment would maneuver by bicycle and dismount to fight. The regiment became known as the 14th Mobile.

The 10th Aviation Regiment proved a more difficult problem. The regiment didn't have many operational helicopters left. After agonizing over the decision for many weeks, I finally concluded that the regiment was not sustainable. I disbanded it and in its place created the smaller 110th Aviation Battalion. Two-thirds of the helicopters were dismantled in order to supply parts for the remaining third. This also alleviated my aviation fuel situation somewhat, as we continued to draw supplies for an aviation regiment. The surplus men were transferred to other regiments in the division or sent to train at the Light Fighters Infantry School on the base.

As part of my renewal program for the division, I reopened the specialized training school that my predecessor had closed. From my days at West Point, I understood the positive effect that quality training had on the morale of the men. I ordered the curriculum to have more emphasis on urban fighting. Many of the graduates were posted to the newly formed 10th Urban Assault Battalion—another creation of mine.

Two years after I first took command, the Tenth Mountain Division had once again become a combat-ready division. Morale was high, and the men were confident that the Tenth could do whatever was asked of it—as was I.

– Chapter 7 –

New York City

Once it became apparent that I had gained control of the Tenth Mountain Division, the Army focused its attention on other troubled divisions and I was left alone with my command. The Army never realized what a superb unit I had created, but it would find out.

On the morning of August 15, I was sitting in my office with my deputy, Brigadier General Tuckhoe, Lieutenant Colonel Joyita, my supply officer and the commander of the 10th Urban Assault Battalion. We were working on the requisition paperwork for obtaining more urban tanks for the battalion. The tank was the same ten-wheel urban tank that saved me in England. During my previous assignment in the Army Procurement Office, I worked hard to ensure that this tough, versatile tank would make its way into the Army's inventory. Now as the commander of the Tenth, I had procured three urban tanks for the division's urban assault battalion through an agonizingly bureaucratic process. My efforts were greatly assisted by the fact that I had many contacts in the Army Procurement Office. This second order was for another three of these precious and expensive combat vehicles.

While Joyita was explaining the complex requisition procedure to Tuckhoe, my telephone rang. I snapped up the receiver. My civilian secretary wouldn't have disturbed us unless it was something important.

The efficient-sounding voice of the division's meteorological officer announced that a hurricane was heading our way. It had unexpectedly veered northward and gained in strength from the warm waters of the Atlantic.

Hurricane Nicole was going to hit New York City. At first, it had been predicted to hit South Carolina near the Myrtle Beach area with Category Five strength. Now it was predicted to make landfall on the Delaware coast with Category Six strength. Mexico had been hit by two Category Six hurricanes last year. The destruction had been terrible. The year before that a hurricane had devastated Houston, and several years ago the first of the new Category Six hurricanes had laid waste much of the Caribbean.

The meteorological officer said that the hurricane was gaining in strength, and that it was going to be the first Category Seven hurricane. It was to hit New York City and the adjacent New Jersey and Connecticut coasts. The Weather Center was predicting winds in excess of 190 miles per hour. Gusts, he said, could reach 245 miles per hour or more. The urban canyons in the city would funnel the wind. Winds might reach as high as 300 miles per hour! The storm surge would be at least thirty feet. Probably more.

"When," I asked.

"Eight hours," he said. "Maybe seven."

That meant the storm was moving fast. After New York, it would track right up the Hudson Valley. It would hit Albany and then move north into Canada. By then, it would weaken to a Category One or Two at most. Fort Drum would miss most of it, but would get heavy rain, flooding and destructive winds.

"How bad will it be," I asked.

"You remember what the last one did to Houston," he said. "That was a Six—this one's a Seven. Damage will be geometric."

I was not exactly sure what he meant by "geometric" but it sounded bad. I thanked him for the warning and slowly replaced the receiver in the cradle. There's going to be chaos.

I had to speak to Governor Waverly—personally. And I needed to speak to the Mayor of Watertown and the commander of the First Guard Division. I had my secretary arrange the calls

"Colonel," I said to my supply officer, "I want you to requisition every operational vehicle in the area and as much fuel as you can find."

"But—," he started to say.

"As of this moment," I cut him off, "under the authority granted to me under Article 15 of the 44th Amendment, I'm declaring martial law in Jefferson County. After I speak to Governor Waverly, he'll declare martial law throughout eastern New York, and all of the state."

The phone rang. My secretary had the commanding general of the First Guard Division, Eva Micklebridge, on the line. I told her the situation and strongly suggested (as I couldn't give her an order at this time) that she mobilize her National Guard division and get them ready to enter Syracuse.

I started to lay out my plan to the assembled officers: the 1st Brigade would guard the base, patrol Watertown and assist the First Guard Division in Syracuse, while the 2nd Brigade would travel down to Albany to maintain order in the State's capital. I temporarily switched the 1st Infantry Regiment over to the 2nd Brigade, as I felt that I would need the extra men in Albany, and the 317th Cavalry Battalion over to 1st Brigade. The horses would be difficult to transport and leaving them in this area meant that 1st Brigade would have some fuel-free mobility. I also left the 110th Aviation Battalion on the base as my reserves, ready to join us as soon as the weather had calmed sufficiently for them to fly.

The phone rang again. I snatched up the receiver. Governor Waverly was on the other end.

"Walter, what is it," he said. "I'm a little busy right now."

Waverly sounded angry, distracted and flustered all at the same time.

"Mike," I said, "do you know what is going to hit this state?"

"Yes," he replied, "I do. I've just been informed. How do you know?"

"Never mind that," I said. "You must declare a State of Emergency and impose martial law."

"Not you too!" he said. "Look, I have just declared a State of Emergency. I'm not prepared to declare martial law at this time."

"You must," I said. "There will be chaos in the cities. The Tenth is mobilizing, and so is the First Guard. My division can be in Albany within three hours after the hurricane has passed."

"Walter," he said, "I'm not declaring martial law at this time. Prepare your division, by all means, but let's see how bad it is first. ... What is it now?"

Suddenly the phone-line went dead.

"Damn!"

With my officers assembled, I announced that the governor had declared a State of Emergency, but had not yet declared martial law.

"He'll be forced to sooner or later," I said. "Nothing changes. My declaration of martial law for Jefferson County stands."

I ordered them to prepare to move out at first light in the morning. I intended to sit in our vehicles at the county border if we had to, but we would be ready for the emergency to come. I dismissed them.

* * *

Outside, rain continued to pour down—I had never seen anything like it. The morning sky was dark and ominous. Visibility was poor. I sat quietly fuming in my command vehicle on Interstate 81 at the southern border of Jefferson County. A long column of vehicles were lined up behind me with their engines turned off. I had reached the limits of my jurisdiction and now waited for orders allowing my division to move forward. I felt somehow idiotic. I knew what had to be done but was powerless to do anything.

Hurricane Nicole hit New York City, moved up the Hudson Valley and departed. At Fort Drum, we experienced very heavy winds and torrents of rain, but little more. The Adirondack Mountains had shielded us from the worst of the hurricane. The only damage to the base was to the roof of the Sergeant's Mess, which was blown off, and one of the communication towers was bent to one side so badly it was inoperable. Luckily, the backup tower was working. My men had prepared the base well.

"Anything from Albany yet," I asked my communications officer. "What about the Pentagon?"

"Not yet, sir," the officer said.

But in a few minutes he was calling me excitedly to look at his console. A message was being delivered to me by courier from Fort A.P. Hill in Virginia.

I stood up and peered over the officer's shoulder at the computer screen. Martial law had been declared throughout New York, New Jersey and Connecticut. I was ordered to proceed to Albany and then on to New York City where I would restore order and report on the situation.

Finally! The orders were clear: restore order. But now not just in Albany; I was now ordered to continue on to New York City. I gave orders for the division to get underway, and the command vehicle lurched forward.

I informed General Micklebridge of our new orders, contacting the general in charge. She said that she had already deployed the First Guard Division in Syracuse. The city experienced only light damage and was now under tight control.

When we reached Syracuse I met briefly with Micklebridge, and she informed me that the situation there was under control. This allowed me to keep my division together and not leave any of my men in Syracuse.

My division entered Albany on Interstate 90 and drove into the heart of the city. Glass and debris were everywhere. People roamed aimlessly, while others climbed over fallen homes or dug through rubble. Looters quickly scurried away when they saw my column of vehicles.

I reached the State Assembly Building and rushed upstairs to meet with the governor. Mike Waverly was in his office. When he saw me, he rushed over and almost embraced me.

"Thank God you're here," he said. "Albany's a mess. I need your help."

I refrained from saying that I could have been there two hours earlier.

"The storm," he said, "was a Two when she hit here. She was a Seven when she hit New York."

He had no idea what was happening in New York City. But he wanted me to get down there and find out. He wanted to place the Eighth Guard Division under my command, but no one could contact it. It was off-line.

I told him that I would leave immediately. The meeting took less than a minute.

After ordering the 1st Infantry Regiment to remain in Albany and restore order, I led the rest of my men south along Interstate 87. With me I had the 14th Mobile Regiment, the 10th Urban Assault Battalion (with its three tanks) and the 132nd Infantry Battalion from 1st Brigade. In total, including support units, I commanded less than two thousand men when I started down the Hudson Valley toward New York City. The only reinforcements available were my 110th Aviation Battalion—if the winds subsided sufficiently for it to fly—and the missing Eighth Guard Division—if I could find it.

* * *

Because debris covered the highway, our progress along Interstate 87 was very slow. At Catskill, I considered dividing my force and sending some of it across the bridge and along the east side of the valley, but in the end I decided to keep my force together. At Poughkeepsie and Newburgh, the bridges across the Hudson River had collapsed, so I couldn't change my mind.

Just before five o'clock that evening, my communications officer handed me an electronic notepad with a Level Black, Alpha-One-A priority message ordering me to secure a secret Army facility in Lower Manhattan: I had never received such a message before in my career, nor was I to do so again. It was the ultimate priority message. The Army didn't want whatever was in this facility to get outside of its control.

"Who has seen this," I asked the communications officer.

"No one, sir," he replied. "When I saw it was a Level Black, I sent the technicians to the front of the truck."

"Good work, Lieutenant," I said. "You can't repeat this message to anyone or acknowledge its existence. You never received it. Understood?"

"Yes, sir. Understood."

I began to regret my decision not to cross the Hudson River earlier at Catskill. My force was on the wrong side of the river. I had to find a way to cross it. I hoped that at least one bridge farther south still stood.

My force entered the outskirts of the New York urban area in a couple of hours. The bridge at Nyack had collapsed so I was forced to continue south into New Jersey. Large areas along the shores of the Hudson River were flooded from the storm surge. The river itself was swollen with runoff. It had not stopped raining since the hurricane hit and fierce winds blew debris around like shrapnel.

A few brave souls braved the wind and appeared in our path from out of the evening gloom. They wanted help and saw us as their saviors. My officers told these people to stay in their homes or whatever shelter they could find. Relief for them would come the next day.

We reached Fort Lee on the New Jersey side of the river. By some vagary of the hurricane, the George Washington Bridge still stood. It was heavily damaged and useless for vehicles, but there was a continuous link across the river which my soldiers could use.

I called a command meeting to inform my officers that the 14th would secure a small local airport at Teterboro, while the 10th Urban Assault Battalion would push on further south towards Newark International Airport. Aid was most likely to flow into these airports before anywhere else. They would become our center of operations. I would take the 132nd across the George Washington Bridge and enter Manhattan from the north. I couldn't tell my officers why we were in such a rush to get into the city. The commander of the 14th would take command of the forces that remained on the New Jersey side. I left him to make his arrangements while I examined the bridge with the commander of the 132nd.

It was pitch black. Except for our vehicle lights and a spotlight illuminating the bridge, there were no other lights anywhere. The officer with me was pointing out features of the bridge to me when suddenly the spotlight beam moved from the bridge and pointed into the black sky. My flash of anger at the men operating the spotlight quickly changed to horror. The river bank had collapsed and the spotlight and its trailer had fallen into the raging water. I ordered a nearby truck to shine its lights where the spotlight had just passed and its crew of four had been. The officer and I rushed to the edge of the river and peered into the churning water. Below us, one side of the spotlight trailer stuck out of the water. Three men clung on to it for dear life, but the forth man had been swept away into the raging river.

I grabbed a rope from the truck and over the screaming wind shouted to the commander of the 132nd to tie it on the truck winch. The other end, I tied around my waist. When secure, I ran a short way upriver and jumped into the raging water. I was driven toward the wreckage of the spotlight trailer. I grabbed hold of it, and signaled for the nearest man to hold onto me. Once he had a firm grip, I signaled him to winch us in. We let go of the trailer and were quickly swept down river. The rope snapped tight and we were slowly pulled to shore. The water flowed rapidly past us and our heads often disappeared underwater. Once we were safely ashore, I repeated the process a second time and then a third.

What made me do it? I don't know. I certainly didn't think about the possible consequences before I leapt into the river. I had lived on stimulant and nutrition pills for over thirty-six hours. I felt I could do anything. Men of the 132nd who had congregated around were impressed. News of my actions that night swept through the division over the next few days. I achieved a loyalty from the men of the Tenth Mountain Division that would never have been given to another commander.

The three soldiers owed me their lives. Two were good men and I feel good about saving them. I don't know what to think about the other one, Private Kellerman, a man from the penal regiment that I had integrated into the regular forces. The psychiatrists had classed him as intelligent-but-not-dangerous. They were right about the first part, but not the second. Kellerman was a solitary man of medium height who had read widely and held several engineering degrees. He was very intelligent, cunning, patient—and a killer. He had been an inmate of the 10th Penal Regiment until I integrated most of the regiment into my regular forces. Neither at the time nor later did he show any remorse for his crime—nor any reaction at all. Whatever emotions he felt were kept deep within him. However, because of my actions that night, Kellerman gave me his absolute, unwavering loyalty. He was like my personal pet attack dog. You felt uncomfortable in his presence but you liked him somewhere nearby. He was an extraordinary assassin. I'm not sure I could have achieved what I did without his occasional services. He repaid his debt to me many times over.

A second spotlight unit was located and brought through the line of trucks. Once it shone on the wreck of the George Washington Bridge, I ordered the commander of the 132nd to start his men across on foot. Under no circumstances would I have attempted the crossing during darkness and with strong winds, but I had an Alpha-One-A order that couldn't be ignored. I saw to it that the lieutenant who led the way was awarded the Army Achievement Medal for his actions that night.

Once the officer and half the men were across, I followed them. It was a terrifying journey. The high winds made the bridge sway. Large sections of the bridge had collapsed, with only bare support beams providing a way across. These beams were wide enough to walk on, but the men preferred to crawl across on all fours. I followed their example. Below me, I could see only black water shimmering from the light of the spotlight. Above us, on each side, there was only a dark void.

The men of the 132nd managed to make it across without any serious incidents. Once all three hundred men were across, I ordered the march south. We had just what we could carry. We had no vehicles, but they would have been useless anyway because rubble and glass filled the roads making them impassable. We followed the river along the Henry Hudson Parkway until we reached West 57th Street. Flooding forced us to turn into the heart of Manhattan. It was difficult to make progress. Many streets were blocked by fallen buildings. Those buildings that had survived only served to funnel the strong winds, making them even stronger. Several of my men were wounded by flying debris. I didn't see any civilians on the streets that night.

Using my hand-held positioning unit (which fortunately functioned well for once), I led the men through the maze of streets. My men knew we were there to locate and secure an important Army facility, but they didn't know what that facility contained—and neither did I. Eventually we reached the building, which had partially collapsed. It took over an hour to locate a way through the rubble to a stairway down. I left the battalion commander and most of the men to guard the outside of the building and look for survivors. I took fifty men down into the underground levels of the building. Once we were below Sub-level Three, there was no rubble and we rapidly descended to Sub-level Ten. A solid-looking metal door blocked our way. I had a corporal bang on it. A few moments later, we heard a bang in reply. The corporal banged out a message stating who we were and offering assistance.

The door opened and light flooded out. A colonel appeared and snapped a salute.

"General," he said, "thank God you're here. Communications have been down since the hurricane hit."

I explained my orders and started through the door.

"I'm sorry, General," he said. "You can't come in."

After all the effort my men and I had gone through to get here, I was angry about this rebuff. I told this colonel so in no uncertain terms.

The colonel didn't back down.

The facility was secure, certainly, but he insisted that he have the use of my communication system. The colonel wanted to talk to Army Intelligence. He asked that I escort him to the surface and that my men guard the door and patrol around the building.

Who in blazes was he? I was beginning to wonder who was the general and who was the colonel, but I sensed that I had better do what this colonel wanted—not that I liked it. I never enjoyed being a pawn in someone else's game. Leaving four men to guard the door, I led the rest of my men and the mysterious colonel, with his heavily-armed escort, back up to the surface. I left the colonel with my communication equipment while his escort surrounded him. None of my men could hear what was being said.

Dawn would break in an hour or so. I decided to get some rest. I had not slept in nearly two days. I descended to Sub-level Four and lay on the cool, dry floor.

* * *

I felt a hand shake me. It was a lieutenant. He looked exhausted.
"What time is it," I mumbled.
"Six-thirty," he said. "Orders have come through from Army Ops."
He handed me a small electronic notepad that ordered me to secure the perimeter of the facility and not enter. I was also ordered to provide full assistance to the commanding officer, and report on the situation in the city.

I yawned and struggled to my feet. I ordered him to get some rest and I climbed back to the surface to make my report.

When I stepped out of the building, the gray dawn light showed a scene of devastation. Numerous buildings had collapsed. Of those that remained standing, all of their windows had been smashed. Glass, rubble and debris covered the streets. Rain continued to fall, but not as hard as the previous day, and the wind was weakening. I saw hundreds of civilians scrambling over the rubble. Some were talking to my men. One of my men was carrying a small child.

I went over to the communications equipment and spoke by radio with the commander of the forces that I had left in New Jersey. He sounded tired. He reported that both airports were secure. Rescue operations were underway. The 10th Urban had run into some looters just after dawn, but the looters had fled. I then spoke to Fort Drum. The 110th Aviation Battalion was still grounded by high winds. The battalion's commander hoped to get airborne by late afternoon. The situations in Albany and Syracuse were under control. Watertown and Fort Drum were secure. There was still no word from the Eighth Guard Division. With this information in hand, I made my report to Army Operations. Although I spoke for some time, I think my report can be summed up by the following sentiment: situation very bad, send reinforcements. I was told that reinforcements were indeed moving toward New York, but the roads were clogged with refugees and debris. Bridges were out all over the area and flooding was widespread. Winds were still too strong for aircraft operations. It looked as though I would be on my own for a day.

I took a quick breakfast of energy bars, stimulant and nutrition pills, and washed them down with rainwater. I assigned my men to various duties. Some were kept back to secure the perimeter around the building, others assisted civilians in rescue operations in the immediate neighborhood, while a few were to scout the area. I crossed the road and joined some of my men as they dug through the rubble. Someone claimed to have heard sounds from underneath. My men and I helped the civilians lift stone blocks. It was back breaking work, but after an hour we were rewarded by a shout from below. We renewed our efforts. Finally we broke through. I reached in and pulled out a girl about five years old. I held her as the others pulled out her father. A medic examined and treated them. Both were alive, although the girl was shaking and the father had dried blood all over his face. The father wept and mumbled something about his wife. Ten minutes later we uncovered his wife. She was dead. The husband held the lifeless body of his wife and rocked her gently. He didn't seem to notice anything else around him. I silently touched the father on his shoulder. He looked up with grief-stricken, memorable eyes. I pried away the little girl, who was clinging tightly to me, and gave her over to him. He reached out for his daughter and pulled her close.

I returned to the communications equipment. I had only just arrived when the captain of C Company came up to me.

"Sir," he said. "There is something happening over on the next block."

He led me along a rubble-filled street to the front of a once magnificent old building. Its solid stone facade had faired better than many of the more modern buildings. As I rounded a corner, I saw a dozen soldiers from his company guarding a group of ten scruffy men. My soldiers looked angry.

"What's going on?" I demanded.

"We have captured these men," he said. "They were removing

things from the museum."

"Looters!"

"Yes, sir."

I was outraged. A block away my men struggled to find survivors and a father cradled his dead wife and terrified daughter. And yet here, these creatures were stealing precious artifacts of our civilization just to enrich themselves. I was sickened.

"Captain," I said, "these men are looters. They will be shot immediately."

The captain told his men to carry out my orders. There was little hesitation. The executions were completed in less than five seconds. I looked down at the dead looters. I felt no pity.

"Captain," I said, "All looters will be shot on sight. No exceptions. Understand?"

"Yes, sir," he said.

Half an hour later, he and a major approached me. They led me over to a building that housed a bank on its ground floor. About thirty of my men surrounded perhaps a hundred and fifty men and women who had been looting the contents of the bank.

"Sir," the major said, "the captain tells me we are to shoot looters."

"Yes, Major," I said, "those are my orders."

"Some are fairly young—just teenagers."

"No exceptions," I said.

"Yes, sir," the major said.

My men opened fire. Some of the looters tried to flee but none escaped.

There were other looting incidents throughout the day and into the night. None were as serious, but all were dealt with in the same decisive way. By midnight, there were no reports of looting within the area patrolled by my men. The message had been understood by the citizens of this section of Manhattan. Order had been established.

That morning the situation improved. Aid was flowing into the two New Jersey airports, and the 110th Aviation Battalion had finally arrived to reinforce my small command in Manhattan. Even the missing Eighth Guard Division had been found. Hurricane Nicole had smashed the division's base and killed most of its command staff. A colonel was leading surviving elements of the division into New York from the northeast.

Thirty-seven days later, I led my exhausted men back to Fort Drum. After the first day, no more survivors were pulled from the rubble—only bodies—but order had been imposed. The citizens of New York started to rebuild their lives. I was proud at what my division had accomplished in that devastated city. The Army was also pleased, and it awarded my division with the Army Superior Unit Award. Initially, the Army had wanted to give it to only those elements of the division that had entered New York, but I insisted that all of the men of the division were responsible for our achievements. This was not the same demoralized and degenerate men that I took command of two years earlier. They had now regained their honor.

I was awarded the Meritorious Service Medal for my initiative to take the division south. Some months later, I also received a bronze oak leaf cluster to my Soldier's Medal of Heroism for my rescue of the men of the spotlight unit.

I look back at my command of the Tenth Mountain Division as one of the most rewarding assignments I had in the Army. It was a privilege to command such men.

Part II
At the Gates of Hell

Upon this rock I will build my church; and the gates of Hell shall not prevail against it.
- **Matthew 16:18.**

Mark Tushingham

– Chapter 8 –
Ottawa

Morale was high in the Tenth Mountain Division. The 10th Urban Assault Battalion received its third and final delivery of the urban ten-wheel tanks. The battalion had now a complete complement of ten of these precious specialized tanks. The base's Light Fighters Infantry School was producing excellent graduates in the art of urban warfare. One of the 317th's horses gave birth to the unit's first foal: a pretty little black filly. The Army did me the compliment of copying my methods for rebuilding several other divisions that had experienced major problems with morale or corruption. However, even though the following summer had been cooler than the past blistering summer, there was little rain. If not for the division's arrangements with the local farmers and the soldiers' own private garden plots providing supplemental supplies of food, the men would have had to survive on half rations.

I had not taken any leave since I took command of the Tenth, so I didn't expect any problems when I asked for seven days of leave for a camping trip in the nearby Adirondack Mountains. I liked the wilderness. It refreshed me—and I felt I needed refreshing after four hard years.

I submitted my request for leave through the usual channels. The paperwork was just a formality. The Army rarely turned down a two-star general's request for a few days of leave, particularly one who had worked without a break for four years. Lieutenant Colonel Joyita had efficiently prepared the paperwork, so I was a little surprised that the Army took so long to reply. I had Joyita inquire to the status of my request. First Joyita was told that it was being processed and that it would come in due course, but when he persisted he got the Army runaround. Eventually, the approval appeared. I was at my desk when Joyita informed me.

"I'm sorry, sir," Joyita apologized. "I must have made a mistake."

He handed me an electronic notepad. It stated that my leave was approved for seven days in the Algonquin Highlands in Canada; and it also said that a major would be arriving to brief me on the details of my trip. I was surprised that Joyita had made a mistake about the location, but I was surprised more so that a major would be coming from Washington to brief me on my own leave. Something was not right. I asked Joyita to find the electronic file of my original request for leave. When we examined the file, it was clear that Joyita had not made a mistake. Joyita had submitted my request for seven days in the nearby Adirondack Mountains, but the brass had changed the request to seven days in the Algonquin Highlands in central Ontario, Canada. The major who was to brief me was going to arrive the next day, so I didn't have long to wait for an explanation.

The following day at the appointed time, the major entered my office and saluted halfheartedly. He wore the insignia of the Army Personal Department, but he was unlike any paper-pusher that I had ever met. He was muscular and had a furtive look in his eyes. He fidgeted slightly in his uniform; he seemed not accustomed to military dress. I had seen his type before. He was CIA.

The major stood in silence, waiting for me to dismiss Joyita. When I did so, the major asked to sit.

"Bryan sends his compliments," the major said.

Bryan Cressy, who I had worked with during the Australian-Indonesian War, was now the Director of the Central Intelligence Agency.

"Very well, major," I said. I knew he was not what and who he pretended to be.

The agent smiled and relaxed in the chair.

"What's this all about," I asked. "Since when does CIA brief Army generals on their own leave arrangement?"

"General," he said, "the Canadian military has invited you to visit their 2nd Mechanized Brigade at Camp Petawawa, north of Ottawa. It'll be strictly an unofficial visit. After which, they will transport you to the Algonquin Highlands for your camping trip—compliments of the Canadian Armed Forces. We'd like you to accept."

"Why am I going to Canada," I asked.

"The Canadians want to meet you."

"Again, why?"

"More than that I can't tell you," he said. "They just want to meet you, and I'm sure that you'll give them a good impression."

I folded my arms defensively.

"Here's your itinerary," he said.

It informed me that I would drive to the Canadian border in a civilian car that the CIA would provide. I would have sufficient gasoline rations. An acquaintance of mine from the Birmingham Summit, Brigadier General Robert Deakin, would meet me there. He'd take me to his home in Ottawa where I would spend the night. The next day, I would travel from there to Camp Petawawa, home of the 2nd Mechanized Brigade. After a brief visit, the Canadians would take me to the Algonquin Highlands for a well-earned leave.

"Why would the Canadians go to all this trouble?"

The agent ignored my question.

"You won't be in uniform," he said. "You will be posing as a wealthy businessman. We'll provide you with a passport and a driver's license with the name Norman Edge. Use only that name."

I resigned myself to playing my part in someone else's spy-game.

* * *

As per the arrangements, my Army driver chauffeured me to a deserted location just north of Fort Drum, dropping me off by the roadside. Minutes later, the CIA agent who had posed as a major arrived in a magnificent limousine with a gleaming red exterior and a plush deep red interior.

He provided me with false identification documents, the keys to the luxury car, and wished me a pleasant holiday. He made me uneasy, but I saw no option other than continuing on with this covert game.

The car's onboard computer continually monitored the interior to keep it optimal for my comfort. The model was one of the last luxury cars to be built before the economic collapse ten years ago. Clearly, it had been lovingly cared for in the intervening years. It was irreplaceable now. Whoever owned the car must be very wealthy indeed.

I left the agent standing by the roadside and drove north along Interstate 81 towards the Canadian border. There were a few transport trucks on the highway but no passenger cars. I crossed the narrow Thousand Islands Bridge, which was in poor repair, and soon arrived at the border security station on Hill Island in the northern half of the St. Lawrence River.

The Canadian guard gawked at the luxury car, but once he managed to take his eyes from it he quickly scanned my passport.

"Welcome to Canada, Mr. Edge," he said. "Your friend is waiting over there."

He pointed to a man standing beside two black cars.

I got out of the car and was greeted by my old acquaintance, Brigadier General Deakin.

"Norman," he said, "life seems to have been good to you."

"It's a rental," I joked.

"I heard what you did in New York," he said. "Very courageous."

I thanked him.

"Many important people were impressed," he said. He gestured towards my car. I got behind the steering wheel and Deakin climbed into the passenger seat. Deakin gave me directions. As I drove away, the two black cars followed us. Deakin said that they were for extra security, and assured me that they wouldn't be necessary.

Once we were on the main highway, Deakin started to reminisce about the Birmingham Summit. He was in the rear bus when we left Himley Hall and, like me, only narrowly escaped the mob attack. We chatted briefly about American politics and lapsed into silence.

After two hours of driving on empty highways, we reached the outskirts of Ottawa, the Canadian capital. We were greeted with the usual sprawl of shanty-towns and destitute people wandering around aimlessly. Deakin appeared tense and the two security cars moved closer. I noticed many people staring at our little convoy, but no one made any moves towards the highway.

We came to a security check point and slowed to a stop. Deakin climbed out of the car, walked over to the security hut and went inside for a few minutes. When he emerged he looked visibly relieved. We continued our drive into the central part of the city. Here, behind the security perimeter, the buildings were well maintained and the streets tidy. We drove past Parliament Hill, and a mile or two to the east we drove into the driveway of a large house. We got out of the car and entered the old brick house.

"Welcome to my house," Deakin said. "It's a rental."

There were no photographs or mementos to indicate who lived there. Deakin informed me that a few friends would be showing up for a barbecue, as he left me to refresh myself.

* * *

After a short while, Deakin knocked on my door.

"Some guests have arrived," he said. "Please come and join us whenever you're ready."

I recognized many of the people standing around the barbecue. The CIA agent had provided me with a briefing book full of photos and biographies of key Canadian military officers, insisting that I memorize them. Besides Deakin, there were four other Canadian generals: the commander of the Canadian Armed Forces, the chief of Military Communications, the deputy chief of Operations, and the commander of the Canadian 2nd Mechanized Brigade. The 2nd was the most powerful force in eastern Canada. Everyone was casually dressed; nobody was in uniform.

The conversation was polite and free-flowing, but some of the guests watched me closely in brooding silence. The scrutiny became annoying after a while. Deakin, the most junior officer there, worked the barbecue grilling God-knows-what. In the casual, relaxed atmosphere (which was certainly by design), we discussed everything from American politics and world affairs to my courses at West Point and my achievements in New York City.

We had just started eating when another guest appeared. Luc Arbique, special assistant to Deputy Prime Minister Ijavek, was a young man with long hair. Silence fell on the room for a few moments when he entered. Eventually the conversations around me started up again, but they were hushed and guarded. The new guest lounged on a recliner chair and looked straight at me.

"You taught Tactics for Occupying Armies at West Point," he said. "Why?"

Although his body relaxed casually in the chair, his eyes looked ready to pounce.

I didn't like this man. I gave him a penetrating glare.

"I was offered it," I said.

"How many people did you kill in New York?"

My eyes narrowed. The others looked on with interest at the exchange.

"I didn't kill any people," I said, "—only looters."

"Why did you run away in Egypt?"

He was clearly trying to get a rise out of me. He didn't seem interested in my answers. I rose to his challenge.

"Have you ever been in combat," I asked.

He didn't reply this time.

Score one for me. But he wasn't finished with me just yet.

He suddenly stood up and pressed himself close to me, uncomfortably so. Although a few inches shorter than me, he was able to bring his face within an inch of mine.

"I don't like your kind," he said.

I struggled to control myself. I don't know what he saw in my eyes, but he blanched, turned and left as suddenly as he had arrived.

"I'm sorry about that," Deakin said. "Someone thought it necessary...."

"Is he always so direct," I asked. "Who is he?"

"A political lackey," he said. "No one very important."

"We've arranged a tour of Camp Petawawa for you, Mr. Edge," said an officer.

"I think you'll be impressed with my brigade," said the commander of the 2nd Mechanized Brigade. "I've put into place a number of training schemes that you started at Fort Drum."

I was relieved to change the subject.

* * *

The next day, an officer drove me northwest to Camp Petawawa. The camp commander rolled out the red carpet for me. I was impressed with the 2nd—both with its men and its capabilities. It had managed to retain its mobility in spite of the fuel shortages by slowly stockpiling large quantities of fuel over a long time. Unlike most

Canadian units, this brigade was considerably stronger than a corresponding American unit. The 2nd along with the 1st Mechanized brigade stationed in western Canada were the elite of the Canadian ground forces.

The commander arranged for a corporal to take me to the Algonquin Highlands in a military truck. In the back of the truck was a canoe and camping supplies. We arrived at the weather-beaten dock on the shores of Lake Opeongo, the largest of the Algonquin lakes. The driver helped me unload the truck and pack the canoe. He provided me with a map of old camp sites that were set up when this region was a huge park. He also provided me with a rifle for my protection—not from wild animals but from hunters and drifters. I thanked the corporal and watched him drive away. I had a week to myself.

I canoed for about two hours and found a lovely campsite on an island in the central part of the large lake. The quiet beauty of the lake, the wilderness and the solitude were soothing and just what I needed.

– Chapter 9 –

The Pentagon

The purpose of my trip to Canada remained a mystery to me for some time until three weeks later when all became clear. I was ordered to the Pentagon for a briefing on an undisclosed subject. I handed over temporary command of the division to the Camp General and left for the Pentagon, as ordered.

I entered the familiar wide corridors of the Pentagon and made my way to the main briefing room of Army Operations. A colonel in the Personnel Department greeted me as I approached the security desk. He saluted and offered me his hand.

"Congratulations, General," he said.

Bewildered, I accepted an envelope that he held out to me. When I read the letter inside, I understood his congratulations. I had been promoted to Lieutenant General and was to command III Corps.

I was a three-star lieutenant general. I commanded an Army corps. The only problem was I had never heard of III Corps. The corps structure had been slowly abandoned over the years in favor of a more centralized control of the Army's brigades and divisions. This was necessary for the domestic urban policing operations that the Army had to undertake. Now I was to command a newly-formed corps.

Still stunned by my surprise promotion, I entered the main briefing room and took my assigned seat. Sitting on my side of the large conference table were three other generals. The general in charge of the meeting, the chief of Army Operations General Viktor Stopic, sat across the table in the center chair. Beside him sat the President's National Security Advisor Jan Sykerman, who started the meeting by briefing us on some recent and extremely sensitive political events which were top secret and could not be discussed outside the room.

Two months ago certain elements within the Canadian military approached United States diplomats in Ottawa. The Canadians claimed that Prime Minister Rochon no longer had the support of the Canadian military, nor a small but powerful faction in his own party. Deputy Prime Minister Ijavek and the Canadian military wanted to force Rochon to resign. They claimed that Rochon's policies of appeasing the population were not working. Riots in the major cities were growing out of control. Instead of strengthening the military, Rochon disbanded whole units in order to afford aid packages for the people. The Canadians asked us to help them force Rochon to resign and recover control over the cities. In return, they promised to increase bulk water shipments to the United States which had declined by nearly seventy percent since Rochon took power two years ago. Americans needed that water badly. The President therefore ordered that we were to provide whatever assistance was required to change the leadership of Canada.

The briefing never mentioned that it was a military coup, but that was what we were asked to assist the Canadian military in doing.

When Sykerman finished her briefing, General Stopic read from the electronic notepad before him. He informed us that we were to provide the assistance that the President had ordered. There would be four corps reporting directly to Stopic's office. A marine general was to command I Marine Corps, which had an area of operations on the west coast and in the mountains of British Columbia. He was to link up with the Canadian 38th and 39th Security brigades operating in Victoria and Vancouver, respectively. And his objective was to secure all the ports in British Columbia.

Another general was to command II Corps, which had as an area of operations the prairies from the foothills of the Rocky Mountains to Lake Superior. He was to link up with the Canadian 1st Mechanized Brigade. And his objectives were to secure the oil fields of Alberta and the water pumping station at Thunder Bay.

I was to command III Corps, with the area of operations in southern Ontario. I was to link up with the Canadian 2nd Mechanized Brigade and the 32nd Security Brigade. My objectives were to assist the Canadians in a smooth transfer of power, to establish control over Toronto and to secure the water pumping stations at Collingwood and Peterborough.

The Canadian security brigades were of similar size and function as our urban brigades. Both were armored urban control forces. The 32nd was Canada's most experienced security brigades. It had fought many tough battles on the streets of Toronto.

The remaining general at the table was to command IV Corps. His area of operations would be Quebec and the Atlantic provinces. And he would link up with the Canadian 5th Infantry Brigade and the 34th and 36th Security brigades in Montreal and Halifax, respectively, with the objective of establishing control over Montreal, Quebec City and Halifax. He would also secure the St. Lawrence Seaway and the water pumping station at Chicoutimi.

Each general was temporarily assigned a highly mobile task force which would secure key sites and await their main forces. These task forces would be controlled by Stopic's office and would be withdrawn as soon as their main forces had reached the sites. Elements of these task forces would then secure strategic areas of the Canadian Arctic.

We were to be briefed on our individual commands that afternoon.

Stopic's aide distributed lists of our specific objectives and the forces under our command.

We were dismissed. I got out of my seat and walked to the door. In my hand, I clutched my thin file with the list of my units and objectives. I was just about to take a peek at the file when Jan Sykerman walked up to me.

"Walter, how are you," she asked. "I've heard nothing but good things about that division of yours. Wonderful what you did in New York."

Her cheerful voice seemed at odds with the subject on which we had just been briefed. The United States was going to mobilize its largest force in decades. Thirty years ago, we were a strong and wealthy country, but now our country was struggling and divided.

"No longer my division," I said, waving my file folder a little. I tried to match her cheer (which was easy since I had just become a lieutenant general).

"Oh, don't worry," she said. "We made sure you've still got the Tenth under your command."

She explained that mine was the most difficult assignment, but also the most important. Ottawa was the political heart of Canada. I was there on the spot to make sure the transfer of power went smoothly. The President would be watching developments in Ontario very closely. General Stopic was not exaggerating when he said we needed Canadian fresh water.

"Make sure we get it," she said.

She glanced pointedly at General Stopic as he was leaving.

"If you have problems from that quarter," she said, "let me know."

My mission clearly had priority. She let me know that General Cottick of the Third Infantry Division was being considered, but she had told the President that I was the man for the job. She didn't want me to let the President down or her. And I assured her that she had no worries on either score.

I was pleased that Jan fought for me; however, I was disturbed by the President's attention being focused on my corps. I was worried that there might be political interference with my operations—always a recipe for disaster.

* * *

That afternoon I entered General Stopic's office for my individual briefing. I was disturbed and angry at what I had read in my briefing file, but decided to hold back my temper for a while.

The chief of Army Operations was seated at a small conference table in the corner of his large office. Electronic maps of Ontario were displayed on the table's surface. I sat down and prepared to listen to what Stopic was about to tell me.

"Good afternoon, General Eastland," Stopic said.

He got straight down to business. III Corps has been provided with the Third Infantry Division, the Tenth Mountain Division and the 6th Armored Brigade. Task Force 3, consisting of airborne and ranger troops, was to secure the water pumping stations at positions he identified on the map in front of him.

My main forces would link up with the forces positioned on the map and the Canadian units in Ontario. Together, we would establish control over Ottawa and Toronto. Tenth Mountain would move north to Ottawa and link up with the Canadian 2nd Mechanized Brigade coming down from Petawawa. The Third would approach Toronto from the west, while our armored brigade came in from the east. They would link up with the Canadian 32nd Security Brigade in Toronto.

While Stopic was talking, he briskly moved his hands over the map to indicate the movements of the various units. Typical bureaucrat. He thinks that this will be as easy as waving his hand over the map, I thought.

I had several important concerns and decided to launch into them.

"General Stopic," I said, "I have a number of issues."

The most significant of them I said was the total lack of follow-up troops and the absence of any reserves. He had given me a single missile battery and a single air drone unit for my reserves—that was it—and that was wholly inadequate. I needed some muscle in my reserves to counter the unexpected.

"Eastland," he said, "you will have Canadian forces to assist you. This is not a war, Eastland."

His tone and response was to call rank on me, for he was my superior officer and I was his subordinate. He didn't want me to challenge him. We were, as he said, assisting an ally on an urban security mission. But I had other concerns that he needed to address.

I suspected that Stopic already had similar conversations with the other commanders. He was in a bad mood. I decided that this was not the time or place to fight this particular battle. I switched to my other concerns.

"The fuel supplies," I said, "seem inadequate. It will take time to analyze the requirements precisely, but—."

"We'll do what we can," Stopic said.

This wasn't going well.

I had some concerns over personnel, and decided to switch the discussion to them. I wasn't going to get anywhere on the issue of fuel supplies.

"I understand," I said, "that General Cottick was considered for my command."

Cottick was a tough soldier with an impressive combat record, but he was notoriously ambitious.

"How do you know that," Stopic asked. "It's that damn woman!"

The tension that surfaced in his response was new. Clearly Stopic didn't like Sykerman. I wondered why. I didn't confirm or deny that it was Sykerman who told me.

"I don't want any personal issues," I said, "developing between me and the commander of my strongest division."

"No, he doesn't know," Stopic said.

"Did he get a trip to Canada," I asked, "to be vetted by the

Canadians like I was?"

"Yes, he did," he said, "but he was not told of the reason any more than you were."

That was unfortunate. Cottick was an intelligent officer. He'd soon guess. I'd have to be careful with Cottick.

"Very well," I said. "I see that I have already been assigned a deputy commander, Major General Gregorakis. But has he any combat experience?"

I didn't say to Stopic that Gregorakis was just a paper-pusher, because that was what Stopic was.

"Ionas is an excellent administrator," he said. "And may I remind you again, this is not a combat situation."

I noticed that Stopic used Gregorakis's first name. They were friends. That could be useful, I mused to myself.

I suspected that I was not his first choice for this command. Stopic probably thought that General Cottick would have been a better choice. However, he didn't get to make the final choice on the commander of III Corps. As my deputy commander and chief of staff, Stopic probably thought that Gregorakis would provide some cautious deliberation to the command staff of III Corps.

"Any other concerns," Stopic asked.

"No, Sir,"

I was dismissed. None of my concerns had been addressed. I now understood Jan Sykerman's offer of help. I would take her up on it.

As I left Stopic's office, I chuckled at the irony in my situation: I was a political appointee. Me—a person who had for years reviled and frequently fought against useless political appointees in the military. Clearly, the Cole Administration had chosen me over the Army's first choice. Sometimes even the politicians get one right.

– Chapter 10 –

Wolfe Island

At Fort Drum, the new headquarters for III Corps, I met with General Gregorakis, a large, overweight man, older than me by many years, and a career Army bureaucrat. Nevertheless, almost immediately my prejudices about him vanished. He was a fine deputy commander who cared deeply for the men under his command. More importantly, he knew his way around the personnel departments. True, he had no real combat experience, but he had experience combating Army bureaucracy. He would have made a terrible commander, but as my deputy he was excellent. With his knowledge of senior officers and my knowledge of junior officers from my days at West Point, we created an excellent command team for the corps. With the help of Gregorakis, I obtained promotions for both Sean Wycross and Coronado Joyita and transferred them to III Corps. By this time, I couldn't imagine anyone else other than Joyita dealing with my paperwork.

In late November, I met with Donald Tuckhoe. I had good news for him. He had been promoted to major general and confirmed in command of the Tenth Mountain Division. I had insisted that the division needed continuity of command, and the Army begrudgingly accepted my argument. Immediately after I congratulated Tuckhoe, I had to inform him that I was taking Wycross and Joyita from him. He knew of my long association with those two officers and accepted the news stoically. I then had to tell him that I was raiding his division for my reserves and taking the 10th Urban Assault Battalion. The battalion would still be stationed at Fort Drum, but it would be a reserve unit under my direct command. He was not happy but could do little about it. I sympathized.

The next day I had my first meeting with Major General Hollis Cottick, the commander of my strongest division. It went surprisingly well. The bulky, hard-faced man was all sweetness with me. At that time, I couldn't tell him what III Corps's mission was, but he assured me that he was pleased to be part of whatever was going on. He hadn't yet guessed that he could have had my command. Cottick was proud of his Third Infantry Division. Morale was high in the division, and his men idolized him. Unfortunately, the same couldn't be said about the 6th Armored Brigade. When I met with its commander, Brigadier General Samuel Price, he went into a long lament about fuel shortages, maintenance problems, and the fact that the Army was transferring all his best men to the urban brigades. I promised him that before the mission got underway the Army would provide the fuel and parts he needed. He was not comforted by my empty reassurances.

In early December, I quietly contacted Jan Sykerman to take her up on her offer of assistance. I explained the need for follow-up units to assist my regular troops in establishing control over the urban areas. She asked if I had any ideas on how to get these troops. I told her I wanted the two National Guard divisions in upstate New York placed under my command. The First Guard and Fifth Guard divisions were undersized, poorly equipped, had little transport and the morale of the troops was abysmally low, but they were conveniently placed near Buffalo and Syracuse. They were better than nothing. Jan promised to see what could be done.

A week later, Jan and I met with Mike Waverly, now the governor of New York, in his office in Albany. As a friend and confidant to President Cole, Mike was aware of the impending operation and welcomed the supplies of water that it promised to provide. He agreed to my request for the two National Guard divisions. Little by little, my corps was taking shape.

In December, I was summoned to a secret meeting on Wolfe Island. The large island is located in Canada where the waters of Lake Ontario flow into the St. Lawrence River. It's only a short boat ride from Kingston, Ontario, and an even shorter boat ride from Cape Vincent, New York (a thirty minute drive from Fort Drum). Wolfe Island was the site for a clandestine meeting between American and Canadian officials. The island proved to be a convenient location for all those involved.

The meeting took place on Christmas Day in a big old stone house on the southern side of the island. There was an excellent view of the St. Lawrence River and the New York coast from the front steps. The weather was cold and gray, and thick, dark clouds loomed ominously. After waiting for the last of the Canadian politicians to arrive, we took our seats. Around the table were six Americans and seven Canadians.

UNITED STATES OF AMERICA
Jan Sykerman, National Security Advisor
(representing President Martin Cole)
Timothy Wright, Secretary of Agriculture and Water Supplies
Michael Waverly, Governor of New York
Tanya Sokohiri, Ambassador to Canada
Gen. Hal Gobburu, Chairman of Joint Chiefs of Staff
Lt. Gen. Walter Eastland, Commander of III Corps

CANADA
Philip Ijavek, Deputy Prime Minister of Canada
John Yarker, Minister of Defense

Katrina Cho, Deputy Minister of Internal Security
Wilson Brent, Premier of Ontario
Gen. Scott Thompson, Commander of Canadian Armed Forces
Lt. Gen. Ginette Dumont, Deputy Chief of Operations
Luc Arbique, special assistant to Deputy Prime Minister Ijavek

Luc Arbique, special assistant to Deputy Prime Minister Ijavek, was the rude, arrogant young man at the party in Ottawa who had rudely provoked me. He tried to give the impression that he didn't remember me. His eyes darted around the room as he lounged in his chair, but he eventually focused his attention on Jan Sykerman. He never once looked directly at me.

Philip Ijavek, Arbique's boss, was a shadowy figure in Canadian politics. Somewhere along the way he had acquired the nickname "The Puppeteer," which explained why Ijavek let Arbique do most of the talking during the meeting. Arbique's sycophantic manner irritated me. In a few minutes he perfunctorily announced that Prime Minister Rochon had to be forcibly removed from office because he was a danger to the security of Canada.

No one objected to his proposal. The purpose of this meeting was to set the scope and the parameters of American assistance. The meeting continued with a high-minded patriotic speech by the Canadian Minister of Defense. His speech seemed nervous, halting, and full of appeals to patriotism; it was mostly a justification and an apology for his part in the conspiracy. It showed only that his conscience was bothering him. If I had been Ijavek, I would have not trusted the minister.

After the minister's speech, Ijavek nodded to Arbique and his assistant discussed the details. Some of these details included no American soldiers within three kilometers of Parliament Hill. Canadian forces would enter cities prior to American. If Canadian forces were already in the city, American forces would be escorted in by a token Canadian force. If urban action was necessary, it would be the senior Canadian commander on the spot who would be in command of the action, regardless of the rank of the American commander. The list was lengthy. It included one item that was purely for show. Senior American commanders in Canada would be under joint command of Army Operations and the senior regional Canadian commanders. This meant that I would be taking orders from both General Stopic in Washington and the ranking Canadian general in Ontario. I don't think that even the Canadians thought this would work once the forces were moving.

The American delegation sat listening to this list in silence. Once the Canadians were finished, Sykerman agreed that the details were reasonable and American forces would abide by them. I didn't see how many of these details could work in practice, but I kept quiet.

Mike Waverly asked about how soon the water and electricity transfers would be implemented. This was the first I had heard about electricity being an issue, although it was not a surprise given our frequent blackouts. I had a bad feeling that the number of objectives that I had to secure had just multiplied.

"The equitable sharing of Canadian natural resources," Arbique said, "in a North American context would be the new government's highest priority once the political situation was stabilized."

This bureaucratic reply didn't give me much comfort, but the American politicians seemed pleased with it.

The commander of the U.S. Army asked his only question of the meeting. The crusty old man came right to the heart of the issue.

"What's the level of support," he asked, "within the Canadian Armed Forces for this transfer of political power?"

"Almost all the officers," Arbique said, "are fully behind the Deputy Prime Minister Ijavek."

Arbique was oblivious to his mistake, but everyone else around the table heard him say "almost all."

"The defense budget," added the Minister of Defense, "has been slashed by sixty percent, with more cuts coming soon. Everyone in the military realizes that this can't continue—."

We Americans must have seemed unconvinced, because Ijavek

interrupted the minister.

When the time comes, he said, the Canadian military would be one hundred percent behind the new government. The soldiers would do what their officers told them. He promised that all officers who showed any leanings for the old government would be identified and transferred to harmless positions or otherwise dealt with. There wouldn't be many. The Minister of Defense was right. The military was being bled white by Rochon and his foolish policy of appeasing the people. Rochon had lost control of the cities—even Ottawa was unsafe. Canada's pitifully inadequate forces would be soon completely overwhelmed by the task of wrestling control from the urban gangs. With American help, however, Ijavek believed that Canada could be rescued from the edge of the abyss to which Rochon had brought it. Now, there was no one in the armed forces and few in the country who wanted Rochon to remain the country's leader. Canada needed strong, decisive leadership in these troubled times. And Ijavek offered himself as that leader. No one objected.

Sykerman graciously accepted this statement without serious comment and then smoothly changed the subject.

"When is the transfer of power to take place," she asked. "We will need to know so we can prepare."

Arbique started to reply, but Ijavek cut him off.

"January the thirty-first."

"Why that date," Sykerman asked.

"Rochon," said Ijavek, "plans to deliver his next budget at two p.m. on that day. His budget will provide me with all the justification I need."

The people, he explained, would see the bankruptcy of Rochon's policies. They would revolt, and push for his removal. Once the budget was read in Parliament, Ijavek's forces would strike and overthrow Rochon."

"The United States government," Sykerman said, "will be ready to support you on the thirty-first."

The meeting adjourned. We got up from our chairs, and everyone shook hands. It was all very polite. No one had said the ugly word "coup." The American delegation then left for the boat to take them back to Cape Vincent. I had only five weeks to prepare.

– Chapter 11 –

Fort Drum

There is an old military axiom: no plan survives the first contact with the enemy. My plan didn't even last that long.

Eight days after the meeting on Wolfe Island, I received some good news and some bad—on my birthday of all days. First the bad news. As I suspected, I had a longer list of objectives that I had to secure. Besides the water pumping stations, I had to secure several power stations and a refinery complex. The good news was that Army Operations finally relented and gave me an urban brigade: the 9th. Toronto and its satellite communities had six million people. To control a city of that size, you needed something more than a few foot soldiers and a broken-down armored brigade. Whether it was my relentless arguments or the politicians becoming nervous, I didn't know or care. The 9th was a first-rate urban brigade, which had to be pulled out of Indianapolis. I was told that I was only going to have it until April, because it would be needed to suppress the predictable summer riots in American cities. Nevertheless, I was content. The brigade had a full complement of urban tanks and armored personnel carriers. Its command structure was excellent, and Brigadier General Ulithi was very well respected, at least in most quarters.

Because the rangers and airborne units of Task Force 3 had more objectives to secure, the task force was reinforced with one regiment from the Eleventh Guard Division. A single regiment was all that could be spared from the ongoing skirmishes in Detroit. This regiment would secure the refinery complex at Sarnia, just across the border, which would release the other units of Task Force 3 to secure more distant objectives.

Besides the one extra military police battalion and the two extra engineering battalions that the Army provided at the last minute, there was one other change to III Corps. I reassigned the 1st Special Support Unit from the Tenth Mountain Division to my corps' supporting forces. The SSU was my creation, and I thought it may prove more useful under my direct command. General Tuckhoe didn't mind at all me taking this irregular and often troublesome unit full of ex-prisoners away from his division.

The illusion of joint command over III Corps didn't survive long. Now I was to only keep the Canadian general in charge of Ontario informed as required by operational concerns—which would mean whatever I wanted it to mean.

Rochon's budget was to be read in the Canadian Parliament by Rochon's finance minister that afternoon. We were to move to Ijavek's aid within an hour of the reading. On that day, I was sitting with General Gregorakis and my command staff in the III Corps headquarters, located in a two-story building in Fort Drum and within walking distance of the headquarters of the Tenth Mountain Division. I tried to relax but couldn't. I was too excited. My men were ready, my officers were ready, and I was ready. I had my orders and I had my units. Everyone knew what was expected of them.

Just before the appointed hour I received a call from General Stopic.

"Eastland, Operation ROCKFACE," he said, "is on hold for four hours."

"What! Why?"

"Rochon," he said, "has delayed the budget until this evening. Something to do with some last-minute changes to the budget. Ijavek insists that we can only move after the budget is read."

I sighed and shook my head. I didn't understand the significance that the Canadian Deputy Prime Minister placed on this condition. Nevertheless, the Army complied with his wishes. I called the commanders of my units and informed them of the delay. Cottick of the Third was angry, Tuckhoe of the Tenth was exasperated, Micklebridge of the First Guard said nothing, Stafford of Fifth Guard laughed, Price of 6th Armored sighed with relief as it gave him more time to find the fuel supplies that the Army had promised him, Ulithi of the 9th Urban was stoic about the minor change as he saw it, and Brown of Task Force 3 was impatient to get going.

I reviewed my plan and tried to relax. Everything was set so I had little to do. Late afternoon, I received another call from Stopic; he was quite angry. He cussed profanely, using language I didn't permit my officers to use in my presence. After a long tirade against Ijavek, Stopic informed me that Operation ROCKFACE was delayed until the next day. Apparently there were more last minute changes. Again, I informed my commanders. This time their reaction was like mine: we were all very concerned. Something was definitely not right.

That night I discovered what that something was—at least I thought I did. General Stopic again called me.

"Eastland," he said, "we have discovered what is behind these delays."

He explained that Rochon had discovered the conspiracy to oust him. Now he was starting to mobilize elements of the Canadian military that remained loyal to him. The forces in Toronto and Kingston had already defected. All Canadian military communications were down.

Stopic gave me my new orders.

"Ijavek is panicking," he said. "He wants action now. Toronto is his political power base."

Ijavek could not allow Rochon to control Ontario. Stopic ordered me to move the Tenth west towards Toronto, instead of north to Ottawa. It was vital that our forces controlled that city. The drive to Ottawa could be undertaken by the second-rate First Guard Division. H-Hour was set to midnight. Stopic wanted me to do whatever I had to do to be ready to move at the given time. His orders, he said, came from the top.

I was stunned. The Tenth was in position near the border at Ogdensburg. It was ready to move north. The First Guard was ready to follow behind the 6th Armored Brigade on its drive west to Toronto. The troops were badly out of position for these new orders, not to mention that maps and intelligence data had to be transferred between those divisions. My well-designed plan was in ruins. I was ordered to do what was done. I had no responsibility for switching the direction that the Tenth had to go. My orders were clear.

I arranged for an immediate conference call between my commanders. I relayed the situation to them. They were all alarmed. However, orders were orders and we made the best of a bad situation. I was uncomfortable—to say the least—about the First Guard Division, a second-line National Guard unit, being the sole unit to go into Ottawa regardless of the lack of opposition we expected. The First Guard had little transport and was essentially foot-bound. I decided that prudence demanded that we get into Ottawa quickly. I reassigned the 110th Aviation Battalion from the Tenth to the First Guard. Originally, it had been planned that the 110th would fly to Ottawa and secure the Air Force base just to the east of Parliament Hill. The battalion would still undertake its mission, only now as part of the First Guard Division. I transferred a battalion of the First Guard to the Tenth in way of compensation to General Tuckhoe. This second-line battalion would now be Tuckhoe's lead unit, and the first-line units of the

Tenth would follow it. Tuckhoe was not happy, but nobody was that night.

At H-Hour, the various units of Task Force 3 started out towards their objectives. The 7th Aviation Regiment left from its base in northern Michigan and headed towards sites in central Ontario. The rangers headed across Lake Ontario from their base near Rochester. They had to take several sites on the north side of the lake. In the west, the Third Infantry Division and 9th Urban Brigade crossed the border at Buffalo and Niagara Falls, respectively. The Fifth Guard Division followed at H-Hour plus three, as planned. In the east, events didn't unfold as smoothly. The 110th Aviation Battalion was thirty minutes late in taking off— a delay caused by complications in the transfer of the reporting structure. It also took longer than planned for the 6th Armored Brigade to cross the old, narrow, steel bridge across the St. Lawrence River at the Thousand Islands. At H-hour plus one, lead elements of the Tenth Mountain Division crossed the bridge at Ogdensburg and immediately turned west along Highway 401 to Toronto. At the headquarters of the First Guard Division, confusion reigned. The tasks of transfer of information and objectives and becoming a lead unit swamped the limited capacity of its divisional command staff. The men of First Guard had to get to Ogdensburg from their start position north of Watertown. It was not until the next morning when the First Guard started to cross the bridge into Ontario. I didn't blame General Micklebridge or any of my commanders for problems that night. I placed the blame squarely on Philip Ijavek.

Early morning Tuesday, February 1, my corps command staff and I took stock of the situation. Task Force 3 had secured all of its objectives without any problems. My western forces were poised to enter Toronto. In the east, the 6th Armored Brigade had bypassed Kingston and linked up with elements of Task Force 3 at the water pumping station near Peterborough, and were preparing to move into Toronto from the east. The First Guard was now across the border in force and heading north on Highway 416 to Ottawa. The Tenth had captured and neutralized the forces of the Canadian 1st Aviation Regiment in Kingston. General Tuckhoe had its commander under arrest. Tuckhoe was greedily eyeing the parts that could be salvaged from the Canadian regiment's dilapidated helicopters. Everything seemed to be going well.

During the meeting with my command staff, General Tuckhoe radioed in. He reported that the commander of the 1st Aviation Regiment was swearing his loyalty to Ijavek's movement. What else would he do now that we had him? Tuckhoe also informed me that he had secured a fuel terminal at Maitland, but it was almost empty. In passing, he casually mentioned that he had captured two fully-loaded fuel trucks that were heading north from the terminal. I failed to realize just then the significance of what he was saying.

At noon, General Cottick reported that he had entered Toronto and met with Brigadier General Zhang of the Canadian 32nd Security Brigade. Zhang was demanding to know why we Americans had shut down Canadian communications and had taken such a hostile attitude towards his forces. Cottick said he believed Zhang was still loyal to Ijavek's movement. I grew concerned. If the Toronto and Kingston forces were loyal then who was not? It came to me in a panic: the 2nd Mechanized Brigade had switched its loyalty to Rochon's side. The most powerful force the Canadians had in my area was going to hit my weak National Guard unit approaching Ottawa.

I contacted General Micklebridge immediately.

"Eva," I said. "I have reason to believe that you will run into enemy forces."

She reported that all was quiet and that her troops were progressing well. I warned her to be cautious, but it was already too late. Less than ten minutes later, I received a frantic call from the First Guard Division. The lead troops were coming under serious fire from Canadian heavy tanks. Moments later, the commander of the 110th Aviation Battalion reported enemy tanks were engaging him. He was returning fire.

Rochon had misdirected us and achieved a strategic surprise. It was a masterful work of deception. In addition, the commander of the 2nd Mechanized Brigade had achieved a tactical surprise over the First Guard Division. If the elite 2nd Mechanized could push aside my poorly-equipped, second-line division, it could drive on the Thousand Islands Bridge and cut my eastern forces off from their base of supply. The situation was dire and I had to take swift and determined action if I was to rescue anything from the mess.

Poor Eva. I had to tell her that she couldn't allow the 2nd Mechanized to break through. All my reserves (such as they were) would be heading her way. I ordered the commander of the 110th Aviation Battalion to hold where he was but to withdraw as soon as the situation became untenable. I would need his force later, so I wanted it intact.

I contacted the Air Force's 174th Ground Support Wing to get its ground attack drones to slow the 2nd Mechanized. What a pathetic effort followed. Of the twelve drones that were to attack, six didn't get off the ground, two crashed immediately after take-off and two more on route. Of the two that arrived at the battle, one fired a missile that failed to explode. The sole successful drone attacked and destroyed a single tank. At the time, I was furious at the air force, but upon cooler reflection I put the fiasco down to the massive budget cuts that the air force had experienced. They were far worse than anything the Army had to live with. You don't need an Air Force for riot control operations.

The following day, Wednesday, February 2, the situation became clearer. Toronto was secure and loyal to the Ijavek movement. Ottawa was loyal to Rochon's government. Elsewhere, I Corps had obtained its objectives without problem. Events also went as expected for II Corps. It had achieved what it set out to do, but the Prairies were bone dry. There was little water available, and the men of II Corps had to go on quarter rations. However, IV Corps had run into major problems. It captured Halifax after some fighting, but its drive to Quebec City had been stopped dead by elements of the Canadian 5th Infantry Brigade. The Canadian brigade had destroyed all the bridges across the St. Lawrence River from Quebec City to Trois-Rivières. The two forces sat impotently looking at each other across the wide expanse of the river. In Montreal, a confusing melee raged between IV Corps units with some elements of the 34th Security Brigade on one side and elements of the 5th Infantry with other elements of the 34th on the other. Rival city gangs were also using the opportunity to fight each other and our forces. Rochon had committed his few Air Force units to the battle for Montreal. I wished IV Corps luck with its battles; I had my own to worry about.

At 5:30 p.m., the 110th Aviation could no longer hold the Air Force base in Ottawa. I authorized the battalion to withdraw. Two hours later, I greeted the men when they landed back at Fort Drum.

"Sorry, sir," the commander said, "but we couldn't hold them any more. My boys were no match for their heavy tanks. We had nothing that could get through their armor."

"You did all that you could," I said. "What are your losses?"

"Twelve dead," he said, "thirty plus wounded. We lost four choppers. Two before we even knew there was war on."

"Rest your men," I said. "I'm going to need them soon."

"We'll be ready," he said. "Sir, we picked up some hitchhikers."

He pointed towards a distant helicopter. Four aviators were escorting two civilians. I recognized Ijavek and his assistant Arbique. Ijavek strode towards me, with his head held high. The assistant, however, looked crushed and was quietly sobbing. I heard him whimper who had betrayed them: The Minister of Defense, who was at the meeting to plan the coup, and the chief of military communications had separately warned Rochon.

Ijavek ignored his sobbing assistant and strode up to me.

"General Eastland," he said, "I must get to Toronto. Make the arrangement immediately."

I had to restrain myself from throwing him into Fort Drum's

prison. He would have made an interesting addition to the Tenth's penal regiment. Instead, I dutifully contacted Army Operations for orders and was instructed to make the necessary arrangements. Frankly, I was glad to get rid of him.

When I arrived back at my command center from greeting the 110th home, I was relieved to receive a message from General Micklebridge. It said that her division was holding its ground – but barely.

I resolved to visit Eva before dawn the next morning.

– Chapter 12 –

Kemptville

The morning of Thursday, February 3, was unusually cold. The thermometer dropped overnight to below freezing for the first time in years. As I flew north in one of the helicopters of the 110th, I was amazed to see snow covering the ground north of the St. Lawrence River. I hadn't seen snow in years. As one of the older generation, I can remember actually skiing on Whiteface Mountain near Lake Placid, but that was not since I was in my early twenties. Many of the younger men in the First Guard Division had never seen snow, except in old movies.

When I landed at General Micklebridge's field command center in a field east of a town called Kemptville, Eva came out to greet me. She escorted me to her command vehicle. Off to one side, I noticed two men having a snowball fight near the vehicle, but as soon as they saw me they stopped and saluted smartly (no doubt feeling a little foolish at being caught).

We stepped inside her command vehicle for privacy.

"General," she said, "after being badly mauled yesterday, we managed to retreat in reasonably good order. I've set up a defensive line running from west to east behind the Rideau River and Allen Creek." On the map, Eva showed me her deployment, behind the river and the creek. Her flanks were by the heavily-wooded marshes of the Marlborough Forest to the west and the Winchester Bog to the east.

"Who are you facing," I asked.

"Elements of the Canadian 2nd Mechanized Brigade," she said. "Its 1st Battalion is to the east."

That battalion was the best unit the Canadians had in their Army. There was another battalion to the west, protected by the river, but it had not been identified yet. Eva didn't know where the 2nd's heavy tanks were—and that really worried me. She had run into them yesterday and they mauled her units badly. Then, they disappeared.

The commanders of my reserve units, having arrived during the night, were present in Eva's command vehicle. I ordered the commander of my air drone unit to undertake vigorous reconnaissance and anti-drone operations.

"Find those tanks," I ordered.

In the meantime, it was clear that there wouldn't be much fighting today because of the snow. This would give me time to come up with a battle-plan. I ordered the commanders of my reserve 25th Missile Battery and 10th Urban Assault Battalion units to return with me to Fort Drum. I left Eva to keep her division together and hold her defensive position.

At Fort Drum, my command staff pulled together what information we could find, while I contacted Brigadier General Brown of Task Force 3.

"General Brown," I asked, "what is the status of your aviation units?"

"We've secured the power station," he said, "at Tobermory and the water pumping station at Collingwood."

The Third Infantry hadn't reached him yet, but it should soon. He didn't anticipate any problems. The water pumping station at Peterborough was also secure and the 6th Armored had already relieved his men.

"Thank you, General," I said. "However, there is a situation developing south of Ottawa."

I told him that the First Guard Division had run into resistance, and I would need some of his aviation units for a combat mission first thing tomorrow.

"My men are ready, sir," he said. "Name the time and place—we'll be there." Brown seemed excited at the prospect of combat.

"Excellent," I said. "You'll be contacted later when we have developed the operational plan."

The reconnaissance drones soon discovered the whereabouts of the Canadian's heavy tanks. They were some miles back straddling each side of the Rideau River at a village called Kars. We also identified the various opposing units. The tanks were from the Canadian 11th and 12th Tank battalions. To the east, the Canadian 1st Mechanized Battalion (formed from what was left of the Royal Canadian Regiment and now the elite unit of the entire Canadian Army) held behind Allen Creek, and to the west the other Canadian mechanized battalion, which had been identified as the 322nd, held behind the wide Rideau River before the river turned northward. We clearly outnumbered our opponents, but they had quality on their side. There was nothing in our inventory that could match the firepower of their heavy tanks. It would have been different if the 6th Armored Brigade had been there, but it was not. It was ironic that the tanks were American-made heavy tanks, complete with our advanced armor and smart shells. The Canadians had purchased them as urban control tanks, but rarely deployed them in that role. The newer, lighter and more-versatile urban tanks had superseded the older heavy tanks.

I studied my opponent's deployment. His tanks were deployed to cover attacks to either west or east. However, I discerned that he was worried that we would attack to the east across the minor barrier of Allen Creek. It was a logical place to attack. There was good open ground with few woods or marshes and the terrain opened up to flat farmland north of the village of Osgoode. To cover that contingency, he had deployed his best unit by the creek. The weaker unit, the 322nd, was protected by the large natural barrier of the Rideau River. He hadn't attempted to destroy the bridges in the area, so I surmised that they were necessary for his own plans. The more I studied his deployment, the more I became convinced that he had one critical weakness: the bridge at Kars. If that bridge was destroyed, he couldn't move his forces from one side of the river to the other. The river divided his forces. If the tanks were on the wrong side of the river when the bridge was blown, I wouldn't have to fight them at all.

I first spoke to the commander of the 25th Missile Battery. Eva linked into the meeting on a scrambler radio.

"Can you destroy the bridge at Kars," I asked, "and the one further north at Manotick?"

"If there are no major anti-missile defenses," he said, "we should be able to."

"Can you attack the bridges and not destroy them," I asked.

"What!" he said. "Do you mean deliberately miss?"

"Yes, I want the appearance of a serious attack, but I want the bridges standing and usable by their tanks.

"Missing isn't difficult. I'll do the best I can, sir."

I asked Eva if she held the small bridge far to the west at the village of Burritts Rapids. She informed me that Number 8 Platoon of her 41st Regiment held that position. They had not seen any enemy activity near them. I was pleased and I informed my staff.

"The objective of this battle," I said, "will be the destruction of the 322nd Mechanized Battalion and the removal of all enemy forces west of the Rideau River from Kemptville to Ottawa."

My opponent was worried that we would attack to the east. I intended to increase his concern. I wanted a vigorous demonstration on the eastern half of our line by the First Guard. The 110th would land at diversionary sites on the east side of the river around the village of Osgoode. At the same time, I wanted an unsuccessful missile attack on the bridge at Kars. The Canadian commander of the enemy would see us making a serious attempt to divide his command and he would counterattack on the east side of the river. When he committed his tanks to the east, we would destroy the bridge at Kars and the one further north at Manotick. The 171st Aviation would then land and hold the area around the village of North Gower, while the 10th Urban Assault would drive its urban tanks on a wide swing against the flank and rear of the 322nd. We would surround the enemy, crush him and move on to Ottawa unopposed.

I was very pleased with my plan. My staff was also enthusiastic. They began to work on the details.

Because a lot depended on vigorous and convincing action of the men of the First Guard Division, I decided that I had to be on the spot when the action started. I would leave for Kemptville before dawn.

* * *

During the early morning hours of Friday, February 4, I didn't sleep very well. I had a recurring nightmare that the commander of the 2nd Mechanized would attack first. But an idea pulled my weary body out of my bed and over to the communications room. I ordered the lieutenant-on-duty to contact the 174th Wing. Maybe our air force could redeem itself. I waited while the air force officer-on-duty left to get his commander. Finally, the commanding Air Force general arrived. I explained to him that I wanted the Air Force to strike the fuel depot at Camp Petawawa and the large fuel terminal in the south part of Ottawa. Most of my forces were foot-bound, so I wanted the enemy forces to suffer the same handicap. Even if it had no immediate effect on the upcoming battle, the Canadian commander would have something else to think about. He would have to be careful and husband his fuel reserves carefully. The Air Force general explained that his technicians believed they had fixed the problem with the ground attack drones. He was eager to have another chance to demonstrate what his command could do. I told him that I wanted an immediate attack on the fuel tanks—the sooner the better. If the Canadian commander was going to attack, I wanted him to have to stop to consider his fuel situation first.

I gave up on the idea of sleep and instead went outside. The cold night-air was invigorating. I wandered over to the silent helicopters of the 110th Aviation Battalion. The maintenance crews were busy repairing battle-damage incurred during the fight in Ottawa. I observed from a distance without being noticed. After a long while, I silently slipped from the scene and returned to the headquarters building. I sat in my command chair and quietly brooded over the upcoming battle. Had I missed anything?

My staff reported for duty before daybreak. They were tired but excited. I made my way over to the helicopter that was going to take me to Kemptville. Just as I stepped into it, the communications lieutenant ran over.

"The 174th Wing reports," he said, "that the attacks were successful. The fuel tanks are burning."

I thanked him for the good news. Now the commander would have something else to worry about.

After what seemed to be an endless flight, I arrived at the field headquarters of the First Guard Division. Over the previous day, the snow had melted, leaving the ground soft. This would make it slightly more difficult for the heavy tanks of the Canadian forces, and every little advantage would be of help. General Micklebridge came out to greet me. She quickly explained to me what she had planned for her division. With one regiment holding in the center ready to move against any counter-attack, another would attack across Allen Creek. Her reserve regiment, the 29th, would swing far to the east and hit the other flank of the Canadian 1st Mechanized Battalion. Eva thought that attacking both flanks in an enveloping move would get the

Canadians attention. On the extreme western part of her line, her largest regiment, the 41st, would, at the appropriate time and in conjunction with the urban tanks of the 10th Urban Assault Battalion, attack the Canadian's 322nd Mechanized Battalion. She had assigned all her meager transport assets to the 29th for its flanking move to the east. Afterwards, the transport would be switched to the 41st for the follow-up movement into Ottawa—if all went according to plan. I approved of her deployment. She understood what I wanted.

I asked General Micklebridge to assemble as many officers and men as could be spared. The First Guard had been hit hard by the 2nd Mechanized and I was worried about the men's confidence. I felt it necessary to give them an inspirational speech. At that time many of the officers of the First Guard Division had assembled around the command vehicle. The men of the nearby 29th Regiment were also present. It was dark and a cold wind blew from the northwest. I climbed on to the top of the command vehicle to deliver my impromptu speech. I forget what I said exactly at the beginning of my speech—a lot about me having confidence in them, I think. One of the important points that I stressed at the end of my speech was regarding why they were fighting in the first place. My men had no interest in the confusing political situation in Canada. They didn't hate the enemy, once a quiet, unnoticed neighbor. So why were they here? I had to make it personal for them.

Our families back in the States were suffering. Why? Because the world was changing—and not for the better. What we once took for granted couldn't be taken for granted any longer. Hunger and drought were increasing, and the number of families who were at risk of starvation was increasing daily. Why? Because fresh water to grow food in the USA was now scarce. We all knew that to be true. We couldn't survive without fresh water. Our families couldn't survive. Our society couldn't survive. Our army couldn't survive. Our division couldn't survive. An army could fight for months without fuel. It could fight for a week or more without food. But an army could fight for only hours without water. That was why we were in Canada—for fresh drinkable water. We were here to keep the First alive. We were here to get Canadian fresh water to our families in the States. I told them to get that water. They had their orders for the day. We were going to fake right and then hit with a powerful left hook. The enemy would be looking the wrong way when we hit him. And I intended for us to hit the Canadians hard. I intended to give them Hell!

When I climbed on top of the command vehicle, I didn't know what I was going to say. The focus on water just came naturally to me. Many of the significant events in my career concerned the supply of water—or rather the lack of it. I wondered if the Libyan general spoke the same words to his soldiers when he attacked my isolated regiment on his way to the Nile. Did the commander of the New Central Indian Army refer to water in his speech when he drove his Army towards the Ganges River? I began to see the Canadian campaign in a larger context.

The plan for the Battle of Kemptville was conceived by me alone. I had a worthy opponent, who only two days before had achieved a complete tactical surprise and defeated a larger force. Although I outnumbered my opponent, he had superior weapons. Nevertheless, I got inside his head and deceived him completely. My victory was complete and the casualties among my men were light on that cold February day.

A Sketch of the Battle of Kemptville

Phase One of the battle (the attack on the east side of the river) commenced when the 110th landed at critical intersections of the roads around Osgoode. At the same time, the lead regiment started its attack just to the east of the main highway. The 29th Regiment completed its swing way out to the extreme eastern end of the line and hit the other flank of the Canadian 1st. My National Guard soldiers couldn't make any headway against the elite Canadian troops, but then they were not expected to. The fake missile attack on the bridge at Kars took place as planned. The men of the 25th Missile Battery outdid themselves. I watched, via a tiny reconnaissance drone, as the explosions surrounded the bridge. Smoke covered the scene and I spent some anxious moments until the smoke lifted. The bridge was still standing.

The missile attack was too much for the Canadian commander. I watched with relief as the heavy tanks of the Canadian 12th Tank Battalion crossed over the bridge. The men of the 110th Aviation strained under the weight of the attacks by the Canadian 11th and now the 12th Tank battalions, but they had to hold out for a few minutes longer. The second missile attack took place. This time the bridge blew up in a spectacular explosion. The bridge to the north at Manotick was also destroyed. I gave the order for Phase Two to commence.

The men of the 110th climbed back into their helicopters and retreated to a field south of Kemptville. They would be my reserves for later. Far to the west, the urban tanks of the 10th Urban Assault Battalion started to cross an old, single-lane, wooden bridge at Burritts Rapids. The bridge must have been two hundred years old—a remembrance of a less-troubled time. The engineers of the 41st had worked all night to strengthen the old bridge so it could support the weight of the urban tanks. The bridge eventually collapsed but only after the 10th got all but one of its tanks across. The tank that fell into the river was later salvaged and its crew experienced only minor injuries. The 10th split into two convoys and drove at top speed along deserted rural roads. Five tanks hit the western flank of the Canadian 322nd. On this signal, the men of the 41st forced the bridge just north of Kemptville. Ten minutes later, the 171st Aviation Battalion (brought in from Task Force 3) landed at various locations along the road between North Gower and Kars. General Brown flew in with his men and took command of all the forces around North Gower. Fifteen minutes after that, four urban tanks emerged from the Marlborough Forest and reinforced the men of the 171st. My trap was complete. The Canadian 322nd Mechanized Battalion was finished; it just took them a while to realize it.

The Canadian 322nd fought an excellent rearguard action. One group forced its way through Kars under the cover of the Canadian tanks from the far bank of the river. Others simply swam across the Rideau River and rejoined their comrades, but they lost their vehicles and equipment. However, most were nicely trapped. We captured many prisoners, while our casualties were very light.

By the afternoon, my men on the west side of the river were heading along Highway 416 towards Ottawa. The commander of the Canadian forces had withdrawn north along the east side of the river. My forces captured some shanty suburbs south of Ottawa, but we didn't enter the city. Canadian forces, reinforced by the retreating 2nd Mechanized Brigade, held the city. I was wary of becoming bogged down in a bloody urban battle like the one being fought by IV Corps in Montreal. I ordered my men to hold their ground and dig in. I hadn't the forces to push my way into the city, and my opponent didn't have the fuel left to push me away. The result: stalemate.

The Army never recognized my victory at Kemptville. They viewed the drive on Ottawa as a failure—which in some ways it was because we didn't capture the city. However, since Ijavek had fled to Toronto and Rochon soon moved his government to Quebec City, Ottawa lost its political significance. I stand by my decision not to enter the city. The men of the First Guard Division would have been badly mauled in the urban fighting that certainly would have followed. If the division had been destroyed, I wouldn't have had it available to fight for me when I needed it later.

– Chapter 13 –

Toronto

I stared out of the window of my office at a well-maintained park in the secure government area of downtown Toronto. I watched as a black squirrel scampered through the branches of a nearby tree. All the trees in the park were broad and leafy and the grass was dark green. A lot of water had been pumped into the soil to keep this area lush in the sweltering July heat. The oval-shaped park was called Queen's Park. That was also the name given to the Ontario Legislative Building, which stood at the park's southern end. The squirrel leapt to a nearby branch and went about its business. Nature continued on regardless of our human problems.

I was disturbed from my contemplation.

"Sir," my secretary said, "General Micklebridge is here."

I turned my gaze from the scene outside my window and warmly welcomed Eva. I offered her some water which she gulped down quickly. It was very hot outside, but in my office it was comfortably cool. The air-conditioning system in this building was working—at least while there were no power cuts.

"Walter, how are you," Eva asked. "We haven't seen each other in the flesh in months."

Eva was the only officer that I permitted to call me by my first name—and only in private.

"I'm doing well," I said.

The Ontarians, I explained, had made me very welcome. They liked the security that III Corps was providing. By day, the city was reasonably safe, particularly within the secure government area. At night was another story, but I was working on that.

By this time, I had the 6th, 9th and 32nd brigades inside Toronto, with the Third and Tenth divisions to the west and east of the city, respectively. I had managed to hold on to the 9th Urban Brigade past the deadline initially set by Army Operations, and the Canadian 32nd Security Brigade had now been fully integrated into III Corps. I had disbanded the Canadian 1st Aviation Regiment. Its decrepit helicopters had been dismantled for parts. I gave its men a choice of serving with their fellow countrymen in the 32nd or being assimilated into my other aviation units. Most of the Canadian aviators chose the later option.

I had my secretary bring in another glass of water for Eva, while Eva and I chatted. Finally, the pleasantries were out of the way.

I was concerned about the prisoner exchange. To negotiate an exchange of prisoners with the Canadian commander in Ottawa meant some risk. We would be returning elite troops, mostly from the 322nd Mechanized Battalion, and in return the Canadians would return men from the second-line First Guard Division. However, I wanted my men returned to their families. It was a popular move with the men, and the current situation allowed for it. There had not been any fighting for months—not since the commander of IV Corps followed my example and realized that Montreal was not worth fighting for. He withdrew, as did the Canadian 5th Infantry Brigade. The 5th moved to Quebec City in an attempt to restore order in that city. The ruined city of Montreal was left to the mercy of the rival city gangs.

The political situation had also become less confused. Individual provincial governments made their own peace with American forces. The Ontario government had been very accommodating to me. With respect to the Canadian government, Rochon had fled to Quebec City, only to run back to Ottawa when the Quebec government ordered his arrest. He escaped during the anarchy that followed the assassination of the Quebec premier. Rochon was lucky in the timing of his escape—or was it luck? The province of Quebec went through several premiers after that, but none survived for long.

The Canadian government now only controlled a few square miles around Ottawa. Rochon was ignored outside of Ottawa; Ijavek was ignored everywhere. The ex-Deputy Prime Minister of Canada was under house-arrest in a building not far from my office. Ijavek was an embarrassment to us Americans, and the Ontario premier didn't want anything to do with him.

"How did the prisoner exchange go," I asked.

"As well as we might expect for now," Eva said. "Our opponent at Kemptville wasn't General Mousseau."

"Not Mousseau?"

Eva explained that General Mousseau, the original commander of the Canadian 2nd Mechanized Brigade, had died under mysterious circumstances just before Operation ROCKFACE began.

"Poor Mousseau," I said. "I liked him, but he was out of his depth."

"Aren't we all," Eva said.

Eva said that she had a very pleasant chat with the current commander of the 2nd. He had some interesting things to say about the battle. He conceded that my deception regarding the bridge at Kars was brilliant, and that he hadn't seen the attack on the 322nd coming. He had thought that the river would block us. Nevertheless, he maintained that the Canadians won the battle because my troops didn't get into Ottawa.

"Only because I decided it wasn't worth the trouble," I said. "We also stopped the Canadian's drive south to attack the Thousand Islands Bridge."

The Canadian commander claimed, Eva said, that he was lucky just to have reached Kemptville, his fuel supplies so low and they became non-existent after I blew up his fuel stocks. His brigade arrived back in Ottawa on fumes. His tanks, immobile after the battle, became fixed gun emplacements.

I might have attacked Ottawa if I had known how bad my opponent's fuel supplies really were. Such is the fog of war. Now, events had made such an attack irrelevant. The American and Ontarian governments were happy to leave Ottawa to Rochon—one less urban headache for them.

"What's going on with my division," she asked. "Is it heading back to Syracuse now that the Fifth Guard has gone back to Buffalo?"

"I don't know," I said. "I'm meeting with Mike Waverly later today."

He and I were going to discuss the command of his National Guard units. I told Eva that I wanted to retain overall command even if her division returned home because we needed a centralized military command in the Great Lakes region.

"I agree," Eva said.

"I'll let you know what Mike decides."

With that, Eva returned to her division's headquarters near Kemptville. It was pleasant to see her again. I was comfortable with Eva more than any other person.

* * *

There was a knock at my office door. Colonel Wycross entered.

"Sir," he asked, "may I have a moment?"

I looked at my watch. I was meeting with Mike Waverly in ten minutes to discuss the situation with the National Guard units.

"All right," I said, "you have five minutes."

It would take me the other five minutes to walk across to Queen's Park where I was to meet Waverly.

Wycross sat in a chair opposite my desk.

"General," he said, "I need to brief you on a troubling situation and a possible solution."

"Go on."

"Have you heard of the Sunset Takers?"

I shook my head.

Wycross informed me that this Toronto gang believed that everyone from the older generation was responsible for the social and climatic problems and that they shouldn't be allowed to live. According to the gang's credo, everyone over forty years old was culpable and therefore a candidate for execution. They wanted to get rid of the old day, so to speak, and make a new day for themselves. They had started killing people in Toronto for some years, mostly homeless old people.

"Snuffing—they call it," Wycross said. "However, now it's rumored that they may start targeting our older officers and men."

Even though I was one of those older officers, I was not concerned for myself. My bodyguards were well trained to deal with the dozens of death-threats I received each week. However, many of my officers would make easy targets. They had to be out there in the city and were often highly visible. I had to protect them.

"We don't know much about the Sunset Takers," Wycross said, "but I have a proposal for you."

"I'm listening."

Wycross got up and opened the door. He called for Major Khanan, the commander of the 1st Special Support Unit, to join us. The major entered and saluted. I beckoned him to be seated.

"Major Khanan," said Wycross, "believes he has found an assignment worthy of the SSU. He is proposing—and I support him in this—that the men of the SSU be used to infiltrate the Sunset Takers. Many of them are young and know their way around the underground world of gangs."

I was a little concerned. The SSU was composed of ex-prisoners from the penal regiment of the Tenth Mountain Division—prisoners considered intelligent and dangerous. Wycross and Khanan were proposing to let these men loose and work independently without supervision by officers or military guards.

Wycross guessed what I was thinking.

"The men of the SSU," he said, "know that they have a better life with us than out there. There may be some desertions, but not many."

"My men," Major Khanan added, "have become a tight unit. We've a strict code. No one will break it. If anyone does, the men will deal with the deserter in their own way."

I didn't have to ask what that way would be. I had no doubts that it would be brutal and final.

"My men know the underworld," Khanan said, "and will use whatever methods are necessary to complete their assignments,"

I had been looking for a task for the SSU. This would be it. These were independent men who didn't play by any rules. They would be at ease in an environment where my soldiers would not. They could do things that my soldiers couldn't, or wouldn't, do. I looked at my watch. I was late for my meeting with Waverly.

"Very well then," I said. "Use the SSU to gather intelligence on these Sunset Takers. I'll give you a month to prove your unit."

As the SSU was my creation, I wanted it to succeed.

"Thank you, sir," Khanan said as he snapped a salute.

I dismissed the two officers and left my office for my meeting with Waverly. In those five minutes with Wycross and Khanan, the SSU had been unleashed. The SSU—the dreaded SSU—was to be a very useful tool for me.

* * *

Mike Waverly was in Ontario to meet with other governors of

states bordering on the Great Lakes. The meeting was to take place the next day. The site of the meeting had been the subject of considerable and often acrimonious debate. The governors finally decided to choose the relatively neutral site of Toronto. This site also had the advantage that it was protected by not one but three armored brigades. My units provided the governors with a level of security that they couldn't achieve in their own state capitals.

The Premier of Ontario had provided Waverly with a temporary office in Queen's Park for his meeting with me and others. I arrived at the building drenched in sweat. The well-functioning air-conditioning was a welcomed relief from the heat outside. I went through the security checkpoint without having to show any identification (everyone knew who I was).

I found Waverly's temporary office and entered. Waverly greeted me enthusiastically—a little too enthusiastically. After expressing a lot of interest in my role in the Battle of Kemptville, he finally got down to business.

"Walter," he said, "I think we need to discuss the National Guard issue. You handled the First superbly in the battle. Micklebridge can't speak highly enough of you. Your handling of III Corps and the political situation in Ontario has been perfect."

This was a lot of flattery. I waited for the inevitable. It didn't take long to come.

"However," he said, "I'm taking the First back to Syracuse and Albany. It's getting a little edgy in Albany. I need some soldiers on the streets, but you have done such marvelous job with III Corps that I want both the First and the Fifth to remain under your overall command."

"I would be pleased," I said, "to continuing leading such good men."

"Excellent," he said. He added that he could foresee a day soon when III Corps will be responsible for the entire Great Lakes region and I would be the one to lead it.

This was quite a promotion he was dangling before me, so I became immediately suspicious, although I was experienced enough not to show it.

"The governors," he said, "will discuss the security situation at the meeting tomorrow. I'm inviting you as an observer."

So, I was invited to the big meeting. Interesting. After politely accepting the offer, I returned to my office. I wasn't sure of what to make of Waverly's vision of the future and my part in it.

I entered my office and received another surprise. No sooner had I sat down than Colonel Joyita came in and offered his congratulations. When I asked why, Joyita smiled and gave me a letter, which I took and read.

I was to be awarded the Department of Defense Distinguished Service Medal. This was the highest award that a commanding general could receive for leading his men, and it was only given on the recommendation of the Secretary of Defense. I was speechless.

As my shock wore off, I became suspicious. The tone of the letter was very odd: it was too informal. I had only met the Secretary of Defense three times. Was he signaling to the Army that I was one of the Administration's men? Why did the Administration think that such a message to the Army was necessary? But at the time, those questions were of secondary importance to me. The big question was: why now? Why was I being awarded the prestigious medal at this point in time? I had received medals before that had political overtones to them; I strongly suspected that it was no different on this occasion. Clearly, my work with III Corps deserved recognition, but the timing of this award had to be more than coincidental. I was notified of the award on the same day as being invited to attend an important, high-level meeting. Why? The answer to that would have to wait for the meeting. I was certain that all would become clear then.

* * *

The large mahogany conference table in the center of the room and the matching wood panels on the walls were both old and well polished. The wood had a deep, rich color. A plush red carpet covered the large room from wall to wall. It was a little worn in spots but nevertheless gave the conference room an atmosphere of power. Most of the people in the room were at ease with such opulent decor. I sat between Waverly on one side and the chairman of the International Joint Commission for Great Lakes Water Resources on the other. The Ontario Premier, as host of the meeting, sat at the head of the table. At the meeting, along with the premier, the commission chairman and me, there were the governors of states that bordered on to the Great Lakes. Represented at the table were the states of Michigan, Illinois, Indiana, Wisconsin and Minnesota, plus New York and the province of Ontario. Two states, Pennsylvania and Ohio, were suspiciously absent.

In front of me, a single sheet of paper lay neatly on the table directly in front of my chair. Obviously the third item on the agenda, "Military Considerations" to which Waverley was going to speak concerned me, and I was interested in what he was going to say. As chair of the meeting, the Ontario premier called the meeting to order and invited the commission chairman to provide his status report. It was the usual litany of woes: droughts, evaporation losses, low water levels, ship navigation problems, illegal siphoning, and on and on. The man's heavily wrinkled face projected woe even before he spoke. His flat, monotone voice just emphasized the bad news that his expression had already conveyed. I was thoroughly depressed by the time the chairman finished.

The premier said something about the seriousness of the situation and then invited the governor of Illinois to speak to the second item. The governor was a tall, good-looking, charismatic man. He started into a long tirade on how President Cole was demanding more water from Great Lakes be sent through the aqueducts to southern states. Every time he mentioned Cole's name it was as though poison dripped off the word.

"I was elected," he said, "to look after the needs of my state—and by God I will do just that. The people of Illinois need our water and I'm going to see that they get it. The South can solve its own problems."

"Look," Waverly said, "we all know that the President's demands are excessive. We all agree on that—otherwise we wouldn't be here. The issue before us is how we will respond."

I was stunned. Waverly was a friend and confident of Cole. If Waverly had decided to break from Cole, things must really be bad. I now understood Waverly's flattery and the prestigious medal from the Cole Administration. I was being wooed by the two sides in this political battle. Pennsylvania's absence was also explained: that state was Cole's power base. Ohio's absence was a mystery and always remained so.

"I don't think," said the governor of Wisconsin, "we should be taking a purely selfish stance. I believe—."

"Selfish!" shouted the governor of Illinois, "I'm looking after the people of my state—."

"We can discuss our response under Item Five," said the premier. "Let's hear what Governor Waverly has to say regarding how the military figures into our discussions."

Waverly discussed the basic disposition of III Corps and introduced me with a lot of flattering words. He then went on to note the number of National Guard and urban brigades currently based or operating in the states bordering on the Great Lakes.

"Bottom line," he said, "is that, if push comes to shove, we have just as much muscle as President Cole."

"What are you proposing exactly," asked the governor of Wisconsin. "An armed response? I can't accept that."

"I'm just saying," said Waverly, "that we can't be pushed about."

"What has General Eastland to say about that," someone asked.

I was on the spot now. And I didn't know what I wanted to say. Fortunately, Waverly rescued me.

"General Eastland is here only as an observer," he said, "not a participant. General Eastland is a loyal American officer who obeys orders from those in charge. We are here—."

"We're all loyal," said the governor of Illinois. "That's not the issue. We can't give the water that Cole wants—that's the issue. If we could give it, we would."

"Let us move to the resolution," said the premier, "on formation of the Great Lakes Union"

He picked up a piece of paper from in front of him and began reading it aloud.

"I move," he said, "that it be resolved that the states and provinces represented here today form a political alliance to work together to insure the proper and sustainable use of the waters of the Great Lakes."

"I second the motion," Waverly said.

"All those in favor," the premier asked.

Everyone's hands went up, except for those who couldn't vote; namely the commission chairman and me.

"All those opposed?"

Silence.

"The motion passes unanimously."

And so, the Great Lakes Union was born. I was witness to its birth.

The premier then opened the floor for views on the final item on the agenda: the response to President Cole. Arguments started immediately. The hawks (Illinois and New York) on one side demanding an uncompromising response; the doves (Minnesota and Wisconsin) on the other wanting a vague, noncommittal response that kept their options open. Indiana flipped from one side to the other, while Michigan drifted slowly towards the hawks. Ontario kept quiet. I don't remember all the heated arguments that were shouted across the table that day. Let us just say that during the birth of the Great Lakes Union the parents screamed more than the baby.

As the arguments flew across the table, I found myself staring out of the window. In the distance, I noticed a heavy tank from the 6th Armored Brigade slowly rumble along a quiet street. The urban tanks of the 9th Urban Brigade would be out there somewhere as well. Outside the door to the conference room, soldiers from the 32nd Security Brigade stood guard. Surrounding the city, I had two combat divisions ready to execute my orders. I don't think the politicians gave much thought about what was around them. They saw only their security—not their vulnerability. A single order by me and this meeting would end with whatever result I wanted.

I learned two things that day. The first was that the water of the Great Lakes was a vital resource that needed protecting. The second was that I was a powerful man—possibly more powerful than all the others in the conference room. Now that was a heady thought.

Mark Tushingham

Part III

Hell

The hottest places in Hell are reserved for those who in a period of moral crisis maintain their neutrality.

- **John F. Kennedy.**

Mark Tushingham

– Chapter 14 –

Fort Drum

So at last the cataclysm struck. This was the year that I stepped through a door which didn't allow for retreat. Up until now, I had worked within rules that I had known all my life. But now I changed the rules—not just for myself but for everyone. Once changed, I couldn't go back to how things were. It was a terrible year, but it was also the year that I set myself free.

In the March, following the creation of the Great Lakes Union, I was ordered to Fort Drum to attend a mysterious briefing. The weather was cold, wet and gray, but I had some rare free time before the briefing that morning to wander around the familiar base. I had missed the place. My duties as the commander of III Corps kept me in Toronto most of the time. As I walked past the various buildings on the base, I remembered walking past those same buildings when I was a raw second lieutenant fresh from West Point. The base had seemed so large then. It seemed difficult to accept that this memory was of the same base into which I had led the 1st Infantry Regiment to start my command of the Tenth. It was here that I had greeted the 110th Aviation Battalion when it returned after its battle in Ottawa. I spent over an hour walking along familiar routes, remembering my past.

I became lost in my thoughts and forgot the time. I was late for the briefing—an unheard of event. I didn't accept tardiness from anyone, but especially not from myself. I hurried to the building and entered the briefing room. I had no idea what the briefing was about or who was giving the briefing. It was all very mysterious.

Upon entering the room, I found Lieutenant Colonel Landsholme, the commander of III Corps' 115th Medical Battalion and my personal physician. The only other person in the room was a colonel of the Army's Medical Corps. Both saluted and I returned the salute.

"General," Landsholme said, "The colonel will provide the briefing, but first I need to inoculate you."

"Against what?"

"The colonel will explain," he said, "but only after I have inoculated you. I have my orders, and I must insist on your compliance."

"I think not," I said. "Before I let you put something in me, I must know what it is."

Landsholme reached into his pocket and pulled out a piece of paper. It had a presidential seal at the top. He showed it to me.

It said that I was to comply with any medical staff of the United States armed forces bearing this letter and was signed by the President. I had little choice but to submit.

"What's this all about," I asked.

"General, please," said Landsholme. "I'm your doctor. I have to do this. It's vital."

I had no doubt that Landsholme sincerely believed this to be very important. In the end, I trusted Landsholme more than I did President Cole. I rolled up my sleeve and my doctor injected me.

Once Landsholme had removed the syringe and I had rolled down my sleeve, the other officer started the briefing.

"General," he said, "what I'm about to tell you is not to leave this room. You can tell no one. No record of the meeting must be kept, except for the file that I have already given Lieutenant Colonel Landsholme."

"Go on," I said.

He launched into his prepared briefing. He informed me that five weeks ago there was a battle in a remote location in the upper Yangtze Valley between guerrilla forces of the rival Chinese governments. Shortly afterwards, the South China government secretly informed the North China government that during the battle a biological warfare facility was damaged. The South China government asked for—and was immediately granted—a cease-fire in that area. The two governments worked together to cordon off the area. Through our contacts in Siberia, we had learned that the Chinese believed that they had contained the situation. Both northern and southern governments agreed that there were no releases of any biological agents. However, according to our Siberian contacts, one case of a lung infection was reported in a nearby village ten days after the battle. The man died. The Chinese were adamant that this isolated case was not related. Nevertheless, they cleansed the entire village as a precaution.

"Cleansed," I asked.

"Burnt everything and everyone," he said.

The Chinese, he explained, discovered that the illness was a previously unidentified influenza-type virus. It did seem an unlikely candidate for biological warfare. It could have been just a newly mutated strain of influenza which, I suspected, was brought about by the extreme heat and drought in China. The timing of the man's death could have been coincidental, but either way the virus was a killer.

The virus, he said, was called Alveoli Destructive Pseudo-influenza or ADPI for short. It attacked the tissue in the alveoli of the lungs, in particular the tissue that separates the air we breathe from our blood. It was across this tissue that the exchange of oxygen from the air and carbon dioxide build-up in the blood occurred. The Siberians reported that the dead man died from drowning in his own blood, after the virus damaged the tissue and allowed the blood to enter the gas-parts of alveoli. Because the Chinese destroyed everything, however, we had only a description of its effects, not a sample of the virus.

Even without a sample of the virus, the Army's Biological Warfare Center in Georgia produced a serum that might mitigate the effects of the virus on the lung's alveoli if it ever resurfaced again. Unfortunately, the serum, which was difficult to make and had only been produced in extremely small quantities, didn't yet make one immune to ADPI—it just reduced the severity of the symptoms. The only personnel in III Corps authorized to receive the serum were the commanding general and the senior medical officer. I had just been given this serum, as had Lieutenant Colonel Landsholme.

"What about my officers," I asked. "Shouldn't they be given the serum, too?"

The colonel just shook his head.

"Nothing is likely to happen," he said. "It's just a precaution. I don't want to alarm you."

Too late. I was alarmed.

The greatest concern at the present, I supposed, was panic. The President had ordered that no news of the viral death was to get out. For now, Landsholme and I were to develop plans on how to deal with ADPI if it ever showed up here. More importantly, we had to plan how to deal with the panic if news of its existence ever got out. We could tell no one.

The briefing was over and the colonel left Landsholme and me to discuss the next steps. How do you plan in secret for this? I thought in bewilderment. And, how do I keep order on the streets and in the corps once the news of its existence is out?

– Chapter 15 –

The Pentagon

I was summoned to the Pentagon on short notice to attend a meeting on an undisclosed subject. I entered the meeting room without any files in my hands. I had memorized all the information that I would need. Brigadier General Zhang of my 32nd Security Brigade had secretly warned me that Army Operations was snooping around my units. Zhang had been interviewed at length by a colonel from Army intelligence. Zhang had been shown an order signed by Stopic that required him not to discuss the interview with me. Fortunately, Zhang knew where his loyalties lay and disobeyed that order.

General Stopic and his cronies were seated on the far side of the table, facing the door. Along with Stopic, there was a brigadier general from the Army Personnel Department, Stopic's aid, and an intelligence colonel who I assumed was the same one who had interviewed Zhang. All bureaucrats, I thought.

"General Eastland," said Stopic, "please be seated."

I sat alone on the other side of the table.

"We have received reports," he said, "—alarming reports—from the Ontario government about excessive use of force by units under your command."

I pretended to be surprised about the nature of the question.

"I have information," he said, "that you ordered the illegal use of convicted felons from the penal regiment of the Tenth Mountain Division. These dangerous felons have, by your orders, been set a liberty amongst the general population of Toronto. ... Colonel."

The intelligence colonel read formally from an electronic notepad in front of him.

It stated that on the thirteenth of July last year, contrary to standing orders regarding the use of convicted felons, I had ordered Major Khanan, commander of the 1st Special Support Unit, to send his men on intelligence missions in the city of Toronto. All these men were convicted felons from the 10th Penal Regiment--intelligent, highly dangerous felons with numerous social disorders. I acknowledged that I accepted the facts of the report.

The intelligence colonel continued his summation by stating that on fourth and fifth of November of last year, the SSU, as it was now called by the terrified population of Toronto, massacred one hundred and twenty citizens of that city. Since that date, killings had continued. On the twenty-eighth of January of this year, the SSU with the support of some elements of the 9th Urban Brigade burned three office blocks in west-central Toronto to the ground. People fleeing these buildings were shot or forced back into the flames. On the fourth of February, in some perverse commemoration of the first anniversary of III Corps' victory at Kemptville, the SSU and some elements of the 9th entered camps for the homeless in Mississauga and Brampton, two western suburbs of Toronto. They shot indiscriminately, killing or wounding hundreds of poor, homeless people. Elements of the Third Infantry Division attempted to stop the bloodshed, but General Cottick was ordered by me to keep his men out of the camps.

I didn't challenge a word of the colonel's statement at this time.

"General Eastland," Stopic sad, "these are serious accusations."

Then he dressed me down by stating that United States Army couldn't have commanders who acted with disregard for human life. The Army was the guest of the Ontario government and must respect the lives of its citizens.

"If," he said, "you remain in command of III Corps, your actions will be the subject of close and public scrutiny."

But there it was: the threat to subject me to an inquiry or even a court martial. However, if I resigned, all this would disappear into the Army bureaucracy—including me. Enough of this! I counterattacked. I informed General Stopic that I knew they were serious accusations, but the spin on them was misleading. The colonel should have been sure of his facts before he painted such a picture. I emphasized that the SSU was a superb intelligence-gathering unit. The men of that unit had performed their duties in a manner which would make any men in the Army proud. They were a credit to their commander, Major Khanan, and they had fully justified my confidence in them. If it had been in my power, I concluded, I would have remitted their sentences.

"Then it's fortunate that it's not within your power—," Stopic said.

I wasn't going to let that remark stand unanswered. I reviewed the events that the colonel had misrepresented. The mission I had given the SSU was to find, assess and destroy a gang called the Sunset Takers. Members of this gang blamed the older generation for the social problems that we live with. They were indoctrinated to believe that they must kill anyone belonging to that generation. They wouldn't hesitate killing any of us. What I said made the personnel general aid squirm in his seat.

When the SSU surrounded a large group of the Sunset Takers, the group had just killed over a dozen homeless old people. After a brief battle, the survivors of the gang surrendered. I believed it important to send a message to the leaders of the Sunset Takers that they couldn't continue killing with impunity. That was why I had ordered Major Khanan to conduct a trial on the spot. The gang members were found guilty and executed.

Within a week, the SSU, through excellent undercover work, had found the headquarters of the Sunset Takers. The members were heavily armed, so Major Khanan had called for reinforcements from the 9th. And Brigadier General Ulithi ordered the buildings set aflame to drive the members out. When the Sunset Takers came out firing weapons, my men returned fire. I could produce Brigadier General Ulithi's report on the event, if requested. Stopic knew that Ulithi had prepared a battle-incident report, but I had not forwarded it on to Army Operations. The report remained in reserve and available to me for unforeseen circumstances—such as the one I now found myself facing.

Some months later, the SSU had tracked the surviving Sunset Takers into the camps on the west side of Toronto. With the assistance of the 32nd Security Brigade, not the 9th—the colonel had got his facts wrong—the SSU went into the camp to arrest the few remaining Sunset Takers. The gang members had taken hostages. Through a level of force appropriate to the situation, my men freed as many hostages as they could. Some civilians were killed, but not many. General Cottick had already been ordered not to allow his men enter the camp because I wanted them to set up perimeters around the camps to catch any fleeing Sunset Takers. And they caught several dozen, who were later tried and executed.

"In cooperation with other units of III Corps," I said, "the SSU is responsible for wiping out the Sunset Takers."

I was pleased with my defense. It was a pleasure to watch Stopic and the others squirm. When I returned, I would have to again thank General Zhang for his advanced warning. Zhang had also misled the intelligence colonel as to which unit went into the camps.

Stopic looked deflated, but not yet defeated. He had another card to play.

"General," he said, "we also hear from sources within the Ontario government that the methods used by your men—both the SSU and your regular forces—are extreme."

His argument now turned on whether my actions corresponded to the conduct expected from soldiers of the United States Army.

I resented the general condemnation. I knew that my actions were harsh, exceptionally so, but they were necessary. The men of III Corps, through untiring work, made Toronto far safer than other similar sized cities. Murders and violent crime were down by over sixty percent since I took responsibility for the city. During the day, in many parts of the city, a citizen could walk down the street without fear of attack. They didn't even have to go armed. The same couldn't be said of those in Washington.

"General Eastland—," Stopic said.

The door burst open and a major rushed over and whispered into Stopic's ear. Stopic looked surprised. Without a word he rushed out of the door followed by the major. Those who remained sat there in awkward silence.

After two minutes, I decided that I had had enough. I stood up and left the room.

* * *

Fifteen minutes after leaving the Pentagon, my driver drove through the security checkpoint for the Ronald Reagan Military Airport and pulled up to my small propeller-driven airplane. The airport was busier than usual—much busier. When I had landed prior to my meeting, the airport was quiet. Now, there was activity everywhere. I exited the car and climbed into the airplane. I flopped down in a comfortable seat and said to the pilot in a flat, tired voice, "Let's go home."

"Not a good meeting, sir," the pilot asked.

"About what I expected," I said. "What's going on here? Why is there all this activity?"

"I don't know, sir," he said. "It all went crazy about five minutes ago. I'll see if I can find out."

We taxied to the runway. There was a line of about a dozen airplanes in front of us waiting to take-off. I thought we would have to wait along time, but the air-traffic controllers were getting us off the ground with unusual efficiency. It was soon our turn. We became airborne and left Washington behind us. I was very glad to leave.

"Sir," the pilot said. "They have just closed all airports in the Washington area. Reagan, Andrews, Dulles—all of them. Outbound only. Nothing is allowed to land."

I asked him if he knew why; and he promised to find out for me. With the computer auto-pilot engaged, he had little else to do.

I became lost in reflection on the meeting with Stopic and so forgot about the situation at the Washington airports. About half-an-hour into the flight, the pilot shouted in an excited voice, "Sir! They have just announced. There's been an accident—a nuclear accident!

"What! Where?"

"Just north of Richmond," he said. "There's a large cloud of radioactive material being blown towards Washington. They're evacuating the city."

I got out of my seat and made my way forward. I sat in the vacant co-pilot seat. "Get me General Gregorakis in Toronto," I ordered.

Gregorakis had not heard the news. I told my deputy commander to place III Corps on high alert and then find out what was going on.

By the time I landed at Toronto's downtown Island Airport an hour later, the situation had become clearer. A reactor in an old nuclear power station northeast of Richmond, Virginia, had suffered a catastrophic meltdown. A large cloud of highly radioactive gas had escaped, and prevailing winds were blowing it towards Washington. I realized that this news was what had abruptly ended my meeting with General Stopic. The top politicians and military leaders had given themselves over forty-five minutes to get out of the city before they told the general population. Once the news became public, the panic in Washington was incredible. Those who had transportation fled the city; those who did not, murdered and stole from those who did and then fled.

I was just lucky to have my airplane waiting for me. If I had taken any longer, some higher ranking officer would have commandeered my airplane, leaving me trapped in the doomed city. I too would have become one of those many unfortunates who died a lingering and painful death.

After I returned to my command, I spent the night in the communications room with my senior command staff. We listened to rapid and often unintelligible messages between Army units. It only gave us a faint image of the disaster that befell Washington. The cloud also hit Baltimore before being blown out to sea. In that city, the panic was not quite as great due to the population having a little extra time to react.

The political ramifications of the nuclear accident were enormous. President Cole relocated his government—such as it was—to St. Louis. I don't know why he chose that city. It seemed a strange choice to me, but Cole must have had his reasons. All of his cabinet and most of the Congressional leaders survived, but many of the people who ran the day-to-day affairs of the government were exposed and died within a month. The survivors scattered. Only a few managed to make their way to join the government in St. Louis; the rest melted away into the vast pool of disaffected and starving masses.

President Cole declared martial law throughout the country. By this time there were already seventeen states under martial law, so it was not as big a step as it seemed. Under an obscure provision of the 44th Amendment, Cole also postponed the upcoming November elections to a date suitable for the proper administration of the democratic voting process. I took that to mean never. Cole had governed for eight years and didn't want to lose power. This incident provided him with an excuse to keep that power. I don't mean to imply that Cole arranged for the accident, but he certainly took advantage of it to the fullest extent. Riots started immediately. Toronto was fortunately spared. Its citizens were not Americans and were already under martial law. If anything, the people of Ontario seemed to take a smug satisfaction that Americans had now descended to their level.

The Pentagon still functioned from its underground shelters, but in a greatly reduced capacity. The junior officers who were stationed in the Pentagon were dead, dying or had scattered. For those who did survive in the underground shelters, they did so with the knowledge that their families likely did not survive. Army Operations moved to the underground complex at Cheyenne Mountain in Colorado. With so much else going on, the military forgot about me. I remained in command of III Corps.

The day after the accident, I decided to personally inspect the two nuclear power stations within my jurisdiction. They were at Pickering and Darlington, both on the eastern edge of Toronto. At Pickering, the plant manager showed me around the station. He tried to be reassuring, but anyone could see that the equipment was worn out and the staff exhausted. Monitoring cameras didn't function. There were visible cracks in the cement around the nuclear units. Many systems were jury-rigged. I left Pickering without saying a word. I was very disturbed by what I had seen. At Darlington, a slightly newer station with a more recent refit, the situation was just slightly better. However, during my visit there was a small incident, as the plant manager called it. I was in the control center when lights started flashing. The technicians scurried around and after ten minutes the last of the warning lights turned off. The plant manager seemed unaffected by this routine occurrence, as he called it. I didn't believe him. I had seen enough.

Upon returning to my office, I gave orders that the two stations were to be closed immediately. The Ontario government protested. The power situation was already precarious; closing these two stations would mean daily blackouts. I gave the politicians vague reassurances that the stations would be reopened once the crisis was over, but I had no intention of allowing my jurisdiction to become a contaminated wasteland. For the first time, I demonstrated my authority in Ontario and closed those nuclear power stations over the objections of the politicians. I was in control now.

– Chapter 16 –

Toronto

It is with a heavy heart that I remember the tragic events in Toronto.

To celebrate Independence Day, General Gregorakis had planned some entertainment for the troops. He excelled at boosting the morale of the men. The show was to be held in the relative cool of the evening on a field just west of Queen's Park. The large field was once the central area of the University of Toronto's downtown campus. A wooden stand had been erected for the top officers and their guests. The rest of the men sat on the open grass. There were men at the event from every unit in III Corps in the Toronto area. Attendance at the event was selected either on the basis of merit or by a lottery. I left it to the individual unit commanders to decide how. Most selected a combination of the two: merit for a select few, a lottery for the remainder. All together, about three thousand men of III Corps were on the field. In addition, I invited as my guests the premier of Ontario and his wife.

The show commenced in the evening with a parade by the Third

Infantry Division's band. After the parade, I had the honor of presenting a sergeant in the Third Infantry Division's 53rd Aviation Battalion with his Distinguished Service Cross. The soldier had single-handedly rescued five of his fellow soldiers from a mob attack. The event occurred last January when his helicopter was shot down over one of the homeless camps in Hamilton (the westernmost satellite city of Toronto). After the crash, this muscular giant of a man disconnected the machine gun from the downed the helicopter and protected his wounded comrades from the mob. One by one he carried his men to a nearby ruin, while also providing covering fire for the ones still in the wreckage. Once his men were all safely hidden, he stormed back to the helicopter and held his position until the other helicopters of the regiment managed to secure the area and extricate the trapped men. General Cottick had recommended the prestigious medal for the sergeant, and I had added my support. III Corps had received the medal on the day before the nuclear accident in Richmond, but because of that event I never got around to presenting it to the brave soldier. The Independence Day show provided an excellent venue for such a presentation.

    I walked over to the soldier, who snapped a smart salute. I returned the salute, pinned on his medal, and shook his hand. He looked bashful and embarrassed when the men cheered enthusiastically.

    After the brief ceremony I walked back to the stand, but before I could take my seat Colonel Wycross intercepted me.

    "Sir, we must talk," he said. Wycross wouldn't bother me without a very good reason. I followed him to a point some distance from the stand. Major Khanan was waiting there for us.

    "Sir," he whispered, "Khanan's men have heard rumors of a possible attack on the leadership of III Corps. I believe the threat is real."

    "Details," I said.

    "Sorry, sir," Khanan said, "we've nothing more than rumors. We're not even sure what is meant by leadership. Is it a threat against you or a more general attack on the command staff? We don't know the nature of the attack, who's behind it, or when it's planned for."

"What makes you think this rumor has any substance," I asked. "What makes it different than all the other whispers of discontent?"

"The SSU agent," he said, "that reported the rumor is reliable."

The agent had contacts inside several of the most secretive gangs in the city. His contacts had provided valuable information in the past. I had a hunch that the agent could be correct.

"I would like to meet the agent, if possible."

"It's difficult, but it could be arranged—," Khanan said.

"Sir," Wycross said, "it may be too late by then. Look behind you."

Wycross pointed to the stand.

"The leadership of the corps," he said, "is seated on that stand. It's a tempting target. Shouldn't we cancel this event?"

I looked at the stand and could see my empty seat. My officers were watching a comedy sketch performed by two soldiers from the 6th Armored Brigade.

"I can't cancel it now," I said, "on the basis of a vague rumor and a hunch."

What message would that give to the gangs? What would the Ontario government think? An armed attack here was highly unlikely. I asked Wycross whether the field been swept for bombs.

"Twice, but—."

"But, a third time wouldn't hurt."

"Yes, sir," Wycross said.

"Very well," I said. "Do it discretely and start with the stand. Tomorrow, we'll figure out how to verify this rumor."

I dismissed the two officers and headed back to the stand and the laughter of the crowd at the comedians. And then …

And then …

And then, my world disintegrated.

I remember lying on my back looking up at the evening sky. I couldn't hear anything. I couldn't move. I was unsure where I was.

Confusion swirled through my mind. I struggled to clear my head and after considerable effort the confusion left me. My mind was clear and in a panic I attempted to stand up, but a sharp pain in my leg stopped me cold. I propped myself up and surveyed a scene of bloody carnage. Some of my soldiers were struggling to their feet while many others lay moaning. Yet others didn't move at all. I looked towards the stand. The wooden seats were covered with blood. There was no movement—just still bodies.

"My men!" I cried out.

A soldier rushed over to me.

"Don't worry, sir," she said. "I'll get you some help."

She then shouted to others. I soon found myself being carried away on a stretcher. I don't remember anything after that.

* * *

I struggled to get my eyes open. My mind felt a little woozy, as though it was working only at slow speed. I tried to focus on a blurry image of a woman sitting beside my bed. She was wearing a uniform.

"Eva," I asked.

"Yes, Walter," she said. "I'm here."

Eva squeezed my hand and shook her head sadly. My anguish consumed me. Nothing else existed except the emptiness that I felt. I passed out.

When I came to again, Eva was still there. My head was clearer now. I remembered the terrible events on the field. The memories drained me and left me emotionally dead.

"What happened," I asked.

"A splinter bomb," Eva said. "Very sophisticated. Very nasty. Colonel Wycross is investigating how it got past security."

"How bad?"

"Nearly four hundred dead," she said, "and over eight hundred wounded."

General Gregorakis, I learned, was dead. The premier and his wife were also among the dead. And General Cottick was badly wounded but, she said, he should recover.

I struggled to get out of the bed. My right leg felt numb. The surgeon had pulled out one of the bomb's needle-like metal splinters from my leg. The splinter damaged the nerves in my right leg, tore the thigh muscle and chipped the femur. The major artery in my leg was punctured. I had lost a lot of blood, but the blood would eventually be replaced. The muscle and bone would eventually heal, but the nerves would never fully recover.

"Walter," she said, "you can't go anywhere."

"Then help me," I said. I didn't mean to be short-tempered with Eva.

With Eva's assistance, I managed to hobble over to a waiting wheelchair. Eva pushed me out of the room.

How could I let this happen? My men depended on me. It was all my fault. I was racked with guilt.

* * *

The next day, I felt physically strong enough to hold a command meeting. The business of III Corps couldn't wait. I don't know how I managed to function that day. Some emotional defense mechanism within me kept me going. I was simply numb. With crutches and Eva's help, I managed to walk outside the hospital to a communications post that had been set up. Via teleconference, I had most of the surviving command staff on the line.

"What happened," I asked.

"An anti-personnel splinter bomb," said Wycross, "was detonated under the stand."

It was a terrible device for maiming and killing infantry or rioting civilians. The bomb's metal splinters killed or severely wounded most of those within fifty yards. Fortunately the wooden frame of the stand took most of the blast. If it had been an air-burst, the number of casualties would have been far higher. It must have been placed under the stand shortly before the show started—after the second bomb sweep. Wycross said that we had three leads. First, the bomb was definitely of American design. It was the latest version and was not in general use. He was already attempting to track it.

Second, an aide to the premier was missing. She was admitted into the secured area, but had not been seen since.

"We're looking into her movements," said General Zhang of the 32nd.

"Find her."

"Yes, sir," Zhang said.

"Third," said Wycross, "immediately after the bomb attack, widespread and coordinated riots started in Toronto. In my opinion, they were too soon after to be a coincidence."

"Do whatever you have to do," I said, "but I want some answers. Now, what is happening in the city?"

General Tuckhoe, commander of the Tenth Mountain Division, had assumed temporary command of III Corps during my absence. He hadn't been at the show. He and his deputy commander drew lots to decide who would go. His deputy won—or in reality lost since he was now among the dead.

"There are large riots throughout Toronto," Tuckahoe said, "but especially in the western part of the city. Our men are fighting back, but it's hard going and they're badly outnumbered."

"Sir," said Cottick's deputy, "we're hitting them hard. The men of the Third are eager to get their revenge."

I had already decided what I wanted to do.

"No. No more," I said, "We are embarking on a new strategy."

As our forces were being worn down in continual urban battles, I ordered that all units would be pulling out of Toronto completely. Before my officers could object, I emphasized that it was time we flexed our real muscles. We would shut the city down. No electricity, no food, no water. Nothing would be allowed in or out of the city—

including people. We were going to let them stew in their own cesspool.

"The gangs will take control," Zhang said.

"Yes," I said, "and they will fight each other instead of us. They will die instead of our men. It's time we showed the people of Toronto the difference between order and anarchy. Questions?"

The people in Toronto were Zhang's countrymen. So I asked him whether he or his men had any problems abandoning the city.

He assured me that his men would support me in this one hundred percent.

The men of the 32nd had been fighting in Toronto for much longer than us Americans had. It was clear they were tired. Zhang's only concern was that once out, his men wouldn't want to return.

"We'll worry about that later," I said.

Although I didn't tell the others at this time, I had no intention of ever going back in. My men were being wasted in the pointless urban battles. No more. All that was over. I had finished it.

I ordered that the 6th and the 32nd pull back to the northern edges of the city. The Third would cover the west and the Tenth the east. Aviation units of the Third and Tenth would cover Lake Ontario to the south of the city. We would create a defensible perimeter.

"Nothing gets in," I said, "and no one gets out. Shut the city down."

My orders were implemented to the letter. Electricity was transferred elsewhere in the province or into New York State. Water was stopped being pumped in and redirected to irrigate farms to the east and west of the city. Food shipments were halted at the perimeter. My soldiers were permitted to keep enough to bring them back up to full rations—a popular move with the men. Anyone who tried to leave the city was fired on. Thousands made the attempt, but they didn't make it. The city of Toronto was dying and its agony would last a long time. I wanted it to suffer.

– Chapter 17 –
Fort Drum

The men's stomachs were full—and that did wonders for morale. It had been a scorching summer, surpassing even the previous summer. There was no rain at all. Now my decision to close off Toronto paid dividends. Sufficient supplies of lake-water were now available for the irrigation of farmland to the east and west of Toronto and in upstate New York. Despite the summer drought, the region had crops growing throughout the summer for the first time in years. The extra water made all the difference. I controlled the taps to that water and everybody knew it.

Over the summer, I came under pressure to open up Toronto. The pressures ranged from halfhearted words from Mike Waverly (whose state was now receiving many more water shipments than was originally planned) to frantic pleas from the rump of the Ontario government. It had been a mistake to allow the Ontario politicians to leave Toronto and reestablish their capital in Barrie, a small city to the north. I should have left them in Toronto. They had allowed that city to descend into what it had become so they should have suffered the same fate as their fellow citizens.

Orders from Army Operations were confusing and contradictory. There were now three command centers for the Army: the sub-levels of the Pentagon, the depths of Cheyenne Mountain, and the makeshift center in the President's bunker in St. Louis. Each one was sending orders to III Corps. One minute I was to send the Third Infantry Division to Michigan and the next to Pennsylvania. I was to ship water back into Toronto; I was to ship Toronto's water to Chicago. I was informed that I would be soon promoted; I was to be relieved of duty. The last one came from General Stopic, who had scurried away from Washington and hid himself away in the depths of Cheyenne Mountain. I had no time for the man. He was a long way from my command, so I could ignore his orders with impunity. Orders from the sub-levels of the Pentagon were usually out of touch with the actual situation. I laughed when I read the one that ordered me to turn over command of III Corps to General Cottick and assume command of the Army of New England, as the orders called it. The order provided a detailed listing of this new Army, including two units from II Corps (which would never find the fuel to travel east) and one unit that had been disbanded years ago. The orders from the President's entourage in St. Louis were usually along the lines of: send military units to St. Louis immediately. President Cole had made a mistake setting up the government in St. Louis. The city's citizens had the mistaken impression that their lives would improve now that the President was nearby. The scorching heat and the worsening food shortages quickly disillusioned them. From what I could infer of the St. Louis news, Cole was surrounded by some very unhappy citizens. In the end, I ignored all orders, except where they suited me.

Following the events in July, I moved the headquarters of III Corps back to Fort Drum. I preferred the security and familiarity that the base provided. I set up home in the house that I had lived in earlier. The old home was a friend from happier times. My old office was another familiar friend. Within its walls, I felt in control.

I was at my desk when Wycross entered. He was followed by two brawny military policemen escorting a single prisoner. The prisoner was in handcuffs and ankle chains; he looked scruffy and malnourished. I recognized him, but could not immediately place a name to the face.

"Sir," Wycross said.

He sat down. The two MPs stood menacingly behind their charge.

"Sir," said Wycross, "this is Private Kellerman. He's charged with desertion. He disappeared from his unit just after the bombing in Toronto."

When Wycross mentioned the name Kellerman, I instantly recalled the man before me. He was one of the men from the spotlight unit that I had saved from the raging Hudson River. He was once a captain in an engineering battalion before he had murdered a man—ruthlessly and without remorse. Kellerman was in the Tenth's penal regiment when I reformed that regiment and integrated some of the prisoners back into the regular forces. Although I had saved the man once, I now had to end his life. Desertion couldn't be tolerated. As far as I was aware of, Kellerman was the first case of desertion that III Corps had experienced this year. I'd have to have him executed.

"Colonel," I said, "we can't let desertion go unpunished. We must make an example here."

"Sir," said Wycross, "I said Kellerman was charged with desertion. I don't believe that he did in fact desert. Let's just say he went on a mission without orders."

Wycross was being coy. Because of some personal quirk, he enjoyed surprising me. I indulged him because he was a superb intelligence officer.

"Out with it, Colonel," I said. "What's going on?"

"Kellerman," he said, "surrendered to the 83rd Military Intelligence Battalion attached to the Tenth. He just appeared in the center of their secured headquarters near Pickering—an amazing achievement in itself. The 83rd are reviewing their security procedures because of Kellerman."

Wycross dismissed the two MPs. They left and closed the door behind them.

"Kellerman," he said, "has an interesting story to tell. He insists that you must hear it—and I can see why. Go on, Private, tell your tale."

Kellerman stood up straight. As he did so, his handcuffs and ankle chains clanged together.

"Sir," he said, "I want to say that it's an honor to meet you again. Sorry I can't salute."

"Get on with it," I said.

"Sorry, sir," he said.

He started by explaining that he was stationed with his company, Company E of the 132nd Infantry Battalion, on the eastern edge of Toronto. He wasn't at the show when the bomb exploded. He said that he had no interest in attending and didn't participate in the attendance lottery. The next day the news of what happened at the show became known throughout his company. He was outraged. However, the attack and the tragic deaths provided him with a way of repaying his debt to me.

Since I had pulled him out of the river and saved his life, he had felt indebted to me. But how could he, a lowly private and a convicted felon, repay that debt? He decided that his repayment was to find the killers. Kellerman had my complete attention now.

He had left his unit and hid himself in the slums of Toronto, only moving around at night. At first, it was difficult figuring out the underground world, but after I had pulled my units out of the city it became much easier. Without the soldiers present, the gangs became much braver and more open. Street battles between rivals became a daily—even hourly—event. The gangs sometimes left wounded members where they had fallen. By dragging off the wounded or by capturing lone gang members, he extracted a considerable amount of information. Of course, he had to kill them afterwards. Kellerman stated this fact as coolly as one would discuss filling out a military leave form.

The gangs, he said, believed that the disappearance of their members was the work of a rival gang. This escalated the fighting, which worked to his advantage. Over a few weeks, he had unraveled an interesting picture of the gang structure. There were also some tantalizing links to parts of the Ontario government. In particular, in the form of a relationship between the boss of a gang called the Grill-V Crew and a woman in the Premier's Office. It took him over a week to trace the woman. He had to interrogate quite a few members of the Grill-V Crew, but he finally found her.

"The woman," Wycross said, "was likely to be the one we have been searching for."

Was? I thought, but I remained quiet.

The Grill-V Crew, I learned then, was one of the most secretive and best organized gangs in Toronto. They branded their members with a V-shaped mark, usually in the center of the chest, both men and women. The SSU had been trying to get inside that gang for a long time.

Kellerman was sorry to say that one man he interrogated and killed claimed to be a member of the SSU. At the time he didn't believe the man, as he thought all of our forces had been pulled out of the city. But Wycross informed him that this was not the case and one of the SSU men was missing.

I was intrigued by all of this.

"Continue," I ordered.

Kellerman then found the headquarters of the Grill-V Crew. The woman was inside and well protected. He studied the building for some time, and finally found a weak point. After neutralizing several guards, he slipped inside and extracted his target. He took her back to one of his safe houses and interrogated her for two days. She was a tough nut to crack but eventually she talked. She admitted to planting the splinter bomb. It was provided to her by her lover, the boss of the gang, along with instructions how to arm it and where to put it.

"So it was an attack by a gang," I said.

"No, sir," Kellerman said. "There's more."

Kellerman pressed the woman for more information on where the gang boss got the bomb. It seemed to him that the splinter bomb was too advanced for the usual weapons available to the gangs. By now she was in pretty bad shape, and he had difficulty understanding her. She said that the governments supplied the bomb.

"The Ontario government?"

"She clearly said governments in the plural," Kellerman said. "She died before she could tell me which ones."

So I had not one, but two or more governments plotting against me and in collusion with a powerful gang. I don't consider myself excessively paranoid, but even paranoids have real enemies. I felt certain that the rump Ontario government was one of them. Clearly they wanted to depose me and the premier, who they likely viewed as too friendly to me.

"Go on, Private, continue your story."

"Yes, sir," Kellerman replied.

After getting information from the woman, his next logical target was the gang boss. Naturally, after the abduction of his lover, the boss became difficult to track and impossible to capture. Kellerman realized that he couldn't get any information out of the boss. Nevertheless Kellerman decided that the man had to die. To get weapons for the task, Kellerman raided a rival gang's armory and obtained a considerable quantity of explosives. The gang boss moved between houses — a different one each night. Kellerman couldn't be sure which one he would be in, but he believed he knew the location of them all. His solution was to wire them all with explosives. He did this over a period of six nights. On the seventh night, he tracked him to one of his safe-houses. When the boss entered the house, Kellerman triggered the explosives. He detonated the other safe-houses as well to cover his escape. That decimated the leadership of the gang and ended the gang as a force in Toronto. The power vacuum that his activities had created led to numerous battles between other gangs that were intent on taking over the territory of the Grill-V Crew. After that, Kellerman slipped out of the city and made his way back to the Tenth. He surrendered to the intelligence battalion, because he knew its commander would contact Colonel Wycross and that he would bring him before me.

"Thank you, Private," Colonel Wycross said.

I leaned back in my chair and studied Kellerman. I knew he was capable of planning and executing a killing in cold blood, but was his story believable? According to his story, this man single-handedly had evaded gangs, stole explosives from their well-protected armories, and kidnapped a woman—the lover of a gang boss—right from inside the gang's headquarters. He had killed numerous guards without being caught, and had tortured many gang members, including a woman. This man had extracted valuable information that even my SSU had failed to discover. Finally, he got through the lines of my Tenth Mountain Division and appeared in the midst of its intelligence battalion. And supposedly, Kellerman did all this to repay me for saving his life four years ago. Did I believe him? Damn right I did! Fate had presented me with a superb weapon—ready to be wielded on my command. I had need of such a weapon.

"Colonel," I said, "Private Kellerman is to be released immediately. All charges are to be dropped."

Obviously I couldn't assign him to the SSU because he killed one of their own, so I put him with my personal bodyguard. Unspecified duties, reporting directly to me. I promoted him to sergeant, effective immediately.

"Thank you, sir," Kellerman said.

"I thought you'd like Kellerman's talents," Wycross said. He then stood up and led Kellerman (who was still in handcuffs and ankle chains) to the door.

Before they left, I called out to Kellerman.

"Yes, sir?"

"Thank you for a job well done," I said. "I appreciate what you did."

My gratitude made Kellerman's face beam with satisfaction. It was one of the rare occasions that I witnessed any emotion coming from him.

* * *

With Colonel Joyita beside me, I limped from my staff car to the derelict building. My cane supported the weight that I couldn't place on my wounded leg. My leg caused me considerable pain, and the pain reminded me of the terrible day in Toronto—and this caused an even worse sort of pain.

As I crossed the short distance from my car to the building's only door, gray ash rained down on me and covered my uniform. The ash had started to fall earlier in the week and now there was a thin layer covering everything. It gave the landscape a dreary, drab look, made worse by the thick black clouds above. The ash was from the many forest fires that were raging across North America, particularly in the west. From the few reports that had been sent to III Corps from Army Operations, it was estimated that there were over thirty thousand separate fires burning, although that number was probably too high now because smaller fires were combining into single gigantic fires. In my jurisdiction, the forests of the Adirondack Mountains burnt fiercely, as did the forests of the Algonquin Highlands. At night, you could see the sky to the east and to the north glowing orange. It was eerie and ominous.

The building that I entered had once been a munitions depot for training exercises decades ago, but it had long since fallen into disuse. It was in a remote corner of the base—far from prying eyes and straining ears. It was perfect for my needs. As I reached the threshold, I turned to see Major General Tuckhoe's helicopter land. The blades whipped up the ash into a blinding storm. Even so, I told Joyita to order the pilot to keep the helicopter's engines running. The noise would reduce the chance of any electronic eavesdropping.

Inside the concrete room, seated on old crates and empty ammunition boxes, Major General Micklebridge, Colonel Waycross and Major Khanan were waiting. Together with Tuckhoe and Joyita, these officers comprised my inner circle. I trusted them like I trusted no one else. Once Tuckhoe, Joyita and I had entered and found a box to sit on, I started the clandestine meeting.

The single purpose of the meeting was to establish who my enemies were. There were a lot of candidates. The rump Ontario government was surely one of them, but no doubt there were others. Rochon's government could be taking revenge or possibly Ijavek was pulling strings from his house arrest. I wouldn't put it past General Stopic from doing whatever he could to ensure my downfall. However, there were more disturbing possibilities. If General Cottick had not been severely wounded in the bombing, I might have suspected him. On the surface, my relations with the commander of my most powerful division were cordial, but there was something underneath that I couldn't put my finger on. He could have been the commander of III Corps if the Cole Administration had not forced the Army to choose me. Cottick was a notoriously ambitious officer, and I was certain that he resented me for getting command of the corps. I would have if the roles had been reversed. I didn't give voice to this concern in front of the others. I didn't want to imply that anyone in III Corps was under suspicion. III Corps had to be — and seen to be — a unified force in a world breaking apart.

The most disturbing possibility for my list of potential enemies was the governor of New York. Mike Waverly had been my longtime friend and had assisted me when I wanted return to active service after teaching at West Point. Waverly had also been a good friend to Martin Cole, but that did not stop him from turning on the President when Cole demanded more water from the Great Lakes. If Waverly could turn on one friend, why not another? I had to find out.

Colonel Wycross started his status report.

He had traced the movements of the splinter bomb. It came from the munitions storage facility at Lockport Air Force Base, near Buffalo. It wasn't known if the bomb was stolen or found another way out of the base. It wasn't a standard type of bomb to be stored there, nor was it generally issued to the Air Force. Wycross had examined the flight logs from that base prior to the attack. There were two unscheduled flights from Colorado Springs that he could not account for. One on June 23 and another on June 26. They may have not been connected to the bomb and could have been just coincidental, but the bomb must have come from somewhere.

The flights were not coincidental. Stopic was behind this. I was certain of it. More disturbing, I now had to add the commander of the Air Force's 174th Wing to my growing list of potential enemies. It was highly unlikely that the unscheduled flights could have come in without his knowledge.

"Are we investigating the command staff at Lockport," I asked.

"I've got someone on the inside," said Wycross, "working for me. There's nothing to report yet, but we're continuing to investigate."

"Continue your report," I said.

After Lockport, the bomb was next seen on July 1 in a disused laboratory once operated by the Toronto city government. That night the bomb disappeared from the laboratory. It was collected by a gang member of the Grill-V Crew. Three days later the bomb was placed underneath the limousine of the Ontario premier, which implied that some members of his own security forces were involved in the plot—possibly many of them. The limousine went through our checkpoint without inspection. It wasn't customary for our soldiers to inspect a vehicle that had been thoroughly examined by the premier's own security forces. Such a search would have been seen as impolite and insulting to our host government. The conspirators found the weak point in our security and they used it. The woman on the premier's staff collected the bomb from its hiding place and planted it in the stands after the second bomb sweep.

My intelligence officer was careful not to mention that it was by my orders that the premier's limousine wasn't inspected. I had been concerned about the politics of American soldiers searching our host's car. Never again, I thought. From now on, I'm doing what has to be done and damn the politics.

"Thank you, Colonel," I said. "We must now consider our next steps. The woman who planted the bomb is dead. The gang responsible is smashed and its leader is dead."

"Excuse me, sir," Major Khanan said. "My SSU agents confirm that the Grill-V Crew is no more, but how did this happen?"

"Sorry, Major," I said, "we had a special intelligence asset operating in Toronto under my direct orders."

This wasn't entirely true as Kellerman had acted without my orders or knowledge, but Khanan didn't know about Kellerman. Only Wycross and I did—and I wanted to keep it that way. I emphasized the phrase under my direct orders in such a way that Khanan took the hint and prudently didn't ask for details. I suspected that he would have the SSU agents investigate to find out what asset I had, but Wycross had covered Kellerman's trail well. Khanan would have to be careful in his investigation so as not to anger me. I was confident that Kellerman's role would remain a secret.

"It's clear," I said, "that the gang was acting on behalf of someone."

The link with the woman and the complicity of the premier's security staff implied that elements of the current Ontario government were involved. However, the link to the 174th Wing also led to others. We had to investigate whatever connections we could find.

I ordered Major Khanan to pull the rest of the SSU out of Toronto and infiltrate the Ontario government in its new capital of Barrie north of Toronto. Colonel Wycross was to continue to investigate the 174th Wing and if there were connections to any Army units. Also, I wanted

Khanan to contact the commander of the military detachment guarding Ijavek. I intended to draft orders for him to monitor Ijavek closely, but without appearing to do so. If Ijavek was involved, we might be able to follow his contact.

General Tuckhoe would have the Tenth's intelligence battalion infiltrate Rochon's government. I knew that wouldn't easy, but I had confidence in the men of the Tenth. Major Khanan was to render any assistance that General Tuckhoe requested because the SSU had considerable expertise in infiltrating Canadian institutions. I ordered Tuckhoe to take advantage of that experience. Tuckhoe was proud of the capabilities of the Tenth's intelligence team—a team I had created. Nevertheless, he saw the wisdom of learning from the men of the SSU.

"Sir," Joyita said, "it occurs to me that Lockport Air Force Base is located in New York. Could the state government be involved?"

I didn't want to be the one to broach this issue, so prior to the meeting I had asked Joyita to pose this question.

I looked gravely concerned, which wasn't just a rehearsed response; I was really very worried about this possibility and its broader ramifications. Rochon was contained, Ijavek was a minor irritant, the Ontario government could be easily crushed and Stopic was far away, but Waverly was nearby and important. The majority of my men called the state of New York their home. I actively encouraged my soldiers to bring their families to Fort Drum and surrounding Jefferson County. I couldn't take on the governor of New York without serious political damage—both externally and within III Corps. I would have to start subtly conditioning my men for this contingency. Joyita's question was the first step in that conditioning.

I turned to General Micklebridge. Her troops were now stationed around Albany, at the governor's orders, to keep peace in that city.

"General," I asked, "can you investigate this possibility?"

Eva look disturbed, as did the others in the room, but unlike the others she had in effect two commanders. As a divisional commander in III Corps she reported to me, but as the commander of a New York

National Guard division she reported directly to the governor. I was counting on Eva's personal loyalty to me.

"Yes, General," she said, "I'll have some of my intelligence people look into it. I'll have to choose them carefully as this will be a sensitive investigation—to say the least."

"I agree," I said. "I'd prefer that you kept the investigation in the hands of just a few trusted officers. If the investigation takes longer, so be it."

"General," Wycross said, "might I suggest that I make an open visit to the Governor's Office? If there is any complicity in the state government, I might be able to get a sense of it."

I agreed, but I also decided then and there to send Kellerman to Albany. Whereas Wycross would travel to Albany overtly, Kellerman would sneak in covertly.

I had set my intelligence machine in motion, and now I had to prepare contingency plans for what it discovered. There was little doubt that some of these plans would involve decisions and acts that would be unpleasant and irreversible. I resolved that I wouldn't shy away from what had to be done.

– Chapter 18 –

Buffalo

The commander of the military detachment guarding the ex-Deputy Prime Minister of Canada was on the radio explaining to me what he had discovered. Ijavek was indeed in clandestine contact with the rump Ontario government in Barrie. I suspected it all along. The Puppeteer just couldn't leave well enough alone. I ordered the commander to maintain his surveillance and track the movements of Ijavek's go-between, a young man who washed Ijavek's laundry in a nearby river.

I had no sooner given my orders when Wycross burst into my office. He was clearly excited. He forgot to salute, but I let that pass. I signed off the radio and flicked off the scrambler switch.

"Yes, Colonel?" I said.

"Sir," he said. "We have something. The SSU has discovered that senior members of the new Ontario government will be meeting next week. It's to be a secret meeting."

I didn't see the significance of this news.

"Yes?"

"It is to be held in Buffalo," he said. "On New York soil!"

"Oh."

A meeting on New York soil implied that the Ontarians would be meeting with representatives of the New York state government and possibly those of the federal government. However, I doubted this latter possibility as President Cole had many other worries with which he had to contend.

"We've got them!" Wycross said.

"Excellent work," I said. "Do we know where and when exactly?"

"Next Thursday," he said. "In the early afternoon. It's to be in conference room in a hotel that has a view of Lake Erie, but we don't know which one yet."

"Find out," I said.

In the meantime, I told him that I wanted electronic listening devises installed in all such hotels. I also wanted a security team put together from the corps' military police battalions—hand-picked men who are unquestioningly loyal to the corps. I wanted Major Khanan and some SSU men there as well. And he was to keep all that very quiet, giving it utmost security.

"What about General Stafford," he asked. "Buffalo is the headquarters of the Fifth Guard Division."

"I'll talk to General Stafford," I said, "and provide your men with a cover story."

I didn't believe that Stafford would be involved, but I had to guard against that contingency. No, it was more likely that Buffalo was chosen as the meeting location precisely because it was the headquarters of the Fifth Guard. This was my weakest division, and its forces were spread all over western New York. It also had the smallest and least-equipped intelligence group of all my divisions. In addition, the corps' intelligence units focused most of their activities in Ontario—not New York. Buffalo was near the border and far from my headquarters at Fort Drum. Albany was on the other hand close to my headquarters.

Ontario politicians attempting to travel secretly to Albany would have been noticed and, if discovered, I would have become suspicious. Conspirators are always worried about creating suspicions in the ones they're plotting against—as I should know. Ironically, if the Ontarians had traveled openly to Albany, I wouldn't have paid much attention.

I dismissed Wycross to start his tasks, and then I quietly sat at my desk, deep in thought. If events in Buffalo proved me correct, I had to act decisively. My enemies—all my enemies—would have to be crushed at once. There would be no half measures this time and no politics would get in the way. I started to develop my plans. My two top concerns were how much could I tell my senior commanders and how would I justify my actions to my men. I was confident in the loyalty of my men, but if I was wrong and they turned on me, all this would be over very quickly.

* * *

Thursday, September 27, found me sitting in a communication vehicle that was hidden in a deserted area of Buffalo. The air-conditioning system of the vehicle wasn't keeping up with the heat generated from the electronic equipment when added to the heat outside. My uniform was drenched in sweat, but I couldn't leave the vehicle. I had to see and hear what was going on. Events had reached a critical phase.

Throughout the morning, I had watched on the monitor Waverly's security detail sweeping the hotel for electronic listening devises and bombs. They were not as good or as imaginative as my men, so they didn't find any of my devises. It also helped that Waverly's deputy security officer was one of mine—or more accurately one of Micklebridge's.

The choice of the old Delaware Star Hotel was a good one from Waverly's point of view. The old hotel was built four decades ago by Star Corporation when America was at the peak of its wealth. It was a giant pyramid-shaped building of glass and thick external beams. It had the advantages of being well away from other structures, having an easy perimeter to secure, and being defensible if attacked. It was close to the bridge to Fort Eire, so the Ontario delegation could quickly scuttle back over the border if needed. However, as I knew he would have to, Waverly relied on forces from the Fifth Guard Division to provide his outer line of security. Waverly's staff had given General Stafford a false story about the governor meeting with the mayor of Buffalo to discuss the water situation in western New York. Routine meeting, nothing special—that's what they told Stafford. General Stafford agreed to provide the necessary men. Why shouldn't he? His office sent a low priority notification of the event to III Corps headquarters. Because he needed the security forces of the Fifth, Waverly had to gamble that this routine event wouldn't be brought to my attention. It was a good gamble. My administration staff never informed me of the event. If I hadn't already known, Waverly would have gotten away with it.

I was ready for what was about to happen. In Buffalo, trusted men from the corps' 13th and 27th Military Police battalions and from the Tenth's 83rd Military Intelligence Battalion were with me. Elements of the corps' 236th Signals Battalion were also present. The signals battalion had helped the 83rd to place the listening devises, and I was monitoring the proceedings from one of its communications vehicles. The battalion would play a crucial part in helping me manage the fallout from what was about to happen. My reserve unit, the 10th Urban Assault Battalion, was poised in the woods of Darien Lake State Park to the west of Buffalo, ready to move into the city to establish order. And of course, I had Major Khanan and over half of the SSU with me as well.

At 12:55 p.m., Waverly and his entourage arrived. Waverly spent a long time talking to his security chief regarding the security arrangements and the sweeps for bombs and listening devices. It amused me to listen to the security chief assure the governor that no listening devices had been found.

With the arrival of the Ontario delegation two hours later, I put my men on high alert. Many of the Ontarians, as they entered the hotel, looked furtively over their shoulders. They were clearly apprehensive about being on American soil. Two sets of political security forces guarded the various hotel entrances and some were placed on the hotel roof. Inside, the security forces established themselves mainly on the ground floor and the second floor, where the meeting was to take place. Outside the hotel, elements of the Fifth Guard Division established an outer perimeter. The arrangements were all very predictable. Those few civilians in the area quickly took the hint and disappeared back into their slums.

The meeting started abruptly when the Ontarians started to loudly complain about my severe restrictions on them, the situation in Toronto and my cavalier attitude towards the lives of the citizens of Ontario. I had heard it all before. The new premier went into a long tirade about my ignoring him and his office. Once he got on a roll no one could shut him up, but eventually he ran out of steam. When he did, the room was quiet and we turned to Governor Waverly. I had promised myself that I wouldn't act until I had heard my old friend betray me from his own lips.

"I think we must..." Waverly said.

I would like to think that his conscience was bothering him and he was reluctant to take the next step, but it was more likely that Waverly the politician was performing to an audience.

"General Eastland clearly lost it in Toronto," he said. "He's mentally and criminally deranged and I don't think any of us are safe."

I had heard it from my old friend's lips, but I was too stunned to take any action.

"General Eastland is," Waverly said, "in my opinion, no longer fit for command. I have spoken to Army Operations and they agree with me. He must be relieved of command."

The Ontarians were clearly surprised by this statement. It was far more than they had hoped for.

"However!" Waverly said, as he banged his fist down on the table. "However, his troops don't share my assessment. The men of III Corps are fanatically loyal to their general. It isn't clear to me that we can relieve or arrest Eastland in Ontario or New York. We must first get him away from his men. Only then can we act."

I felt a hand on my shoulder. It snapped me back to life. I turned to see Colonel Wycross looking at me. Major Khanan stood behind with a worried expression on his face.

"Gentlemen," I said, "I've heard enough. Let's go."

As the communication vehicle got underway, Wycross lifted his radio to his mouth and ordered my men to action. I would smother this fire before it got out of control.

Events happened very fast. A small nerve gas bomb exploded on the roof of the hotel. The invisible gas rendered all the security men on the roof unconscious. Moments later, snipers from the 13th Military Police Battalion took out the security guards at the front door. Before the men of the Stafford's Fifth Guard Division could react, I arrived on the scene with men of the SSU and the 27th Military Police Battalion. Using my cane for support, I limped quickly over to the commander of the perimeter detail and ordered him to stand down. I briefly explained that there was a situation developing in the hotel and that I was taking command. I ordered him to contact General Stafford and inform him that I needed him here immediately. I knew that Stafford was far to the southwest in Jamestown (where I had sent him). It would take him an hour or more to get to Buffalo. Events would be long over by then.

The officer obeyed my orders and my men entered the hotel unopposed. Inside, the political security men were initially surprised and confused by the appearance of American soldiers. They had not been told what was going on and so were expecting only the usual problems with local rioters. Belatedly, some realized what was going on and fought back. They were quickly dealt with. With the political security forces neutralized, I entered the conference room. The politicians were still seated when I entered. In unison, their heads turned towards me. Their expressions were a mix of surprise, guilt and horror. I stood silently at the base of the table. My men fanned out behind me and forced the politicians from their chairs. The new Ontario premier shouted abuse at me. I ignored him as I had always done. Some of the women in the room and one of the men started to cry. My men forced them from their seats and pushed them out of the room. Colonel Wycross escorted Governor Waverly to the door. Waverly, as he walked towards me, stopped and looked searchingly at me. I wanted to say something to him, but couldn't think of anything. We looked at each other in silence. It was a poignant moment that I find difficult to describe. Wycross pushed Waverly along, and soon I was left alone in the room. I leaned heavily on my cane. My leg ached from all the exertions of the last few minutes, but I attempted to push the pain from my mind. I had other things to think about. The reality of my situation was sinking in. When I entered that room, I had crossed a line and there was no going back now.

I returned to my communications vehicle. The 10th Urban Assault Battalion was already on its way. My next task was to call General Micklebridge.

"How goes it," she asked.

"According to plan," I said. "We have them. Execute your orders."

"Yes, sir," she said.

Micklebridge's National Guard division in Albany captured the State Capitol, the Governor's Mansion and City Hall. The operation was executed smoothly. There were no significant problems. All politicians and staff in the Capitol were arrested; others were tracked down in their offices or homes.

My next call was to Major General Price of the 6th Armored Brigade. Price came on the line.

"General Price," I said. "There has been a development of a very serious nature."

"Oh?"

Price was not one of my inner circle, so I hadn't informed him of the plot against me.

"There's been a plot," I said, "involving the rump Ontario government. We've uncovered it before they could take action and all is well. I'm ordering you to enter Barrie and arrest all members of the government. No doubt some are innocent, but we'll have to work out who they are later."

Given the ongoing investigation into the bombing in Toronto and the clear connections to the Ontario government, Price wasn't all that surprised. In fact, I discovered to my pleasant surprise that Price had, on is own initiative, developed a plan to cover that precise threat.

By the time General Stafford arrived, Buffalo, Albany and Barrie were firmly under my control. Stafford quickly appraised the situation.

"I'm with you," he said. "It's time something was done about this mess. I lost some good boys in Toronto."

I accepted his support, but I wondered to myself what Stafford would have said to Waverly if it was me under arrest.

* * *

I sat in the communication vehicle and pressed the button that turned on the microphone. I was about to start the most important speech of my life. I didn't fool myself: my life depended on what I was about to say. If the officers and men of III Corps didn't support me, all would fail. It was 10:00 p.m. when I started the speech. I had been the military governor of Ontario and upstate New York for nearly six hours. The support of my men, or lack of it, would determine the duration of my governorship. Would it be measured in years or hours? The next few minutes would decide the issue.

I don't know if the men believed all that I said about saving civilization, but they heard the message about saving themselves and their families. In the end, my men were loyal to me. My only doubts were in regard to the men of the Third Infantry Division. If General Cottick came out against me, his sway over his men could have won them over to him. However, the issue was decided not by me but by Army Operations in Colorado. General Stopic denounced me and relieved me on the grounds of mental unfitness. There were also angry accusations of treason. However, Stopic didn't name Cottick as the new commander of III Corps (a mistake for him, I believe), but a lieutenant general from Army Operations headquarters. Obviously, Stopic believed all of III Corps' command staff were compromised. This replacement general (wisely for him) never arrived to take command. If Cottick was uncertain whether or not to support me, Stopic's actions made up his mind.

Although I had appealed for units outside of III Corps to join my cause, I never really expected any to do so. I had only included this so that other commanders would be more worried about their own men than taking action against me. It was a welcomed surprise when the next day the commander of Michigan's Eleventh Guard Division called me to place his division and what was left of the 23rd Urban Brigade under my command. The Eleventh and the 23rd had bled themselves white in Detroit—the commander said as much to me. I realized what he and his men wanted. My first order to him was to withdraw from Detroit. The Eleventh and the 23rd, along with elements of the Third Infantry Division, would shut down Detroit in the same manner as Toronto. Food and water would be diverted to rural northern Michigan and to his soldiers.

After giving this order, I realized that, only one day after Governor Waverly posed the question about which city would suffer the same fate as Toronto, I had an answer for him: it was to be Detroit. The death of that city was long and bloody.

– Chapter 19 –

Fort Drum

Following the arrests in Buffalo, I had to make some very unpleasant decisions, but the most unpleasant one of all lay before me. I sat at my desk in my office at Fort Drum, where I had returned after the events in Buffalo. I re-read the sheet of paper before me and once again pushed it away. Colonel Joyita had personally typed the execution order for me to sign and had placed it before me. Now alone in my office, I couldn't face what had to be done. I had signed so many execution orders over the past two days. Why was this one so different? Mike Waverly was once a good friend. Over the years, we had talked on the state of world affairs for hours at a time. I had laughed at his witty jokes, and he had endured my sermons on how to fix the country. Our long-standing friendship made his betrayal impossible for me to bear.

All the scheming politicians and bureaucrats that had been rounded up in Buffalo, Albany and Barrie had been shipped to the prison at Fort Drum. We also had netted an Air Force colonel and a major from the 32nd Security Brigade among the conspirators at the Delaware Star Hotel. General Zhang disclaimed all knowledge of the major's actions, and I believed him. I had to believe him; I couldn't risk loosing the loyalty of the commander of one of my armored brigades by pursuing the matter too far. I accepted Zhang's assurances that the major was acting alone. Nevertheless, there was a cloud of doubt over the 32nd. I'd have to watch Zhang and his men a little more carefully. They would have to prove themselves. I ordered Zhang to purge his brigade of all those that showed any sympathy to the Ontario government. Zhang did so with ruthlessness that surprised me. Did that indicate a guilty conscience? I hoped not.

As for the Air Force colonel, the commander of the 174th Wing also gave me the same assurances as Zhang, but I didn't believe him. The bomb had come through Lockport Air Force Base. I knew he was involved, but if I arrested him I would send a message to the men of III Corps that their leaders couldn't be trusted. This I couldn't do. Everyone in III Corps needed to believe that we were united in our new duty. If it was an illusion—and I prayed it was not—the illusion needed to be carefully maintained. The 32nd, an ex-Canadian unit, was different, and the men accepted its different status within III Corps. Everyone accepted a purge of that brigade, but I couldn't repeat the same purge in any of my American units. Morale would plummet.

I ignored Waverly's unsigned execution order and decided to focus my mind on the Air Force problem. I walked to my office door, opened it and called to my secretary. I ordered her to get Sergeant Kellerman. My assassin arrived a few moments later. He saluted and stood quietly at attention. My secretary closed the door.

"Sergeant," I said. "I have a special assignment for you."

"Yes, sir," Kellerman said.

"The commander of the 174th Wing," I said, "is involved in the Toronto bombing. However, I can't arrest him. It wouldn't be good for the morale of the men. I'd like you to arrange an accident for him—a fatal accident. It mustn't appear to be anything other than an accident.

Is that clearly understood?"

"Yes, sir," he said. "I understand perfectly."

"Thank you Sergeant, That is all."

"Sir?"

"Yes."

"While we are discussing sensitive matters," he said. "I've a proposal for you."

"Go on."

He told me that the troops suspected for a long time that the Ontario government was behind the bombing, but there were also rumors that the Canadian government in Ottawa was involved. Now, he didn't know if this was true or not, but clearly Prime Minister Rochon had an interest in seeing discord develop within III Corps. Rochon had been and, in Kellerman's opinion, always would be an enemy of III Corps. Kellerman expected that there would be a long series of intrigues coming out of Ottawa if we did nothing. Even if that was not true, at the very least Rochon would provide a safe haven to our enemies."

"Hmm," I mused.

"We should take preemptive action."

"Such as?"

I could see exactly where Kellerman was heading with this.

"Rochon," he said, "is extremely well guarded, mostly from his enemies in Quebec. Think about powerful message that would be sent if we assassinated him. No enemies of III Corps would feel safe."

More than anything else Kellerman wanted the challenge—that much was obvious. Nevertheless, I could see the wisdom in what he was suggesting. I'd be glad to be rid of that particular thorn in my side. With chaos in Ottawa, I could free up some of my troops from covering that city. I slowly nodded my concurrence. I can't be sure but I think a brief smile flashed across Kellerman's face. My assassin turned and left. I knew that I wouldn't see him again until his two tasks were completed. What a weapon! I'm glad that I was fated to wield it and not my enemies.

Alone in my office again, I dragged Waverly's execution order toward me again. I knew I had to sign it, but still I resisted. I had signed so many execution orders since the end of the trials. The military trials had been held in the administration building of Fort Drum's prison. The trials had only taken two days. They were quick because there was little more that needed to be proven; the conspirators had been caught in the act. What more evidence was needed? I had not taken part in the trials (I left that up to others), but I reserved for myself the unpleasant responsibility of signing the execution orders. Waverly's was the last one.

I picked up the pen lying on my desk. I studied it. It was just an ordinary pen, but it felt heavy in my hand. I took a deep breath and poised the pen over the paper. My hand shook. I replaced the pen on my desk and flexed my hand. I picked up the pen and tried again. My hand continued to shake. This time I ignored the shaking. I scrawled my signature at the bottom and pushed the paper away from me. My hand was still shaking when I dropped the pen into the wastebasket beside my desk. I got up and walked out of my office. The execution order was left on my desk for Colonel Joyita to collect.

The execution of my friend Mike Waverly was necessary. If it were not, I would never have ordered it.

* * *

I had not attended any of the executions. I didn't wish to watch the conspirators die. So many of them had to be put against the wall of the prison's exercise yard—Ijavek and his arrogant assistant Arbique were the first. I was told that Arbique cried all the way from his cell, and Ijavek had stared silently and defiantly at his executioners the entire time. More followed: the new Ontario premier and his cabinet, dozens of New York assemblymen, the Air Force colonel and the major from the 32nd Security Brigade, and others. Top bureaucrats in both the

New York and Ontario government were executed, although I released most of the low-level bureaucrats. I needed some of them to help run my government.

The prison commandant had methodically carried out the executions in the same order as he received the execution papers. As I had signed Waverly's order last, he was the last one to be executed. From an empty room on the prison's third floor, I looked down out of the barred window and into the courtyard below. For some reason I felt compelled to witness this execution. Neither the soldiers nor Mike Waverly knew that I was watching from above. No one ever knew.

Four men from the Fort Drum Prison Detachment escorted the prisoner to the wall and then left. The old brick wall was riddled with bullet holes. The fresh holes were clearly visible in the bright sunshine. The holes were not just from executing the conspirators; I had also ordered the execution of the remaining military prisoners of Fort Drum. These men were either mentally deranged or violently dangerous. They couldn't be assimilated into the SSU or the labor battalions. The murderers, rapists, psychopaths and worse were a waste of valuable resources. Three days before I had ordered men of the SSU to execute their one-time fellow inmates. I felt no guilt or uneasiness about getting rid of these criminals, but I did worry about the effect on the men of the SSU. I felt it important that they be the ones to carry out the executions. My worries in this regard were unfounded: the SSU carried out their orders without demurrer. However, for the conspirators, it wouldn't be right for the SSU to carry out the executions; it had to be regular troops, preferably military police.

Five men of the 13th Military Police Battalion stood in a line with their rifles shouldered. Their lieutenant stood off to one side. The prison commandant and an officer from his command stood off in one corner of the courtyard. Mike Waverly, ex-Governor of New York, turned to face the firing squad. He was unbound. From my vantage point, I couldn't see his expression clearly, but he seemed haggard and worn out. I thought at the time that there was one other expression displayed on his unshaven face: a terrible sadness. My heart ached to shout down to the soldiers to let my one-time friend go, but I couldn't. Mike had gambled and lost. I had won—and my victory had to be complete or I would ultimately lose everything.

The lieutenant ordered the men to ready their rifles. Five rifles aimed at Waverly. He didn't move. The lieutenant gave the order to fire and a volley shattered the quiet scene. I flinched. For a moment, Waverly was pinned against the wall by the force of the bullets. Then slowly, his body slumped to the ground. My former friend was dead and I had killed him. It had to be done, I repeated over and over to myself.

As I watched the lieutenant walk over and fire the unnecessary final shot into Waverly's head, I vowed that I would help my friend in the only way that I could think of: I would ensure that his wife and son were looked after and protected. They wouldn't be forgotten and left to starve. I owed my friend that much at least.

– Chapter 20 –

Ithaca

Revolution, insurrection, call for independence—I don't know what I'd call what I did. President Cole and the Army called it mutiny. Their response was slow in starting, but now they were coming at me with everything they could muster. My forces were on the defensive and events were not going well for me.

On the last day of October, a large air battle was fought over Lake Erie. The airmen of the 174th Wing did their best, but my Air Force (if I can use that term for a single wing of ground-attack aircraft and fighter drones) was effectively wiped out. It didn't help that, just as the battle started, the commander of the 174th Wing and his deputy commander were killed in an accident involving a fuel truck. Kellerman could have chosen a better time to carry out my orders, but then again the new commander did get the airmen fighting for me. I doubt the old one would have done that. Fortunately, the air battle exhausted the other side (I couldn't think of them as the enemy). Although they had achieved total air supremacy, they did little with it. I don't know whether it was their losses or the fuel shortages that plagued us all.

On the ground, events also turned against me—at least initially. In the west, their response was badly coordinated. The defection of the Eleventh Guard Division had thrown the other side into disarray, but mounting pressure meant that I had to order the Eleventh and the Third to withdraw from southern Michigan. The Third had pulled back into Ontario and set a defensive line behind the St. Clair and Detroit rivers. The city of Detroit was an effective barrier to the other side. Its units were understandably reluctant to enter the ruined city. The Eleventh held on to northern Michigan, where the fighting became localized and confused.

To the southwest, the Fifth Guard Division, supported by elements of the 6th Armored Brigade, had been pushed back to the outskirts of Buffalo. It looked as if the whole sector was going to crumble, but at the blackest moment the commander of the 9th Urban Brigade defected to my side. The 9th had driven up from Pittsburgh as part of the other side's reserves. My one-time subordinate decided that I was right in what I was doing. He brought his entire brigade into the fight on my side. The 9th hit them from behind, split their forces and linked up with the Fifth. We managed to recapture some ground south of Buffalo before the fighting petered out into a stalemate.

The commander of IV Corps was ordered to drive into my eastern flank. Strangely, no attack came. IV Corps remained inactive regardless of the pressure put on it by Army Operations. To hit my eastern flank, IV Corps would have had to fight its way though Montreal. The year before IV Corps had lost many men in the futile battle to control that city. I don't know if the men refused to re-enter Montreal or whether its commander was carefully watching events to see what would happen. It could be either, but knowing how cautious the commander was I suspected the latter.

In the southeast, however, no such miracles were being bestowed on III Corps. The attack by the other side was vigorous and not the least bit confused. I had no surprise defections to aid my cause. I was in trouble. The Eighteenth Guard (Pennsylvania) and Eighth Guard (New York) divisions, supported by the 1st Marine and the 57th Urban brigades, were attacking. The First Guard Division was being badly defeated in every sector. The 28th and 29th regiments were quickly pushed out of Albany and up the length of the Mohawk Valley. It was only when we retreated into Utica that my forces could hold. Because of the inactivity of IV Corps, I took a supreme gamble and withdrew the 1st Brigade of the Tenth Mountain Division and elements of the 6th Armored Brigade from covering Montreal. If IV Corps moved now, it would only be resisted by one light infantry brigade, which also had to cover against any movement from the Canadian forces around Ottawa. Thank God Kellerman succeeded in assassinating Prime Minister Rochon. The resulting chaos in Ottawa meant that my northeast flank wasn't threatened.

With my forces holding at Utica, the other side switched its center operations to Binghamton near the Pennsylvania border. The 41st Regiment was pushed out of that city and into hills to the north. The terrain suited defense and the 41st managed to hold. The other side then deftly switched its center of operations again. Clearly this was their commander's strategy—and it was effective. Whenever my forces managed to hold, he switched his line of attack. I was continually on the defensive; I hadn't the forces to meet all potential attacks. This time, elements of the Eighteenth Guard Division and the 1st Marine Brigade moved through Elmira and headed towards Ithaca. I rushed the 17th Regiment of the First Guard Division into Ithaca, along with two battalions of the 1st Regiment of the Tenth Mountain Division and six heavy tanks of the 655th Battalion of the 6th Armored Brigade. These were my reserves in the area—all my reserves. I had no other troops available. None. If Ithaca fell, my defense in the hills north of Binghamton would be outflanked and I would have to retreat to Syracuse. My command south of Lake Ontario would be split into two and Fort Drum would be threatened. Ithaca had to hold. It had to.

With a commander's instinct, I knew that I had to be on the spot in

Ithaca. On the night of November 5, I traveled down from Fort Drum with only the brigadier general of the 1st Brigade of the Tenth and my driver accompanying me. I arrived just before midnight. Major General Micklebridge arrived minutes after me. Eva too had a commander's instinct that this was the key battle. We three generals, along with the colonel of the 17th Regiment, who was the local commander, assessed the situation. There were three parallel east-west rivers flowing into a fourth south-north river, which in turn flowed into Cayuga Lake to the north. Between the first and second river, there lay the downtown core of Ithaca. To the north, between the second and third, there lay the sprawling campus of Cornell University. To the north of the third river, there lay only open ground all the way to Syracuse. The colonel of the 17th had set up defensive lines using the rivers. His first line had been breached and fighting was now taking place in downtown Ithaca. We were losing the battle and the colonel was recommending that he pull his men back to the second river.

"My guardsmen," he said, "are no match for the marines. If it wasn't for the firepower of the tanks of the 655th, we couldn't have held for this long. I must pull my men back to my second line of defense."

"If Ithaca falls—."

"My men are dying in there," he said. "I must pull back."

He was angry and clearly exhausted.

"We cannot continue to fall back—," I started to say.

I was about to order that there must be no retreat—a classic order from a losing and desperate general. I wasn't that desperate—not yet.

"Very well," I said. "Fall back to the second line."

The colonel left to give the order to his men. During the night, downtown Ithaca was abandoned by my troops. I toured the new line of defense and talked to the men. I tried to instill in them a confidence that was lacking in me. I fully expected the other side to hit our second line of defense in the morning, and we would have to fall back again. How wrong I was.

At 2:30 a.m., I took a brief nap, with explicit orders that I was to be woken in an hour-and-a-half or if the other side started to attack our second line. I fell asleep quickly, even with the certain knowledge that I was losing this battle and the war. An hour later, I was shaken awake by my driver. A miracle had happened while I slept. I was saved! But at first, I didn't see it that way. My driver told me that the colonel of the 17th needed to see me immediately. Thinking that our lines had been pierced, I hurried over to the regiment's command center, a basement room in the Fine Arts building at the northernmost edge of the university. As I rushed over, I noticed several of the university buildings to the south burning, presumably from shelling by the other side. I entered the Fine Arts building and descended the stairs. In the command center, boxes containing paintings leaned up against a wall. Piles of art books were scattered carelessly around the room. An exquisite piece of sculpture sat on a desk acting as a paperweight. Broken glass covered the floor. I was horrified at the casual damage being inflicted on our cultural legacy.

Men were running everywhere. I noticed the colonel in the corner talking to another officer. He saw me and waved me over.

"General," he said, "something bad is happening. This is the ranking medical officer with the 17th. Captain, give General Eastland your report."

"General," said the medical captain, "the first one was reported yesterday before breakfast. Now there are hundreds. Everywhere."

The woman looked exhausted and wasn't communicating very clearly. Obviously something was going on and I needed to know what. I became impatient.

"Captain," I said, "what are you talking about?"

General Micklebridge entered the command center and hurried over to us.

"Sorry, sir," the captain said. "I haven't slept for a while."

She managed a weak smile.

"Sir," she said, "our men are falling sick. First one, then dozens, now hundreds. Whatever it is, it's spreading like wildfire—."

The colonel interrupted her.

"General," he said, "at this rate, by tomorrow I won't have anyone capable of fighting."

At that moment, a soldier in the doorway coughed loudly. It was a terrible, barking cough. I watched him double over, wretch and then cough again.

The medical officer pushed her way past me and ran over to the sick man. She quickly examined him and then gave orders to a nearby soldier. The sick man was led away, but no one had time to clean up the vomit.

"It starts," the captain said, "with a tickle in your throat, then a gentle cough, but within four or five hours the cough becomes violent. You ache everywhere and have a high fever. Soon you're too sick to do anything."

I needed a moment to absorb this. I turned away from the officers and looked across the room. Several men were gently coughing; one was stretching his arms in a way that indicated that they were aching. Coughing, coughing, coughing, I pondered. Something was there in the back of my mind, but I couldn't reach it. Then it hit me in a flash. Because of the events of the summer, I had forgotten the briefing on the incident near the biological warfare research center in China. Was this the same? I tried to remember. What were the symptoms? Blood!

"Captain, has anyone started to cough up blood?"

"No, sir. ... Not yet anyway."

The others looked at me inquiringly. They suspected that I knew something. Before I could say anything, the colonel abruptly coughed. He looked momentarily embarrassed but then he realized that he too was sick with this illness. As the realization registered in his mind, the eyes of this brave soldier showed fear—a deep, primitive fear.

"Colonel," I ordered, "Get me your communications officer. I want an urgent, top-priority message sent to Fort Drum. Get Lieutenant Colonel Landsholme of III Corps Medical down here at once. Tell him to bring the ADPI file."

Once this was done, I took the group of officers into a private room. I told them what I knew about the Chinese incident and what symptoms to look out for. I ordered them not to tell anyone, although I permitted the captain to brief her medical staff on the symptoms. I hoped I was wrong; I hoped the Chinese plague had not reached my men.

* * *

Twenty-four hours later, all fighting around Ithaca had stopped. My troops weren't the only ones suffering. The marines and Pennsylvanian guardsmen opposing us were also sick. I listened to the desperate pleas for help from the commander of the other side's forces. The replies made it clear no help would come. The other side had quarantined Ithaca. I had no one left to help me decode and interpret the flow of calls, but from what I could gather on my own many other sites in the United States had been similarly quarantined.

My forces in Ithaca were reduced to two active men: myself and Landsholme. Thanks to our inoculations back in March, neither of us became sick, although we both had a slight tickle in our throats and coughed occasionally. A few resilient men managed to overcome their symptoms and look after their comrades, but the rest were too weak to even look after themselves. Landsholme and I were everywhere. We were both completely exhausted. The task of looking after so many men and women was overwhelming, but it was too important to stop. Landsholme administered to their medical needs, and I did what I could. My men took me not catching the illness as a sign: in their eyes, I was invulnerable. I did nothing to dissuade them of that belief. If any of my men in Ithaca doubted my cause before, none did now.

The illness was violent, but fortunately no one had coughed up blood and no one had died yet. Landsholme believed that this was either not the same illness or the Chinese virus had somehow mutated since the incident in the upper Yangtze Valley into a less-virulent form.

He didn't have the time to do any research into the matter; he was far too busy looking after the men.

I too was busy. Besides doing what I could for my men, I had to run the affairs of the rest of III Corps. The commander of the other side's forces took the opportunity to switch his center of attack back to the Mohawk Valley. The fighting was not going well, and the 28th and 29th regiments were in danger of being dislodged from their defensive positions. I had to stop these attacks and I believed I had found the weapon to make that happen. I remembered the look of fear in the colonel's eyes. That fear could be used.

Taking half-an-hour out from helping my men, I sat in the deserted command center and drafted a speech to III Corps. I re-read it once. It was full of misleading facts, half-truths, falsehoods and down-right lies, but it would do very nicely. I prepared to broadcast to III Corps in an open-air transmission. As there was no one left in the command center to turn on the communication equipment and the portable generators, I had to do it myself. The other side would be listening to my broadcast, but that was precisely what I wanted. My speech was really for them, not for the men of III Corps.

I provided details of the China incident and the ADPI file, and I blamed Army Operations for the cover-up. I ordered my soldiers to remain where they were and not come into contact with other units. There was to be no offensive operation and no prisoners were to be taken, as they might be carrying the plague. I promised my men that I would get them through this ordeal.

After my speech, I turned off the communication equipment and leaned back in the chair. I had now done all that I could to stop the fighting. There was nothing left to do but wait—wait for the inevitable panic. Other commanders would demand a copy of the ADPI file. When Army command refused, it would confirm the commanders' worse fears. If in the unlikely event that the Army released the file, the details in the file would become unimportant; only the confirmation of its mere existence would be remembered.

I let out a big sigh and lifted myself from my chair. With my cane, I limped out of the deserted command center. There was nothing left for me to do there. I returned to helping Doctor Landsholme look after my men.

* * *

Eva was pale, but she managed to give me a pathetic smile from her sick bed. She had been particularly hard hit by Adepi, as the coughing plague had become known among my troops. Thankfully, her fever had broken and her coughing fits had subsided. Eva was on the road to recovery. She was one of the last to recover. I confess that I had spent much more time looking after Eva Micklebridge than I had any of the other men or women under my command. She had helped me after the bombing in Toronto, tending to both my physical and emotional wounds. I owed her a great debt and I was pleased to repay it.

Eva struggled to sit up. I helped her place a pillow behind her back. She reached for a mirror that I had laid beside her and, while holding the mirror with one hand, she fluffed up her short, brunette hair with the other. I smiled: I interpreted it as a sign of recovery.

"I look like hell," she said in a weak voice. "Thank you for looking after me, Walter. I know you had many other demands on your time."

She reached out and held my hand. I squeezed it and then we let go. A moment later and with surprising swiftness, Eva the woman disappeared and Major General Micklebridge, commander of the First Guard Division, appeared in her place.

"I hate being sick," she said. "What has been going on? How many of my men have died in this plague? What's happening with III Corps? Are we still fighting in Ithaca? Has the plague spread? What's—?"

"Whoa," I said. "Hold on. One question at a time."

"I feel so out of control," Eva said. "I hate being sick,"

I provided Eva with a full debrief of what had gone on in the week that she had been stricken with the plague. The men in and around Ithaca had faired very well. I had only lost ten men, although another fifteen were so weakened by the illness that they couldn't return to active duty. They would be looked after and found some administrative duties—I would make sure of that. The death-rate amongst the well-fed, otherwise healthy soldiers was very low, but the same couldn't be said about the civilians in the Ithaca area. They were starving and weak before the plague hit. Amongst the malnourished civilians, the death-rate was possibly as high as one in twenty, but no one bothered to keep count. True to what I had promised in my speech, I kept the rest of III Corps fully informed of the situation in Ithaca. When one of my men died, I announced his or her name over the air, which helped to maintain my credibility.

My speech had the desired effect: fighting all around the perimeter of III Corps ceased almost immediately. Commanders on the other side isolated their commands and all offensive operations stopped. At first, generals in Army Operations denied the whole thing. No one believed them. Next, they said illness was completely unrelated to the incident in China, that it was completely contained and dealt with by the Chinese. This announcement had made things worse for generals in Army Operations. By denying a connection to the Chinese incident, they had confirmed that such an incident did in fact take place. They lost all credibility. This was highlighted to me early on when the commander facing my units in the Mohawk Valley contacted me for details and not his commander in Army Operations.

Two days after my speech, the commanding general of IV Corps finally made up his mind. He announced that IV Corps would follow the example of III Corps. It would become isolated and independent. He renamed his corps the Northeast Army. I resisted the temptation to change the name of III Corps to, say, the Army of the Great Lakes Union. It remained simply III Corps. Two days later, units in Fort Bragg, North Carolina, announced their independence. They called themselves the Army of the Carolinas. I couldn't guess what mix of miscellaneous units were thrown together to form that new Army.

Maybe they were units from Army bases in Maryland and Virginia that had escaped the radiation fallout from the nuclear accident earlier in the year. The following day, the Army of Kentucky came into existence, and this was immediately followed by the units opposing me in upstate New York. Their commander called his collection of units, the Army of the Appalachians. After that, I stopped taking any notice. Independent armies popped up everywhere. Most were brigade-level units; some were just single regiments. I doubted that many of them would survive in the long-term, because they had neither the organization in place nor the resource base that III Corps had.

Army Operations had lost control. It continued to issue orders but they were ignored. President Cole had become isolated in his bunker in St. Louis. A few hours before I debriefed Eva, my now partially-staffed command center intercepted a desperate call from Cole's bunker. A woman announced, in a voice rank with fear, that a mob had entered the bunker and were making their way down to the President. The woman pleaded for any Army units nearby to come to the President's aid. The call ended abruptly, and that was the last we heard from President Cole's bunker. I didn't listen to the call, so I couldn't identify the woman's voice. I hope it wasn't my old friend Jan Sykerman. I wanted to believe that she had left Cole long before, but I doubted she did. She was loyal to a fault, and now I feared that she was dead.

"Walter," Eva said, "you've done it. Everything we once had is gone. Only III Corps remains. You've saved it, and you've saved us all."

"I had to save something," I said, "from the wreckage that was once our great country."

"What a year," she said. "But, you've managed to get us through it. We've had plagues, riots, nuclear accidents, forest fires, famines, droughts. It's been a year from Hell — worse than Hell."

"Yes. Yes it has."

Part IV
Purgatory

To Purgatory fire thou com'st at last.

- The Lyke-Wake Dirge
(an old English funeral ballad).

Mark Tushingham

– Chapter 21 –

Toronto

An idea came to me during the weeks that followed the plague in Ithaca. With my men in Ithaca recovered but the plague spreading to other units in III Corps, my stay order remained in place. There wasn't any fighting around the perimeter of III Corps, so I had little to do. I took to wandering the ruins of Cornell University. I was greatly saddened by the sight of its destroyed libraries. The libraries in the southern half of the campus were burnt to the ground; their books gone forever. The libraries in the northern half of the campus (physical sciences, music and fine arts) were heavily damaged; however many of the books were salvageable.

As part of my independence speech in Buffalo earlier in the year, I had announced that III Corps' new mission was to save civilization. At the time, it was simply an expedient rallying call, but I now saw a way to realize that mission. With my men recovered and no fighting to keep them busy, I was looking for activities to employ them and now I had found something. I ordered the men to rescue books and other documents from the libraries of Cornell. It started slowly: a truckload here, a truckload there. The fuel situation was bad, but with little prospect of renewed fighting I could afford the modest expenditure of fuel to operate the trucks. Books were collected together in an abandoned warehouse on the northern edge of Ithaca. Two months later, after I lifted my ban on movement, I transferred the books to Fort Drum.

My rescue program grew. Most of the men saw it as a noble undertaking and supported it enthusiastically. Throughout the following year, men and women of III Corps collected books, documents, maps, paintings and other works of our once rich civilization. These works were placed in warehouses, stored in mines and caves, and distributed to farmers to secure on their farms. I scattered these works throughout the area of III Corps, so that no single disaster could destroy the cumulative achievements of centuries. Some of the works were available to be used, but others I hid so that they won't be found for decades or maybe even centuries. In the collapsing world in which it is our lot to live, much knowledge will be inevitably lost, but I have ensured that this knowledge will be found again one day.

Within the jurisdiction of III Corps, many libraries had been lost to fires, looting or exposure to the elements, but I had saved many others: public libraries and libraries once belonging to universities, governments and corporations. Only two major libraries remained and both were located in Toronto: the Toronto Central Reference Library and the vast depository of the University of Toronto's Robarts Library, along with several satellite libraries on the university grounds. There were over twenty million books and other documents to be rescued.

Since my closure of Toronto two years ago no troops from III Corps had entered that city, except for a few SSU agents on reconnaissance missions; however, that would now change. I was about to lead elements of the 14th Mobile Regiment into Toronto, supported by five urban tanks and a single heavy tank of the 32nd Security Brigade. The powerful force would enter, collect the books and leave quickly.

We were to be in the city for no more than twelve hours. This sort of in-and-out operation used to be called a thunder run, but only older officers like me remember that name. The operation is now called a hell run. This particular hell run was about to start.

The last of the Army trucks was being filled with diesel fuel—if you can call the dirty, foul-smelling liquid that. The fuel that was being pumped in to the truck's fuel tank was a long way from the clean-burning, carefully-refined liquid fuel that the truck had been designed to use. My men had to strip the emission control equipment off the trucks just to make them work.

My fuel situation was precarious. There were some supplies still left over from before the collapse two years ago, but these were very precious and used only in dire emergencies. Most of the corps' needs were now supplied from the once-abandoned oil wells of southwestern Ontario near the towns of Petrolia and Oil Springs. The viscous dregs of the virtually depleted oil reservoir were my only sources of new fuel. The 31st Engineering Battalion, along with some civilians, operated the oil wells and the sole surviving refinery of the once vast Sarnia Refining Complex. The Third Infantry Division provided heavy protection for this invaluable and irreplaceable resource. If III Corps was to lose this single source of fuel, the corps would be foot-bound—not a pleasant prospect. As it was, the helicopters of the aviation battalions of the Tenth and Third divisions hardly ever flew, and most of the heavy tanks of the 6th Armored Brigade had been immobilized and made into strong-points guarding various vital facilities.

The immobilization of most of the 6th Armored Brigade had forced me to make some personnel changes within the corps' command staff. The 6th was disbanded and its tanks were either immobilized at key facilities or in a limited number of cases distributed to other units in the corps. Price was promoted to major general and given command of the First Guard Division. Eva Micklebridge became the corps' deputy commander. I had been without a deputy since the bombing in Toronto killed Major General Gregorakis. Eva had never quite recovered from the plague. She wheezed often and her voice had become husky. After any physical exertion, she would cough. Sometimes it would be gentle, hardly-noticeable coughs, but at other times it would be prolonged fits of barking coughs. I felt that she was no longer up to the physically-demanding task of commanding a front-line division, but she would make a superb deputy. I trusted her like no other and I liked her nearby.

Price and Micklebridge were not the only changes. I completely restructured my intelligence apparatus. I never wanted to be caught unawares as I was on Independence Day in Toronto. I placed all corps and divisional intelligence units and military police units under one unified command. I gave the command to Wycross and promoted him to brigadier general. The role of the SSU was expanded, and Khanan was promoted to a full colonel. I permitted him to recruit a limited number of civilians into the SSU—mostly ex-gang members but also some ex-civilian police. My personal security detachment remained under my direct command, and Sergeant Kellerman continued to be my personal and very secret tool for fixing delicate problems. Wycross was the only person who ever knew what Kellerman really was. I never even told Eva.

When the final truck had been filled with diesel fuel, its driver started the engine and the truck roared to life. Thick, black soot streamed from the truck's twin exhaust pipes. We were ready at last to continue our noble mission of saving the treasures of our civilization. It was a hot but overcast morning when the large convoy got underway. Forty-five trucks and my command vehicle were strung out in a line. Fifteen of the trucks carried men from the 14th Mobile Regiment; the remaining thirty were empty. Two urban tanks led the way, with one urban tank and a heavy tank bring up the rear. The other two urban tanks were mixed in with the trucks. I was in my command vehicle with my driver, three of my bodyguards and Colonel Luna Malaloff, commander of the 14th.

Malaloff was a strange woman. Her middle name was Zoggata.

Who would name their child Zoggata? Her dark eyes were set far apart and separated by a large, beak-like nose. She had taken to wearing her jet-black hair in dozens of tightly-wound braids (not regulation but so much had changed since the Toronto bombing. Since that day, she never wore a helmet or even a cap over her braids.) On that day, her helmet had stopped a metal splinter from killing her. In some bizarre act of defiance, she now wouldn't allow anything to be placed on her head. The braids and her unusual features made her look quite alien. The woman was however the perfect choice for saving books from oblivion. It was rumored that Malaloff was a gifted speed-reader and that she read a book every night. She could recite poetry by heart— and often did to emphasis one point or another. She switched from Shakespeare to Russian masters to more modern works without skipping a beat. The more depressing the poetry, the more she enjoyed it. Malaloff was an avid supporter of my program to save civilization's treasures, and because of that I used the 14th more often than other unit in this endeavor.

The convoy followed a route previously mapped out using small reconnaissance drones. We entered the city from the east and stayed on the main expressways until a destroyed bridge over the Don River blocked the way. The convoy turned on to the city streets and made its way through a maze of debris and abandoned vehicles. I was in a buoyant mood until we entered the deserted city streets. Then, I saw sights that I wish I hadn't seen. There were partially-clothed skeletons everywhere—some still clutching weapons. More than once, I noticed packs of large feral dogs running away with bones in their mouths. The convoy momentarily halted while some debris was cleared away. Not ten feet from my command vehicle, I noticed a skeleton of a woman (judging from the faded clothes covering most of the bones). The woman's skull had been crushed and lay in dozens of fragments. Protruding from underneath her clothes was the skull of an infant. I didn't want to look, but I couldn't take my eyes from this one tragic scene in a city full of such scenes.

"Out, damn spot!" said Colonel Malaloff. "Out, I say! One, two, why, then 'tis time to do't. Hell is murky! Fie, my lord, fie! A soldier, and afeard? What need we fear who knows it, when none can call our power to account? Yet who would have thought the old man to have so much blood in him?"

I was puzzled for a moment, but then it became clear.

"What!"

I startled the others in the command vehicle. Malaloff gazed straight ahead and said nothing more. I recognized the passage, at least the beginning part of it: it was from a scene in Shakespeare's *Macbeth* in which Lady Macbeth could not wash her hands clean of the blood of one she had murdered. Malaloff's inference was clear: all this death and destruction around us was my doing. Seconds before Malaloff quoted this passage, I was thinking precisely the same thought. Somehow this strange woman had read my mind. I would never be free from the image of the skeletal woman and her child. My hands would never be clean—no matter how much of civilization I managed to save. For one terrible moment, guilt flooded over me. Yes, I caused all this, but what could I have done differently? I did what had to be done. My men couldn't have remained in Toronto a day longer. The city was dying and taking us with it. What suffering there must have been. Tears welled up, but I forced them back. These people killed so many of my soldiers, that they deserved to suffer.

The command vehicle jerked forward; we were on our way again. Twenty minutes later, the convoy entered from the north the old government security area around Queen's Park. Only blackened stumps and dead grass remained of the lush park where I had once watched a squirrel scrabble through the trees. My old office was just off to the left. The building was now just a burnt-out shell, as was the nearby Ontario Legislature Building. Was it only three years ago that I had met Mike Waverly in that building?

Colonel Malaloff set up a command center at the front of these ruins. Her men split into four unequal groups. The smallest group headed south to the Ontario Art Gallery. The others headed for the Royal Ontario Museum just to the north, the Toronto Central Reference Library further to the north, and the university's Robarts Library and its satellite libraries to the west.

After a while, I left Malaloff to work with her command staff. Long before I entered Toronto, I had decided that I must visit the site of the bombing. It was in a field just to the west. In my command vehicle and with one urban tank providing protection, I traveled to the site. The shattered wooden stand remained were it had fallen two years ago. I climbed out of the vehicle and walked with my cane up to the stand. My leg hurt more than usual. The stains where the blood had soaked into the wood were only just visible. With a shaking hand, I reached down and touched the place where my men had died. I said goodbye to them. I turned and slowly went back to my command vehicle.

"Sir, are you all right," asked one of my bodyguards.

It was then I realized that tears were running down my cheek. I quickly wiped them away and continued on without a word.

* * *

My driver pulled up in front of the giant, fortress-like building that was the Robarts Library. Twelve trucks from the 14th were parked outside, with a tank guarding them. I could see a few of my men carrying boxes out of the main doors. Twelve trucks—or one hundred and twelve—couldn't remove all the books, maps and documents out of this vast library. We could only take a small selection. Four of the trucks carried the men, two trucks were dedicated to the collection of rare books located in the basement, and each of the remaining six trucks was assigned two or three floors within the main library. I sought out the major who was in charge of this part of the operation. After asking several soldiers, I was directed to the tenth floor. Immediately after exiting the stairway, I saw the officer talking to a civilian woman. A soldier had his rifle pressed into this woman's back. The woman's rag-like clothes draped off her stooped, emaciated figure. Her face was heavily lined and her cheeks were sunken; her gray hair hung listlessly over her shoulders.

"Major, what's going on," I asked.

"Hello, sir. Welcome to Fort Book. That's what this woman calls it."

"And who is this woman?"

"She claims to be the librarian."

"Claims!" the woman said. "I am the deputy-chief librarian in charge of social studies and the humanities, but for a long time I've had to take over responsibility for all the departments."

Then she muttered crazily to herself about how soldiers just didn't understand, and asking herself what she was to do about them. Why were the soldiers here? Why were they taking her precious books? Maybe she ought to have stayed hidden. After this mumbling monologue with herself, she finally decided to talk to me.

"Why are you here," she asked. "What are you doing with my books? They belong to the library. Get out!" She had a violent gleam in her eyes.

"What's your name," I asked.

The woman looked puzzled. "My name? ... I should know that."

Clearly, this woman was only hanging on to her sanity by a thread. How she'd survived so long was a mystery. In a gentler tone, I asked her, "What are you doing here?"

"Looking after the books," she said with suspicion.

"My soldiers are here to rescue the books," I said. "The library is in danger and the books must be taken to a safe place."

"In danger?"

"Yes, in danger. We must take the books to safety."

"Yes, yes, we must."

"But we can't take them all. I've only a few trucks. Can you help us decide which books should be taken?"

The major with me looked surprised by my request to the woman, but I ignored him.

The woman hesitated.

"You can come with them," I said. "We'll need someone to look after them and organize them in their new home."

"What should we do," the woman mumbled to herself. "He appears to be telling the truth," she said, "but what if it is a trick? The soldiers are taking the books. They're moving them somewhere. Maybe it is to safety. We should go with the books and find out. Yes, we ... I mean I will go with you. The books are very important."

"They contain our civilization's wisdom and follies."

"Yes! That's right," she shouted. "You do understand. I will help you."

Whether it was therapy for my troubled soul or to help forget the blood-soaked wooden stand or the skeletons of the woman and child, I spent the next hour wandering through the labyrinth of bookshelves with this wraith of a woman. She pointed out important books and I ordered nearby soldiers to add them to our growing collection. I offered her my rations, which she greedily accepted and gobbled down with gusto.

Just then, the major came up to us.

"Sir, Colonel Malaloff is on the radio," he said. "She says there seems to be some trouble brewing over at the Central Reference Library."

The woman became agitated.

"Central! Don't go there. It's a trap. I know."

She nodded her head violently.

"What do you mean," I demanded.

She stood up on her toes and whispered confidentially into my ear, "Cannibals."

I stiffened and shouted.

"Major, where's the radio," I asked. "I must speak with Colonel Malaloff immediately."

The major and I dashed down the stairs to the fourth floor (at least as fast as my bad leg could carry me). The woman trailed along behind. I grabbed the receiver from the soldier operating the radio.

"Colonel, what's the situation over at the central library?"

"My men," Malaloff replied, "have reported some civilians in the area. They're elusive. At first, only a few were observed, but now there seems to be many."

"I want the men out of there now."

"But we haven't finished loading."

"I don't care," I said. "I have intelligence that they're in a trap. Send the heavy tank and your reserve urban tanks to help the men out of there. I'll bring over my tank and meet you there. Move!"

"Yes, sir."

I handed the receiver back to the radio operator.

"Major," I said, "speed things up. I don't know how long we'll remain in the city. And Major, bring this woman along when you leave."

"Yes, sir."

I descended to the ground floor quickly, and got into my command vehicle. I gave some quick orders to the commander of the tank and to my driver, and then we were off. We careened through the streets, heading in the direction of the central library. We arrived just as the first shots were fired. Many hundreds of poorly-clad men and women charged my soldiers with suicidal abandon. The mob blazed away wildly with guns of all description: machine guns, rifles, pistols. Some just wielded baseball bats. My tank fired with its machine gun at the mob. Dozens fell, but dozens more replaced them. The mob kept coming. Colonel Malaloff arrived with her reserve tanks. At the sight of these reinforcements, the mob turned and fled. Within moments, the streets around the central library appeared deserted, but I knew we were being watched. I called on my radio over to Malaloff and ordered everyone back to our base at Queen's Park. So far we had been lucky. There were no serious casualties, except for one truck that had its engine shot up and had to be abandoned.

We soon got back to our base. The trucks from the museum and the art gallery arrived just before us, but they carried disappointingly light loads. At the museum, most items small enough to be carried had already been removed by someone else; at the art galley, the roof had partially collapsed and rain had damaged most of the paintings.

I ordered Malaloff to move out. We were going to leave the city after we had gone by the Robarts Library to collect my troops there. We arrived at the huge library within fifteen minutes of my order to move out. The soldiers were still in the process of loading the trucks. I was torn between saving more books and getting my men to safety. With no one visible but my men, I decided to risk a few more minutes to complete the loading. Any attempt at selecting the best books was abandoned. Soldiers just gabbed what was nearby and filled their box. My men were understandably hasty and several boxes were dropped and their contents spilled into the street. Some books were thrown loose into the backs of the trucks, while others were just left in the street where they fell. I became increasingly anxious to leave and began to pace beside my command vehicle. Then, I heard an explosion to the north. It sounded a long way off, but it was the last straw. I ordered my men back to the trucks. We were leaving. The sound of the explosion worried me. It reminded me of the mob in Albrighton, England. There, the mob had set a trap by blowing up a building. Could this mob be setting a trap? I decided not to find out and ordered the convoy to take the back-up route out of the city. We wouldn't take the same route that we had used to enter the city.

The convoy headed south to the lakefront and then made its way eastward. The route was slower and windier, but we made it out of the city without incident. We drove by a large number of people, particularly near the lake. Shanty buildings lined the lake shore. The civilians gawked at us as we streamed by, but none of them made any aggressive moves against us. It was with great relief that I entered the 2nd Brigade's security zone. It had been a busy, eventful day.

* * *

The next morning, I inspected some of the units of the 2nd Brigade. This brigade, the mobile half of the Tenth Mountain Division, was a personal favorite of mine. Various units within the brigade had played significant roles in my career. The 110th Aviation Battalion and the 10th Urban Assault Battalion were instrumental in my victory at the Battle of Kemptville. I personally established the 10th Urban Assault Battalion and build it up from nothing. The 14th Mobile Regiment had accompanied me most of the way into New York City after Hurricane Nicole, and had often assisted me with my mission to save the knowledge and treasures of civilization. The horses of the 317th Cavalry Battalion had started me on my way to rethinking mobility in an age of fuel shortages.

My inspection of the first unit was depressing. All the helicopters of the 110th were non-operational, save for three lone survivors. Equipment had either been damaged in the fighting or had been stripped off to repair one of the other helicopters. Most of the men had been reassigned to the 14th or, if they were adept at riding horses, to the 317th. I gave the remaining men a short pep-talk, hoping to boost their sagging morale.

My visit with the 317th was a much happier affair. The men were active on reconnaissance missions, both for the brigade and for the division. They reveled in their important status and clearly enjoyed having their mobility. The troopers of the 317th doted on their horses. Nothing was too good for their working pets (for that is what the horses were to them). The troopers often gave some of their own rations to their horses. The commander of the 317th, Lieutenant Colonel Sheflin, had turned it into a first-class unit that had successfully adapted to the new order. It was a pity that their uniforms were so ragged.

Back when I took command of the Tenth, Jan Sheflin had surprised me with the use of horses to recover her battalion's mobility. She was about to surprise me again. Once again, the petite, energetic woman would force me to expand my thinking.

After an exciting display of horsemanship, Sheflin invited me to inspect her new project. She refused to give me any description of what it was. I followed Sheflin to a large warehouse on the perimeter of the security zone. I thought this mysterious project would be a demonstration of some novel cavalry tactic, so imagine my surprise when two soldiers pushed open the warehouse door and I was greeted by the roar of an elephant.

"Tiny says hello," Sheflin said. "He's welcoming you to the Ark."

I looked around the warehouse. Tiny the Indian elephant was tied up near the door with a heavy chain. Close by, a tiger was lying down in a cage that was far too small for it, and facing the far corner two camels stood motionless beside each other. Lining one side of the warehouse, cages were stacked upon cages—dozens of them. Each one containing one or more small animals: iguanas, lemurs, gibbons, beavers, otters, snakes, and many others. A sad-looking chimpanzee looked down at me from the uppermost cage.

In shock, I stammered out, "What's going on?"

"The troopers and I," Sheflin said, "took your call to save civilization to heart. We just expanded the concept a little."

Sheflin informed me that there used to be a world-class zoo nearby called the Toronto Metro Zoo. When the 317th arrived here, she undertook a reconnaissance through its ruins. Most of the animals were dead, but some had escaped and were living in the nearby valley of the Rouge River. Civilians were hunting them for food, but the proximity to our front lines had deterred all but the bravest or most desperate of the hunters. These animals had survived solely because of our presence here. Sheflin and her troops thought that saving civilization meant more than just saving books and libraries, and decided to save something just as precious—the planet's genetic library. The animals needed our help. If what was going on here was being replayed elsewhere in the world, there would not be many large animals left.

Sheflin firmly believed that we must preserve these poor animals as they may be the last of their kind.

I must have looked skeptical, because Sheflin added that she knew how to look after them. She had found herself an expert. I followed her to get an introduction. There was no stopping this woman, but I figure it was a harmless diversion for the troops.

Sheflin led me towards the camels. As we went around the back of the docile beasts, a large woman of about forty-five came into view. She had very dark circles beneath her eyes and her skin sagged noticeably from what once had been a round, plump face. A chimpanzee infant draped itself around the woman's thick neck. On a nearby rickety wooden table, a medical case laid opened flat. The case was battered and worn, but inside the contents were well organized and, if not new, at least well maintained. Sheflin introduced the woman.

"General, this is Doctor Adlan. She was once a vet with the zoo. Doris, this is General Eastland."

A strange mix of emotions flashed across the woman's face. I almost believed that she was going to cross herself in a religious fashion.

"Doctor Adlan and I have some plans we'd like to discuss with you," Sheflin said, oblivious to Adlan's reaction.

The vet found her voice at last. It was a deep, booming voice.

"General," she said, "these poor animals must be saved. They're irreplaceable." When I said nothing, she explained that the baby chimp and his mother were possibly the last ones left on the planet. There hadn't been any observed in the wild in thirty years, and if what had happened to the Metro Zoo had happened to other zoos, there would not be any chimpanzees left. The vet also informed me that the female camel was pregnant and she insisted that the baby must be allowed to be born.

"You know, General," Sheflin said, "long ago the Army experimented with a cavalry unit composed of camels. I think it was in Texas in the 1850s. Camels are very useful in hot, dry conditions. Last summer, some of my horses died from the heat. Camels could be used to replace our losses. And Tiny the elephant, he can be trained to move loads. He's very sweet and—."

"Relax ladies," I said, "I don't need convincing."

I stroked the camel beside me. I had always liked animals.

"If anything," I said, "I think your efforts need to be expanded."

Sheflin beamed and a wave of relief swept across the vet's face. For a moment, I thought the vet was going to hug me.

Over the next hour, Sheflin, the vet and I discussed plans for the animals. I enjoyed myself immensely. The two women planned to scour the old zoo and the nearby river valley for more animal survivors and then turn the warehouse and two others nearby into a makeshift zoo. This was clearly inadequate. We had to think bigger. The animals couldn't continue to live in these tiny cages. We needed to build a proper zoo in a safe location. The vet became so excited with the prospect that she insisted that the new zoo be called the General Eastland Animal Refuge. I laughed at the idea, but the woman was earnest in her desire to show this small measure of thanks.

We spent most of the time deciding on where we should locate the new zoo. I ordered for a map of Ontario and we three poured over it. In the end, we agreed on a site on the Isle of Quinte, the large island that juts out into Lake Ontario. It was out of the way but not too far from our current site, which would ease transportation logistics. It was rural and so the surrounding farms could provide food, and more importantly it was near the Picton Wind Turbine Power Station. That station and the ones at Tobermory, Sackets Harbor and Olcott were the only sources of electricity that I had remaining. It was important for the new zoo to have a reliable electricity source nearby; particularly if we were going to keep the penguins that Sheflin swore she had seen swimming in the nearby river. The vet would set up and manage the new zoo, while Sheflin took a select group of volunteers from the 2nd Brigade and rounded up as many escaped animals as she could find.

Yes, it was a very enjoyable hour. My time in Toronto was satisfying. In a way—in a very small way—it eased some of the terrible memories that I had of that city. I had saved many truckloads of books from Toronto libraries, and now I had saved dozens of animals from death and, in some cases, from extinction. Yes, very satisfying.

– Chapter 22 –

Rochester

The following April, the corps was rocked to its very foundation.

In that month, I called for a full face-to-face meeting of the corps' command staff. Such meetings were becoming increasingly rare due to the desperate fuel situation. Around the large table in the main conference room in my headquarters at Fort Drum sat the familiar faces of the generals under my command. We had each brought assistants, who sat along the wall. In all, more than thirty people were in the room. There was no formal agenda; each unit commander provided a status report and raised issues of concern. Unless there was a high-priority issue to discuss, I generally liked to take the commanders' reports in a geographical order: that is, moving from unit to unit from either east to west or from west to east. At the last meeting we went from east to west, so this time we went in the opposite direction. I turned and asked for a status report on the Eleventh Guard Division, my westernmost unit located in northern Michigan.

The young major general started his report in his signature quiet voice. By the end of the report, he would be nearly shouting, particularly if he had some demand or other or if events were going badly. The quieter his voice in the beginning, the louder it would be by the end—or so I had observed in the past. For this report, he began very quietly so I expected a bad report. He reported that his division was coming under increasing pressure from the surviving gangs of Detroit. There were continual raids into the farmlands north of Flint. Several had attacked as far as Saginaw. In the west, it was a no-man's land. South of Grand Rapids, the Chicago gangs and the so-called Army of Northern Indiana are busy battling it out. They had made a wasteland of southwestern Michigan. He saw no point in getting between the two, so he had withdrawn north to Mount Pleasant and White Cloud. Even then, he was going to need help. His base at Grayling was secure for the moment, but he wanted to keep it that way. With dramatic flare, he hit his fist on the table.

"General Cottick," I asked, "can you spare any units from the Third?"

I didn't expect an affirmative, because in the past Cottick had always been very protective over keeping his units together. I was surprised by his positive reply.

Cottick gave me a broad smile, which transformed his otherwise hard features. He ran his fingers through his thinning hair (a peculiar habit of his).

"Yes, sir," he said, "I think I can spare the 67th Regiment. The gangs of Detroit have been attacking north, not east across the river. The unit is looking for employment."

"Excellent," he said. "How can you get them there?"

Cottick shrugged.

"They'll have to walk," he said. "We've experienced some problems with fuel production which I'll brief you on during my report."

I wasn't pleased to hear of more problems with fuel production.

"Very well. Get your men moving."

"Yes, sir," Cottick replied, "but I think we should view these problems in southern Michigan as an opportunity."

"How so?"

"Once the other two forces have exhausted themselves," he said, "we should move into northern Indiana. We should expand our zone of control into the rich farmland that will be wide open for us to take."

Cottick and I had had this debate before. He wanted to expand III Corps well beyond its original boundaries, while I wanted to keep my command manageable.

"No, we won't move south," I said.

I knew that both our flanks would be open to attack. Even if we managed to hold the farmland, it would need irrigating, and that would reduce the water supplies available to the farms we currently had.

"We have to expand or die," he said

"No," I said. "We work with what we have. III Corps is functioning and I want to keep it that way. Now, you were going to report on the fuel situation."

Cottick wasn't happy, but he decided to drop the argument for today. Instead he ordered a colonel from his 31st Engineering Battalion to provide an update.

The colonel stood up and came to the head of the table. He launched straight into his briefing. It was full of technical reasons why it was becoming increasingly more difficult to extract crude oil out of the underground reservoir. In addition, once the crude was extracted, it was of such poor quality that only a small fraction of the crude could be made into gasoline or diesel fuel. The residual was used in the refinery's boilers to produce the necessary power to operate the refinery.

At the end of the briefing, I thanked the colonel.

"We're all relying on your efforts," I said. "We need that fuel, so get every drop you can."

Cottick then concluded that he had nothing else to report.

General Stafford, the commander of the Fifth Guard Division informed me that all was quiet in his command, so I moved next to

General Zhang, of the 32nd Security Brigade.

"Sir, I would like to defer to General Tuckhoe."

"Very well. General Tuckhoe?"

"Sir," said Tuckhoe, "everyone in my division and General Zhang's brigade, and indeed throughout III Corps, supports the efforts to save what we can of our civilization. It's a worthwhile cause. It makes us stand apart from the brutal urban gangs and self-serving so-called armies operating outside of III Corps."

"But," he said, "the continual hell runs into Toronto have got to stop."

The last one, he said, was a disaster. He had lost twenty-two men. General Zhang lost eight men and two tanks. The mission before that hadn't been much better. These hell runs were using up men, machines and fuel. It was the end. He wanted to stop the mission.

I sat quietly for a moment and reflected. After the first successful hell run into Toronto, I had ordered another. And then, another and another. There were so many books left in the University of Toronto libraries. They all had to be saved. Tuckhoe just didn't understand our cause. None of the men around this table really understood what we were doing—what we were saving. However, our movements had become predictable and the gangs in Toronto had prepared traps for our return. The high losses from the last run affected me deeply. Colonel Malaloff had been killed. Such a terrible loss. Her men were very distraught. The new commander of the 14th Mobile sent to me, as per Malaloff's instructions, her personal copy of *Macbeth*. It was a badly worn paperback in which she had underlined Lady Macbeth's soliloquy that she had quoted to me on the first hell run into Toronto. I now thought that I better understood what she was trying to tell me. I focused not on the first part of the passage ("Out, damn spot!"), but on the middle part: "A soldier, and afeard? What need we fear who knows it, when none can call our power to account?" The blood on my hands was put there by necessity and would never come off. I accepted that. No, Malaloff was telling me that I was powerful and need not fear what had to be done. Nevertheless, it was clear that the men of the Tenth and 32nd were exhausted. They needed rest.

"Okay," I said, "the runs into Toronto will be put on hold temporarily."

I told them that I would make no plans for returning, but would store what we have already rescued and then see what the future brought. Realistically, I doubted that I could get Tuckhoe or Zhang to agree to another venture into Toronto. If I pushed forward and ordered another hell run, the men wouldn't act with the same enthusiasm that they did on the first one. Such an order would be bad for morale.

I moved on to hear General Price's report.

"Sir," he said, "there's little activity along our borders. However, there's something disquieting occurring within them."

It was, he said, a small incident, but about a month ago a woman in the First Guard had died from dehydration. His medical officer concluded it was suicide. He ordered the First's medical team investigate. It was supposed to be a routine investigation, but apparently his officers turned up something.

Price reported that the private had joined some religious cult called the Church of the Sun (that was "sun" as in the star, not the Son of God). This sun-worshipping cult promoted suicide for its members. Price's medical officer suspected that one or more of the woman's friends in her unit were also members of this cult. He put a watch on them and his efforts paid off. Another woman, a friend of the first, left her unit without permission. The medical officer ordered a soldier to follow the woman. She walked over forty miles from Geneva to Rochester without resting for food, water or sleep. It nearly killed the soldier trying to follow her. In the end, he had to abandon the chase.

"What do we know about this Church of the Sun," I asked.

"We're aware of it," Wycross said.

It was one of dozens of suicide cults that had sprung up within III Corps. Most were tiny. No more than fifty members. For obvious reasons, they usually disappeared quickly. The Church of the Sun was larger than most. Its leader was a charismatic man who called himself the Redeemer. Wycross had no intelligence on the man's real name. His followers, after giving what they could to the church and finding as many new followers as possible, were persuaded to commit suicide. Their doctrine was that the Sun was taking retribution on us for our sins. It was drying out the planet to make way for a new world. Accordingly, if you wanted to be part of this new world, you had to dry yourself out by not drinking. Those who managed with their last ounce of strength to cut their wrists and drain their blood would be, according to their dogma, truly blessed and be reborn in the new world as a priest of the church. The Redeemer, however, had not chosen to dry himself out. Our intelligence was that he lived very well in a large compound just west of Rochester. Wycross stated that he had not paid much attention to this cult, because it had not recruited any soldiers.

"Clearly that's changed," I said. "Rochester is within your command, General Stafford. Are you aware of any recruitment of soldiers from the Fifth into this cult?"

It was an innocuous and obvious question, but General Stafford's initial reaction was disconcerting. For just an instant, I saw something flash in his eyes. I don't know what it signified. A faction of a second later it was gone. Did I imagine it?

"We've had some isolated cases," said Stafford, "but I didn't think them to be of any significance."

"What do you know of the church and its leader?"

"Not much more than General Wycross has told us," he said. "My attention has been on Buffalo and the area to the southwest. But if it's important, I can have my men investigate."

"Yes," I said, "please do. We can't have cults spreading through the men of III Corps. It will undermine our authority over them."

After a long list of routine housekeeping items were discussed, the meeting was finally adjourned. As I walked back to my office, I asked General Wycross to accompany me. A little voice in my head was telling me that I needed to put more resources into investigating this cult than just the meager intelligence assets of the Fifth Guard Division. I ordered Wycross to undertake a separate investigation of this church and its leader. He asked permission to send in some SSU agents as well. I approved his request.

The results of Wycross's investigation took just over two months. His findings shattered III Corps.

* * *

My driver drove rapidly towards Rochester along the deserted Route 104, adeptly avoiding numerous potholes. I sat in the back of the staff car holding the thick file tightly in my hand. Beside me in the back seat, General Wycross sat quietly—he had said enough already. When I awoke this morning, I thought I commanded a strong, united corps; now I didn't know what I commanded. In the car, I didn't need to re-read Wycross's report. Its words had already seared themselves into my memory. You don't forget words like "widespread plot," "significant recruitment amongst officers," "Guard divisions compromised," and "imminent danger of a coup."

The investigation undertaken by General Stafford into the Church of the Sun had been completed over a month ago. I remembered his conclusion that the cult offered no threat to III Corps. He told me that vigorous efforts had been made to identify soldiers within the Fifth who were members. Those few who were members had been confined and were receiving psychological assessments. Wycross's investigation, on the other hand, had found that there were strong links between the Church of the Sun and many high-level officers of the Fifth Guard, including General Stafford. It also noted some elements of the First Guard appeared to be involved, although no link to General Price was found. You can guess which report I believed. Even so, General Wycross insisted on showing me definitive proof before I took any action. This proof was secured in an old, disused police station in an eastern suburb of Rochester.

Wycross insisted on haste. I left Fort Drum with only my bodyguards and a platoon of Wycross's military police trailing behind me in a truck. We arrived in East Rochester in what must have been record time. My bodyguards fanned out around my car, and when all was set my driver opened my door and I got out. I strode past two SSU men who were guarding the police station and entered the dilapidated building. Stale and musty odors assailed me; they weren't pleasant. I followed Wycross down the dark, claustrophobic hall to a door. We passed through the doorway, while my bodyguards arranged themselves outside.

I found myself in an observation room looking into an interrogation cell. Colonel Khanan was already in the observation room and turned to salute. Without saying a word, Khanan beckoned me to look into the cell. Through a large window of one-way glass, I saw a naked woman sitting on a metal chair in the center of the cell. She sat before an old wooden table, with an empty chair opposite. The woman's hands were tied behind her. Her legs were bound with ropes that had cut into her ankles. The woman's head bent forward and her long blond hair covered her face. Blood was everywhere: in her hair, running down her chest between her exposed breasts, covering her feet, pooling on the floor. In the corner, a muscular man lounged up against the wall. He was wiping his fists on a blood-stained towel. The blood on the towel was not his. The whole scene was sordid and ugly. I didn't want to see this.

The door to the interrogation cell opened and a woman entered. She was short, with shoulder-length brunette hair and a well-developed bust. Her dress had a cheery flower pattern on it that was incongruous with the surroundings. She carried a tea tray, with two china cups and a white teapot. A blanket was draped over one arm. After the woman entered, the man ambled out of the cell and closed the door behind him.

"Carla is excellent," Khanan said, "especially with women."

As he described the process, her assistant would soften them up and Carla would get them talking. The system never failed. Carla used to run a brothel in Niagara Falls and the man was her bouncer. Khanan had used the team often since he recruited them. He felt that it was a treat to watch a master at work—and Carla was a true master at her particular art.

I didn't share Khanan's enthusiasm. This was awful. I didn't want to watch, but at the same time I couldn't take my eyes from the horrible scene in front of me. Now Carla was speaking to the woman.

"Hello, my dear," Carla said. "Sorry I'm a little late. You look a little chilled. Here, I brought you a blanket. Let me put it around you."

Carla draped the blanket around the woman's stooping shoulders, and then she undid the rope that bound the woman's hands.

"There. You must feel better now."

"Yes, much better," the woman mumbled. "Thank you."

We could barely hear the woman's response, so Khanan adjusted the volume of the speaker.

"Oh it's no problem, my dear. I'm glad to help. Would you like some dandelion tea? I've made it fresh."

"Yes, please. I'd like that. You're a good friend, Carla."

A wave of shame washed over me. Watching this pathetic, broken woman being played with like this made me feel dirty. I turned away from the scene.

"Why am I watching this," I asked. "Who is this woman?"

"General," Wycross said, "this is Carrie Waverly. Governor Waverly's widow."

Disbelieving, my head turned rapidly back to the window. Just as I did, the woman raised her head to look at the cup of tea in front of her. The blood-soaked hair fell way from her beaten face. I could barely recognize Carrie's once beautiful features, but it was her.

"How? Why? What's going on? She's supposed to be under house-arrest in Buffalo. What's she doing here?"

In a low, flat, unemotional voice, Wycross explained that he had picked her up yesterday morning, along with General Stafford. The two just come from a visit with the Redeemer, the leader of the Church of the Sun. They were over-confident and careless, and Wycross had caught them red-handed. There was no doubt, or any room for misinterpretation. Over the last few months, Waverly and Stafford had manipulated the cult and the cult leader for their own purposes. They wanted to create a religious movement that ensnared my soldiers, particularly the men of my two New York Guard divisions. They wanted to use the control that this provided to topple me from my command. They had a lot of assistance from other officers in the Fifth Guard, and were slowly gaining some support in the First Guard.

"Where's the proof?" I demanded.

"Listen," Wycross said as he nodded towards the window.

I turned back to the pathetic scene on the other side of the one-way window. Carla had poured the dandelion tea, and she and Carrie were sipping it slowly.

"I'm very upset with you," Carla said.

Carrie looked terrified.

"Why?"

"I'm your friend," Carla said, "and I don't like to hear you running yourself down. When I was here last, you said that you were sinful. I can't believe that. You're such a nice person."

Carrie remained quiet.

"We're friends, are we not?"

Carrie nodded.

"Then you tell me how you have sinned. I can't believe it. I won't believe it."

"I have sinned I tell you," Carrie said. Her voice was now slightly louder.

"Tish," Carla scoffed. "I bet it's no worse than forgetting to say your evening prayers. I do that sometimes."

Carrie started to cry.

"I've worked with evil men to do evil things," Carrie said. "I've let them use my body."

"Don't cry," Carla said. "God shall wipe away all tears from your eyes."

"He won't forgive me," Carrie said.

"Tish," Carla said. "The Good Book says 'her sins, which are many, are forgiven, for she loved much.'"

"I did love him," Carrie said. "My husband was a good and honorable man. The Devil took him from me—and I want my revenge. Is it wrong to do evil when you fight a greater evil?"

"What is this greater evil?"

"The Devil. The Devil on Earth."

"Who is the Devil?"

"He walketh about, seeking whom he may devour. He is the Devil!"

"Who, dear? Who?"

"Eastland!"

Hearing my name used with such violent hatred stunned me. The force of Carrie's voice hit me and I nearly lost my balance. It took me a moment to recover my composure. I turned and left the observation room. Wycross followed me out, while Khanan stayed to watch Carla extract more information.

I had seen enough. Mike Waverly had plotted against me. He knew the risks. I had only done what had to be done. I had to maintain the order that my men had spilt so much blood to achieve. Did Carrie want the anarchy that existed outside III Corps to seep inside? I had cared for Carrie after her husband was executed. She wasn't thrown out into the hard world. And this was how she repaid me: plotting with my enemies to get revenge for her dead, traitorous husband.

"I never pictured her as a Bible-thumper," Wycross stated.

"Nor I," I said. "I am not a strongly religious man, but I remembered one quote from the Bible. 'For the wages of sin is death.' See to it, General Wycross."

Wycross led me to the other prisoner. Unlike Carrie Waverly, General Stafford had not been beaten. Wycross told me that there was no need. Stafford had told all: names, activities, plans, everything. I observed Stafford through the bars of his cell. His face was as white as a sheet; his eyes were wide. Fear oozed from the man. He wasn't made for conspiratorial games. Carrie had led him and he had followed, but reluctantly. How had she persuaded him? That question was soon answered.

Stafford summoned up his failed courage for one last time. "General, how is Carrie?"

That told me all. It was simple and sad. She had used him to get her revenge upon me, but he had simply loved her. He had betrayed me for love. They both had.

* * *

A month later and it still wasn't over. Carrie Waverly and General Stafford were dead, but the purges within the Fifth Guard and the First Guard divisions continued. The senior officers of the Fifth had been virtually wiped out. How was I going to replace them? The rounding up of members of the Church of the Sun continued as well. The Church's leader, the so-called Redeemer, was dead. Kellerman had solved that problem very handily. When I ordered Kellerman to assassinate the man, I told him that I wanted it done in a way that would discredit the church leader in the eyes of his followers. I didn't want to create a martyr—you can't fight one of those. The Redeemer's body was found floating in his own swimming pool. The members of the church no doubt suspected that I had ordered the assassination of their leader, but they had to reconcile themselves with the fact that the Redeemer, who espoused death through dehydration as a way of reaching paradise, owned and used a swimming pool. I burst out laughing when Kellerman told me that tidbit of information.

I sat at my desk in Fort Drum. Colonel Joyita had just brought me the latest list of church members that we had arrested. They would all be executed, but I offered them a choice of which methods. They could be hung like common criminals, commit suicide through dehydration like their dead Redeemer promoted, or follow the example of their once-beloved Redeemer and be drowned. None took the latter option, but I was surprised how many chose to dehydrate themselves. Their belief that the Sun was cleansing the old world in preparation for a new one was unshaken. So be it.

Joyita fidgeted nervously in front of my desk. I had worked with him for such a long time that I knew that something was wrong.

"What is it," I asked.

"Sir, please examine the list carefully."

"Why? What's in it?"

Joyita didn't reply. He snapped a salute and left without waiting to be dismissed. He closed the door on his way out.

Alone in my office, I took Joyita's advice and read the list closely. With his usual efficiency, Joyita had arranged the names alphabetically. I saw nothing that warranted my attention until I reached the 'W's. There it was. I couldn't believe it. Waverly, Alan, arrested in Rochester. Mike and Carrie Waverly's teenage son. Will my trials never end?

I put my head in my hands. My mind whirred around wildly. I didn't know what to do next. Finally, I decided that I had to see him. I had to talk with him. I got up and flung open the door. Joyita looked up from his desk. "Where is he?"

"Rochester, sir," he said. "Your driver is getting the car ready, and your bodyguards are being assembled."

Joyita was his usual efficient self.

I don't remember the drive to Rochester. It was just a blur. Wycross had placed Alan Waverly in a well-guarded house, not far from Lake Ontario and too close to where his mother was once held for my comfort. I entered the house and a captain directed me to a bedroom. I opened the door and entered the room alone.

Alan lay on a mattress on the floor, staring at the ceiling. He rolled over listlessly to see who had come in. When he saw that it was me, he sat up on the mattress and looked at me sullenly.

"I knew you'd come," he said.

"I promised to look after you," I said.

Without knowing why, I felt defensive.

"Yeah, like my parents."

I ignored the jab.

"What's going on," I asked. "Why are you messed up with the Church of the Sun. Surely you don't believe the nonsense they preach?"

"Oh sure, why not?"

"You're the son of a bright man. You have your father's intelligence."

"Yeah, whatever."

I studied the teenager in silence for a while.

"So, you're not a believer. Then why did you become involved. What did you think you could achieve?"

Alan stood up in front of me. He was as tall as me. He looked me in the eyes.

"To kill you," he laughed. "To succeed where both my parents failed. You and your kind wrecked this world for us, and now you're doing everything you can to hold on to the wreckage. The order that you hold so dear is just a fantasy—a figment of your imagination. When they enlisted me to help them, I saw the opportunity to overthrow all that. There should be no order."

"You're an anarchist," I asked.

"Everything should be destroyed. We should start again. No rules this time. No order. Just freedom to do what we like."

"You're wrong. Order is essential for us to function. If someone doesn't fight to keep it then there will be nothing."

"Then let there be nothing!" Alan yelled.

There was a moment of silence as we both calmed down.

"Alan, what am I to do with you? I promised myself that I'd look after you, but you've plotted against me."

"What would your precious order demand of you?"

"That you be executed for your crimes," I said as I looked at the ground. "But you're just a boy."

"You have your answer," he said.

He spat at me defiantly.

"No, I promised myself that I would look after you."

"Then you've failed. I'll have no part of the world you are trying to keep. I need to be free to do whatever I want—not to live by your rules. I'll find another way of bringing down you precious order. I will be free."

I turned and fled the room. The captain appeared and closed the door behind me. I had failed in my promise to protect Mike Waverly's family, but Alan, like his mother, was beyond all hope. He would bring down everything I had managed to protect. So many had died in my quest to save the remnants of our once great civilization, so what was one more? I looked over at the waiting captain and nodded slowly. The captain opened the door and entered. A second later, a single shot rang out. Alan was dead.

I limped back to the waiting car. I felt sick.

– Chapter 23 –

Kitchener

Brigadier General Sean Wycross, my trusted intelligence chief, was dead—murdered. I couldn't believe it. It was all so stupid. Wycross had become involved with a woman in the Third Infantry Division's brothel by the name of Rosy Dish (not likely her real name).

Rosy was mentally unstable and had killed Wycross before committing suicide. Maybe Wycross had been trying to end the relationship, maybe she'd thought he was seeing another woman, or maybe she was an agent working for someone. Maybe, maybe, maybe. There were too many possibilities and too many unanswered questions. Major General Cottick's report on the tragic incident was too brief. Although the report noted in detail how the murder-suicide took place, it didn't discuss why. A single statement that Rosy Dish was known to have mental problems was insufficient for me to let the matter rest.

After I read the report, I decided to visit Cottick and discuss the matter in detail with him. The death of III Corps' chief intelligence officer warranted my personal and immediate attention. I authorized a rare use of my personal helicopter. Fort Drum's operations officer arranged for an immediate departure. I would take only my normal bodyguard detail, which in this instant included Sergeant Kellerman.

Kellerman's special talents had not been required since he assassinated the cult leader three years ago. Since then, my command over III Corps had been unquestioned. The brutal purge of the two New York Guard divisions had crushed any internal dissension. As for the civilians living within III Corps, they had accepted their lot. By comparison to those outside III Corps, our civilians led a good life. They were safe from the roaming bands of desperate men and women that plagued those outside III Corps' area of control. Food, while not plentiful, was at least available to most. Order was maintained. The civilians accepted my commands and summary justice as the price they had to pay for security. It isn't like that outside of III Corps. The so-called armies had all disintegrated. No organized unit larger than a regiment existed out there. No forces of order were operating outside III Corps—none at all. It was complete anarchy. The corps' signals battalion only picked up a few radio messages from outside III Corps' borders, but they clearly indicated the horrors of life out there.

I'd like to believe that Alan Waverly would have become disillusioned with the utopia of anarchy that existed outside III Corps. But maybe he wouldn't have. I should have given him the chance to grow out of his fantasies. I should have found a way to save him from himself—and from me. I should have let him live. He was too young to die. I had failed Alan. My guilt over his death washed over everything that I have done since, even more than Carrie Waverly's death. She had seen life; Alan had not. The first heady days of saving what I could from the old civilization had faded. I received no satisfaction from the work. The work continued but without my active participation; others had taken up the noble calling. Maintaining order—that was all that mattered to me now.

During the helicopter trip to Kitchener, headquarters of the Third,

I had three hours to quietly brood upon my regrets and upon what I had become. To me, everything seemed colorless. I was empty inside. I didn't like what I had become: a soulless machine barking out orders and making snap judgments. I was a tyrant. There was no joy anymore. No happiness. Maybe that was why Wycross's death hit me so hard. He was a friend from my past. He had helped me rebuild the Tenth Mountain Division, and he had fought with me in Egypt. My helicopter touched down on a makeshift pad outside the headquarters of the Third. The bump forced me out of my brooding and back to the present reality. My men exited the helicopter and formed an armed perimeter. I climbed out and walked towards the low, squat, fortress-like building that served as Cottick's command center. It was far bigger than my own command center.

I arrived at the building's security desk. The sergeant-on-duty informed me that General Cottick hadn't been informed of my visit. I was surprised at this because Fort Drum should have contacted the Third. It was routine procedure. For some reason, someone had neglected to send the message. How strange are the whims of fate? What would have happened if the message had been sent and Cottick knew I was coming? But that was not the case; fate hadn't finished playing with me. Cottick didn't know and I surprised him.

"Never mind. I'm here now," I said to the sergeant. "Where's General Cottick?"

"Er … In his day-quarters with Colonel Khanan and er …"

I made my way up to Cottick's day-quarters. As I walked down the long hall, officers of the Third seemed to scramble out of my way with a guilty nervousness. There were also many women dressed in flimsy outfits—women from the Third's brothel. Unlike all my other units in III Corps, the Third didn't come from the Great Lakes area. Originally, the Third had been based in Georgia. Although I encouraged the soldiers to move their families into III Corps' area, Cottick had never pursued this very actively for soldiers in his division. As a result, the brothel of the Third had blossomed into the largest in III Corps by far.

I had left the management of the Third to Cottick. If he found that prostitutes kept his soldiers happy, so be it.

As I walked down the hall surrounded by my bodyguards, one woman attracted my attention. She smiled and pretended to flirt, but the moment that our eyes met, her expression changed to a serious one. She subtly put her finger up to her temple and then shook her head slightly. Once she was certain that I had seen the gesture, she smiled again and resumed her flirtatious actions. I didn't know what to make of the clandestine gestures. I carried on without looking back at the prostitute.

The corporal guarding the door to Cottick's day-quarters saluted but made no movement to open the door.

"Corporal, open the door. I'd like to see General Cottick."

"Yes, sir. See General Cottick. Yes, sir."

The corporal finally opened the door, but with an exaggerated slowness.

I entered the room. Colonel Khanan was standing in a corner of the room. Maps adorned the walls and a large table occupied the center of the room. Half a dozen comfortable chairs lined the wall on both sides. At the head of the table, a tall chair dominated the others along the sides of the table. There was no doubt where Cottick usually sat. Seconds later, Major General Hollis Cottick, son of a general and grandson of a general, emerged from a back room. He was doing up the buttons to his shirt.

"Sorry, but you know how it is."

He tried to look embarrassed.

Clearly, Cottick wanted me to believe that I had caught him in the middle of an escapade with a prostitute from the brothel. It was a little too easy an explanation. It was also out of character for Cottick—not the part about him being with a prostitute, but the part about him looking embarrassed. Cottick's sexual escapades were the stuff of legend within the Third. He reveled in the notoriety.

I decided that it would be wiser to accept Cottick's explanation for now. Changing the subject, I commented on his lack of hair.

"I see your barber got carried away," I joked.

Cottick had shaved off his thinning hair and was now completely bald. It made him look younger, which I was sure was the intent. It also made him appear harder and meaner, which may have also been the intent.

"Yeah. What do you think?" Cottick replied. "A surprise visit, General. We weren't expecting you."

"Surprise visits are like that," I said.

I decided not to mention the communications foul up and to keep up the pretense that this was intended to be a surprise visit. I dropped the humor and got down to business.

"I'd like to discuss General Wycross's death," I said. "Your report is very thorough in the details of how Wycross and this woman died, but I'd like to get a better understanding about why this woman did what she did."

Cottick showed me to one of the comfortable chairs. Khanan joined us.

"Rosy was always a little peculiar," Cottick offered. "She just went crazy."

"Was Wycross in love with this woman?"

"Maybe," he said. "Whenever he visited the Third, he used her and no other—at least in the last six months."

"So for six months, they got on well. And then?"

"And then one day," Cottick said, "she went nuts. Who knows why? She shot him for some irrational reason, and then turned the gun on herself. She put it to her head and blew her brains out."

Cottick put a figure to his temple and mimicked Rosy Dish's last act.

An icy cold shiver ran down my spine. The woman in the hall had made the same gesture and then shook her head. Was she a friend of Rosy Dish? Was she trying to say that Rosy didn't shoot herself? If that was true, had Cottick killed Wycross? Had my chief intelligence officer discovered something and died because of it. Was Rosy one of Wycross's agents? What had Wycross discovered that would make Cottick have him killed? Plans for a coup? Or was I being overly paranoid? Did the woman in the hall mean something entirely different? All these disturbing questions flashed through my mind in an instant. If Cottick was planning such coup, I had just delivered myself to him. I was in his headquarters with only a handful of bodyguards and surrounded by hundreds of men that would do Cottick's bidding without question. I was in big trouble. My only advantage was that I had arrived unannounced and had surprised Cottick. He was unsure of himself and what I knew. I had to stay calm, but I had to get out. I continued the conversation by asking him why General Wycross didn't notice that this woman was acting irrationally.

Cottick shrugged.

"I don't know," he said. "Maybe he did. Maybe she was just that good and he didn't care."

"Hardly. General Wycross was an experienced intelligence officer. Just a moment."

I waved to Sergeant Kellerman. He came over and I whispered in his ear, "Trouble. Get my helicopter started."

Kellerman reacted with his usual calm. He turned and walked slowly out of the room.

I turned to Cottick and lied.

"I've just asked the sergeant to get Wycross's personnel file," I said. "I seem to remember something in his file about a mentally ill sister or cousin."

Cottick took the bait.

"Sure that might explain sympathy for the bitch," he said. "Maybe he thought he could help her."

"Maybe," I said. "Let's skip over that until we have Wycross's file in front of us. Your report wasn't clear where this Rosy got the gun. Was it hers?"

Cottick looked blank. Khanan came to the rescue.

"It was General Wycross's gun," he said.
"The report didn't say that."
"An oversight," Khanan said. "But it was his. I recognized it,"
"I'd like to see the gun and the bodies."
"Certainly," Cottick said. "The corporal outside will show you the way to the morgue. I've just got to finish some business with Colonel Khanan and then we'll join you there."
We were both in a hurry to get out of that room.
I left the room followed by my bodyguards. I didn't ask the corporal to take me anywhere; instead, I walked briskly down the hall and towards the exit. I gave my men a hand signal that told them all they needed to know. With my right hand I casually touched my ear followed by my shoulder. This simple signal meant we were surrounded by enemies but might be able to escape without trouble. The sergeant-on-duty snapped a salute as I strode past him. Out of habit, I returned the gesture. Across the field, my pilot had my helicopter powered up and ready. Kellerman had successfully passed on my instructions. I noticed Kellerman casually draping his arms over the helicopter's machine gun.
I was halfway across the field when there was a sudden commotion behind me. Armed soldiers poured out of the command center. I'm not sure who shot first. It may have been one of my men, but the soldiers of the Third shot back. I had the answer to all my questions. My men and I ran. I ignored the pain in my leg. One of my men was shot, but managed to limp along. Kellerman then opened up with the machine gun. The soldiers behind us probably dived for cover, but I can't be sure because I didn't look back. I kept my eyes focused on Kellerman and the helicopter. We reached the helicopter just as another of my men was hit. I helped one of my bodyguards pull the wounded man into the helicopter. My pilot took off very quickly. Fortunately, we hadn't left anyone behind. Kellerman continued to fire the machine gun at the soldiers on the ground. The helicopter flew towards the city of Kitchener and left the command center of Cottick's Third Infantry

Division in the distance. I say Cottick's division, because it was clearly no longer mine.

I was still trying to absorb the ramifications of the defection of the Third when the helicopter banked sharply. "Incoming missile!" the pilot shouted. I owe the pilot my life. The woman pushed the helicopter through acrobatic movements that I didn't know helicopters could do. As she turned violently and dived steeply, I could see two helicopters flying towards us. By this time we were over the ruined office towers of Toronto. The pilot took us into the deserted street canyons. The incoming missiles struck an old office tower and exploded. The two faster and more powerful helicopters of the Third followed us in. She moved expertly through the maze of office towers. The other pilots were not up to her level of skill. They became cautious and started to fall back. They split up: one continued to follow us while the other tried to cut us off. More missiles. Again, a nearby building exploded. My pilot flew out of the maze of towers and went into a dead run eastward. If she could get us to the base of the 2nd Brigade of the Tenth Mountain Division, we'd be safe.

Suddenly, two missiles flashed by, but they were going in the opposite direction. Behind us, one of the Third's helicopters burst into a ball of flame. The other turned and fled back into the maze of towers. In front of us, two helicopters of the 110th Aviation Battalion turned and escorted us to the 2nd Brigade's base. Kellerman had sent a message to 2nd Brigade.

Everyone onboard my helicopter was cheering and shouting, except me. I was devastated. What I had fought against for so long had happened: III Corps had come apart. The unity and order for which I had sacrificed everything was gone. I had held III Corps together longer than any other force left in North America, possibly even the world. But in the end, I had failed. The civil war that I dreaded had begun.

– Chapter 24 –

Fort Drum

Cottick's well-laid plans for the conquest of III Corps were delayed every step of the way by an unexpected foe: the weather. It had gone mad—and that had saved me so far. The traitor had to contend with torrential rains in December and January, frigid temperatures in February, a blizzard in March, and a hurricane in April and another in May. The winter had been the coldest in my memory, and the summer had been hotter than it was in the year of the Toronto bombing. In July, the temperature reached a staggering 136°F during a month-long heat-wave that was consistently above 125°F. Throughout the winter and spring, Cottick's soldiers waded through flooded fields and seemingly bottomless mud. During the scorching summer, sustained movement was only possible at night and for a few hours after dawn. As the air-conditioning units of Cottick's vehicles had long since ceased to function, it was impossible to operate them during the day. The weather, my unlooked-for ally, had helped my soldiers defend against ever-worsening odds.

My early discovery of Cottick's traitorous intentions gave me some time to establish a defense. This—combined with the weather—meant that Cottick's offensive had dragged on for ten months instead of a few weeks. The civil war had irretrievably damaged III Corps. Both sides had suffered terribly. What I had sacrificed so much to preserve Cottick had destroyed just to feed his insatiable ambition. I had always suspected him coveting the command of III Corps, but I had overlooked another side of his character. General Cottick was a very patient man. He gave no outward clues of this. It was a serious misjudgment on my part not to appreciate that side of him. I had always believed that if he acted against me it would be the rash actions of a bull-headed man. Not so.

The best-kept secret in III Corps wasn't kept by me; it was kept by Cottick. For four years or more, I later learned from my spies, Cottick had secretly siphoned off fuel from the refining operations in southwest Ontario. He had stockpiled a plentiful supply of fuel for his vehicles. Cottick's treachery didn't end there. He quickly won over to his side the command of the Fifth Guard Division. After my brutal purge of that division's officers I had no friends there. Recruitment to Cottick's side was easy. Cottick had also courted General Zhang of the 32nd Security Brigade. I don't know what Cottick offered Zhang, but whatever it was worked. Early in the offensive, while the soldiers of the Tenth were holding off those of Cottick's Third, Zhang slammed his fully-fueled armored brigade into the Tenth's flank. My men were forced to retreat from their base near Toronto all the way back to east of Kingston. It was only the rugged terrain of the Canadian Shield and the crazy weather that allowed my men to regroup and set up defensive lines.

South of Lake Ontario, the Fifth Guard Division, reinforced by elements of the Third, had pushed against the men of my First Guard Division and the 9th Urban Brigade. Unlike Cottick, I didn't have the fuel to operate the urban tanks of the 9th as they were supposed to be operated; instead, I had to use them as immobile strong-points. These strong-points bolstered up my defenses and I contained the Fifth. Neither side could breakout of the stalemate that developed.

Once again, Cottick had displayed his patient qualities. Instead of frittering away his fuel reserves in small battles, he had replenished them ready for a knock-out blow. Unlike Cottick, I had no source of fuel to replenish my supplies. My divisions moved by foot, bicycle and horse. With the end of the summer heat wave, I could no longer contain his more mobile forces. Disaster fell upon disaster.

On the twenty-fifth of September, I was woken at dawn by my orderly. Rubbing the sleep from my eyes, I made my way over to the command center in Fort Drum. General Micklebridge greeted me with the bad news.

"Sir," she said, "we are getting confusing reports from the First Guard Division. General Price claims that elements of the 9th Urban Brigade are mobile and are attacking his men."

"He must be mistaken," I said. "Get General Ulithi on the radio."

"We've tried. There's no response."

At that moment, an excited communications officer rushed over to us.

"Sir, we've made contact with the 9th," he shouted.

Eva and I rushed into the communications room.

"… 717th and 790th have gone over," a panicked officer blared over the speakers as we entered. "All battalions in the south have. … Command center bombed. The general is missing. We need orders. Help us!"

I ordered the officer to hold on and told him that help would be coming from the First Guard. I then raised General Price on the radio.

"What's going on?" I demanded.

"Dammed if I know," Price shouted back.

He informed me that Ulithi's tanks were hitting him hard on our southern flank. He didn't know where he'd get the fuel to move anything. Just then I got a report that there was fighting on my northern flank as well. What was Ulithi doing? Cottick, I surmised, must have bought him off. If both my flanks collapsed, I knew that I would be surrounded. Price said that he wanted to pull back.

"That's premature,' I said. "Find out what's going on first. Our intelligence indicates that only two regiments in the south have defected."

"What about in the north," he asked. "Both my flanks are being forced. I must pull back."

Price was panicking. He was uncertain what forces he could rely on.

"General Price," I said, "do not pull back unless ordered by me. Understood?"

There was no reply. Moments later the radio went static. I had lost contact with General Price.

"Get him back!" I said. The communications officer tried unsuccessfully to reach the First Guard Division.

Just when it was looking really bad, it became even worse. Another communications officer called out, "Sir, General Tuckhoe is calling."

I reached for the microphone.

Tuckhoe stated that he was getting reports of helicopter troops landing around the Thousand Islands Bridge. The small detachment defending the bridge was being overwhelmed. If Cottick could hold that bridge, the Tenth would be cut off from Fort Drum. I told him I was sending the 317th to reinforce him.

"Just a moment, General," he said, "I've just received a report that the 32nd has swung down from the north. Cottick's going for the bridge in a big way."

I needed a few moments to digest this. If the Tenth was trapped on the north side of the St. Lawrence River and Price's forces collapsed to the south, Fort Drum would be wide open. For the first time since this terrible civil war started, I saw defeat in front of me. Cottick had out-thought me, out-waited me, and out-maneuvered me. He had all along. While I had dallied with saving some trinkets of civilization, Cottick had kept his eyes firmly focused on his objective: command of

III Corps.

Ulithi was either dead or a traitor. Price was panicking and Tuckhoe was in danger of being cut off. I had to act decisively to rescue anything from this situation. I looked around the communications room. All eyes were silently watching me.

"General Tuckhoe," I said. "Get your men back to this side of the river. If you can't hold the Thousand Islands Bridge, blow it up and use the bridge at Ogdensburg. Swim if you have to. Get everyone to this side and hold the river."

There was long pause before Tuckhoe acknowledged, "Yes, sir."

I then contacted General Price and ordered him to pull back to Syracuse. My order was unnecessary. His lines were melting away. The men of the First Guard and those of the 9th who remained loyal to me were already streaming eastward. The end was near and getting ever closer. Price had lost control over the situation, but I couldn't be too critical of him because so had I lost control.

* * *

My decision to pull back the Tenth across the St. Lawrence River and abandon the territory to the north bought me a reprieve of only six days. With both the Thousand Islands Bridge and the bridge at Ogdensburg blown up, the wide river formed a difficult barrier for Cottick's men to overcome. With the Tenth's 2nd Brigade holding the river, I moved the stronger 1st Brigade south to fill the void formed by General Price's surrender of the remnants of his force. Cottick had offered generous terms, and Price would have been a fool not to have accepted them. Cottick wanted my head. All other considerations were secondary. He could deal with Price later if he wanted to.

Cottick's forces were now closing in on Fort Drum from the south. The depleted and demoralized 1st Brigade couldn't hold them for long. I knew that within hours—or days at most—of Cottick's forces capturing me, I would be executed. If events had been reversed, I certainly would have executed the traitorous General Cottick. He knew the risk when he started his treachery and had taken the gamble nonetheless. He had won; I had lost. It was that simple.

I had to decide what to do. There were only three options open to me: commit suicide, stay and fight and die with my men, or flee. I never seriously considered the first option. Suicide would be the defeat of everything for which I had fought so long. Throughout my ceaseless struggle to maintain order in a dying world, I always had hope. My suicide would send only one message: in the end, I had lost hope.

The second option was tempting. It was heroic and what was expected of a losing commander. I was sixty-four years old. How much longer would I live in this hard world? Ten years? Less? My death would be spectacular and would be remembered for a long time afterwards. Cottick would have to battle the memory of me for years. However, in the end, I decided not to die with my men. There were two reasons for this. First, many good men and women would die with me. They had loyally served me to the end. I owed them more than a glorious death; I owed them a chance of living. Second, if I died with my men, it would be over. Cottick would have won completely. I wanted to cheat him of the complete victory that he sought. I wanted to continue to fight him in some small way.

No, it would be the third option. I decided to flee. But to where? One night as I lay awake in the dark I remembered how happy I had been during the week in the Algonquin Highlands. I could go to the same island. The more I thought about it, the more I warmed to the idea. It was an out-of-the-way location and completely unexpected. Cottick would search in the urban centers for me—not in an isolated and vulnerable wilderness. I laughed at the vision of Cottick become more and more frustrated at my disappearance. I started to entertain the hope that Cottick's reign as commander of what was left of III Corps might be short lived. Perhaps his men would tire of him. Maybe after a suitable period of time I could return from the wilderness and reclaim my command. It was a pleasant dream, but in reality it would take years to overthrow Cottick. I could survive in the wilderness for a month or maybe two at most. And why would the leader of the coup against Cottick want to take all the risks just to award me with command? No, the leader of the coup would keep command for himself.

I decided to flee to the wilderness of the Algonquin Highlands. With my plan set in my mind, I put things in motion. Quietly, I ordered Sergeant Kellerman to secretly arrange my transportation and supplies. I told no one else of my plans. I placed the last remaining helicopter on standby. It was refueled with the last few gallons of fuel available on the base.

In the early evening of October 1, I received a cryptic message from Kellerman that all was ready. I called General Micklebridge, General Tuckhoe and Colonel Joyita into my office for the last time. They saluted smartly and I returned the gesture. Dropping formalities, I smiled weakly and reached out to shake their hands.

"Eva, Donald, Coronado," I said, "you have been true and loyal friends. You must live through these days. If I stay here, you won't. Make whatever peace you can with Cottick."

"It's been an honor to serve with you, sir," Tuckhoe said as he shook my hand.

Joyita, from years of habit, saluted again. He choked with emotion and couldn't speak.

Eva Micklebridge embraced me warmly. I returned her embrace. She began to sob. If things had been different, maybe I could have found some happiness with her, but events hadn't turned out that way. All I could give her now was a chance to live.

I picked up a briefcase that I had filled with a few important files, my medals and Malaloff's copy of Macbeth. I walked to the door of my office, turned, saluted my friends, and then left. The walk to the waiting helicopter was mercifully short. Remembrances of better times flooded over me. My pilot started the helicopter's engines. The blades quickly accelerated to a blur. I climbed in and the helicopter took off. I couldn't bear to look out of the window at the familiar scene of Fort Drum.

We flew low, barely above trees. The sound of a helicopter's blades cutting the air can be heard for miles, so we expected some reaction from Cottick's forces north of the St. Lawrence River. Our helicopter burst out from the trees flanking the river and darted between the many rocky islands that make up the Thousand Islands. As the sun set, we crossed the river and entered enemy territory. We had left the river a few miles behind when the helicopter suddenly lurched to one side.

"Missile!" the pilot shouted, as she flew the helicopter under a bridge of a deserted road. The missile impacted the bridge and exploded. We suffered no damage from the near miss.

Without further incident, we arrived at the rendezvous where Kellerman was waiting. The pilot landed the helicopter and I climbed out. I turned to the captain and thanked her. She smiled and shouted over the noise of the spinning blades, "Anytime, sir."

"Save yourself, Captain," I shouted back.

"I plan to, sir," she said. With that assurance the pilot took off and flew away into the darkening eastern sky.

Kellerman was standing beside a battered, old van.

"Everything's ready, sir," Kellerman said.

I nodded in acknowledgment.

I climbed into the passenger seat and waited for Kellerman to get underway. He placed an old pair of night-vision goggles over his eyes and then started the engine. It was unnerving to careen through the darkness without any lights. Kellerman turned corners and swerved around potholes that went unnoticed by me. Over then next, two-and-a-half hours, Kellerman drove along disused rural roads towards our destination. We saw no one.

We arrived just after midnight. I peered through the darkness of the night at the same decrepit dock from which I had left nine years ago. Kellerman helped me unload my supplies and a battered canoe that he had found. He was a remarkable and resourceful man. I would miss him and the power that he implied, but the time had come for my last soldier to leave me.

"Take care of yourself, sir," Kellerman said, looking like a dog that had lost its master.

"Sergeant, I have one last mission for you," I said. His expression perked up immediately. "I can't order you on this mission. It's entirely up to you."

"Yes, sir," he said.

"I don't think General Cottick or Colonel Khanan should profit by their treachery. Do you?"

"No, sir."

He had the terrifying expression of a python about to swallow his prey.

I don't have any illusions about the mission that I just gave my assassin, and I don't believe that Kellerman did either. Cottick and Khanan would be extremely well guarded, and Kellerman's face was known to both of them and their men. The chance of Kellerman killing them both and surviving was precisely nil. I had sent him to his death. I know Kellerman didn't see it that way; he saw it as the ultimate challenge to his craft. I wished him luck. The traitors deserved to die.

After Kellerman drove away, I stood there in the dark beside my pile of supplies. All I possessed was a canoe and some boxes. I had no army. I commanded no men. I was alone—alone and in the dark.

– Chapter 25 –

Algonquin Highlands

I camped on an island in the middle of a wilderness—the last refuge of a tyrant. I'd been here for two weeks. The moon was new when I arrived and now it was nearly full. Frankly, I was amazed that I hadn't been found yet. Either my flight north had deceived Cottick or he had decided that it was better for him if I simply vanished.

My sanctuary was a pleasant place. There was fresh water in the lake and the trees on the island had been spared from the many forest fires that annually consumed the wilderness. On the far shore, new growth was slowly hiding the charred stumps of the once proud forest. On my island, I had made two new friends. There was a chipmunk that came to visit me each time I ate. I found it comforting to have some living thing to be with in my solitude. I shared my dwindling supplies with it and often talked to it at great length. My other companion was a loon that serenaded me each night. Last night, during the loon's haunting calls, I distinctly heard another loon return the call. I was so overjoyed at the prospect of the loon finding a mate that I scrambled out of my tent and stood there in the dark for hours listening to the two of them. At dawn, I saw them in the distance swimming side-by-side. I was so excited. I didn't understand why until I realized that this pair of loons represented hope—hope of survival and renewal.

I was not the same person who I was when I arrived here. Gone was my anger at Cottick and my pain and regrets. This quiet place has healed me by ways I didn't understand.

I had done some terrible things, but they were necessary to preserve order in a decaying world. Should I have done nothing, even when I knew what had to be done?

No flash of insight came to me until this morning when I noticed Malaloff's copy of Macbeth. I found the passage that the strange woman had quoted to me when we were surrounded by horrific scenes of death and destruction. Was it my guilty conscience or my ultimately fragile power to which Malaloff was referring? I don't know. I never will. I decided to take my own message from the passage. In the middle of the passage, Lady Macbeth laments, "Hell is murky."—I think that sums it up nicely. I did what I believed necessary at the time, but how could I predict what would happen in the end. I came to power because it was inevitable given the environmental disasters that caused the economic and social collapse. If it was not me, it would have been someone like me. The necessary conditions were there for me to step in and take power. I didn't create those conditions; I just took advantage of the opportunities they gave. After that, Hell indeed became murky. I blindly led where no one had gone before and others blindly followed. At least I had the vision to save something of the old world. Would any other person with my power have bothered? Do men like Cottick concern themselves with the needs of future generations? No, I think not.

* * *

I heard a helicopter yesterday evening. They're getting close. I expect to be captured or killed today. I've decided that I won't offer any resistance. They will either kill me immediately or they won't, but I refuse to make the decision easier for them. My plan is to stand defiantly on the big rock at the tip of the island and wait for them to arrive.

It's a beautiful day today. The sun is warm but not too hot, and white puffy clouds float serenely in a light-blue sky. A cool breeze is blowing from the north, forming tiny ripples in the smooth surface of the lake. I feel more alive today than I have for years. If I'm to die, today is a good day to do so.

They're coming. I'm ready.

Dr. Mark Tushingham has worked on climate change and other environmental issues since 1981 and continues to do so today. In obtaining his doctorate in 1989, he demonstrated a strong link between climate change and the rise in sea level. He has watched the issue of climate change grow from an obscure subject of interest only to a few academics to an issue that today unsettles governments. As a hobby, he has collected a personal library of over eighty books on military matters. Mark was born in 1962, when the world's population was only three billion—half that of today.

APPENDIX I

ORGANIZATIONAL CHARTS

TENTH MOUNTAIN DIVISION
(At the time of Hurricane Nicole)

Command Staff

Commanding General	Maj. Gen. Walter J. Eastland
Deputy Commander	Brig. Gen. Donald D. Tuckhoe
Operations	Col. Oliver P.D. Holcomb
Supply	Col. Marum Omar
Intelligence	Lt. Col. Sean B. Wycross, Jr.
Administration	Lt. Col. Coronado J.H. Joyita

Fighting Forces

1st Brigade (Light)	Brig. Gen. Paul Sorensen
1st Infantry Regiment	Col. Gifford V. Gulas
31st Infantry Regiment	Col. Mario L. Sorrotti
132nd Infantry Battalion	Lt. Col. Edward C.T. Hunt, Jr.
2nd Brigade (Mobile)	Brig. Gen. Sorel L. Dillabaugh
14th Mobile Regiment	Col. Luna Z. Malaloff
10th Urban Assault Battalion	Lt. Col. Bradley Seybaplaya
110th Aviation Battalion	Lt. Col. Zig Meshfeld
317th Cavalry Battalion	Lt. Col. Jan Sheflin
Division Artillery	Col. Anthony Reitano
15th Missile Battery	Lt. Col. Tran Vihn
62nd Air Defense Battery	Lt. Col. Maud E. Allen
333rd Air Drone Unit	Maj. Kyle T. Smith
10th Penal Regiment	Col. Liam W.I. Malley
Fort Drum Prison Guard Detachment	
Military Guard Detachment	
10th and 11th Labor Battalions	
1st Special Support Unit	

Supporting Forces
    10th Transport, Logistics and Support Group
    10th Signals Battalion
    10th Medical Battalion
    10th Military Police Battalion
    47th Engineering Battalion
    83rd Military Intelligence Battalion
    1215th (Fort Drum) Garrison
    Light Fighters Infantry School

Total Strength   10,155

III CORPS
(At the time of Operation ROCKFACE)

Command Staff

Commanding General	Lt. Gen. Walter J. Eastland
Deputy Commander	Maj. Gen. Ionas Gregorakis
Operations	Brig. Gen. Raymond Sack
Supply	Brig. Gen. Alice K. Kneffel
Intelligence	Col. Sean B. Wycross, Jr.
Administration	Col. Coronado J.H. Joyita

Main Forces

Third Infantry Division	Maj. Gen. Hollis Cottick III
Tenth Mountain Division	Maj. Gen. Donald. D. Tuckhoe
First Guard (New York) Division	Maj. Gen. Eva Micklebridge
Fifth Guard (New York) Division	Maj. Gen. Jonathan Stafford
6th Armored Brigade	Brig. Gen. Samuel T. Price
9th Urban Brigade	Brig. Gen. Maka Ulithi

Task Force 3   Brig. Gen. Sam Brown
   7th Aviation Regiment of 102nd Airborne Brigade
   19th Ranger Regiment
   27th Regiment of Eleventh Guard (Michigan) Division

Corps Reserves
   10th Urban Assault Battalion
   25th Missile Battery
   341st Air Drone Unit
   174th Ground Support Wing (Air Force)

Support Units
   III Corps Transport, Logistics and Support Group
   III Corps Civilian Liaison Unit
   236th Signals Battalion
   18th, 19th, 30th and 31st Engineering Battalions
   115th Medical Battalion
   13th, 24th, 26th and 27th Military Police Battalions
   1st Special Support Unit

Canadian Units in Ontario	Lt. Gen. Ginette L. Dumont
2nd Mechanized Brigade (Petawawa)	Maj. Gen. Michel P. Mousseau
32nd Security Brigade (Toronto)	Brig. Gen. Daniel Zhang
1st Aviation Regiment (Kingston)	Col. James R. McInnis

Total Strength   89,832